PR

VALLEY OF THE DEAD

THE TRUTH BEHIND DANTE'S INFERNO

"The zombie roll call has grown long over the past few years, but with *Valley of the Dead*, Kim Paffenroth has put himself at the top of the list. He is our poet of the apocalypse."

—Joe McKinney, author of *Dead City*

"That rare work that can appeal to fans of splatter and classic literature at the same time."

—*Dark Scribe*

"Dares to get intellectual about flesh-eaters, faith and the human condition... some seriously smart horror fiction, with plenty of gore to boot."

—*Rue Morgue*

"A masterwork of horror, with the living-dead adrift on the darkest horizons of our nature."

—Kevin P. Spicer, Stonehill College, author of *Hitler's Priests: Catholic Clergy and National Socialism*

"A clever and engaging take on a classic work. Plenty of action and gore for the zombie fan. Paffenroth is at his best here."

—Scott A. Johnson, author of *Deadlands*

"An exciting read in alternative literary history, weaving Dante's masterful vision of hell with a new voice in zombie fiction. Gripping from the first pages, this is a book you'll read more than once."

—Douglas E. Cowan, author of *Sacred Terror*

OTHER BOOKS FROM KIM PAFFENROTH:

Dying to Live
(from Permuted Press)

Dying to Live: Life Sentence
(from Permuted Press)

History Is Dead
(from Permuted Press)

The World Is Dead
(from Permuted Press)

Gospel of the Living Dead
(from Baylor University Press)

Orpheus and the Pearl
(from Magus Press)

VALLEY OF THE DEAD

THE TRUTH BEHIND DANTE'S INFERNO

Kim Paffenroth

A PERMUTED PRESS book
published by arrangement with the authors

ISBN-13: 978-1-934861-31-8
ISBN-10: 1-934861-31-6

Cover art: Garret DeChellis

10 9 8 7 6 5 4 3 2 1

Such torment and sadness
That overwhelms like madness
So fearful and intense
It burns inside

- Judas Priest,
"Revelations"

Timeline of Dante's Life

1265	Born in Florence, Italy
1274	Sees Beatrice Portinari for the first time
1283	Marries Gemma Donati; they have four children
1289	Fights in the Battle of Campaldino
1290	Beatrice dies
1292	Begins writing *The New Life* (*La Vita Nuova*)
1295	Joins the guild of apothecaries and becomes active in Florentine politics
1302	Banished from Florence; sentenced to being burned alive should he return
1302-1319	**Exact whereabouts unknown**
1321	Dies in Ravenna, Italy

Acknowledgments

Once again, my primary beta reader has been Robert Kennedy, who never failed to give prompt and detailed comments on each chapter as I progressed. A new beta reader this time was Christine Morgan, a fine author in her own right, whose feel for action scenes and dialogue is keen and exacting; she offered many improvements.

Certain fact checking, answering of technical questions, and general encouragement was generously provided by coteries of the knowledgeable and charming, within both the academic and horror communities—Jerrod Balzer, Mike Brendan, Brian Brown, Phil Cary, Teresa Delgado, John Goodrich, Karen Koehler, Michele Lee, Michelle McCrary, Bryon Morrigan, Mark Orr, Elena Procario-Foley, Paul Puglisi, Rich Ristow, Mark Samuels, John Urbancik, and Doug Warrick.

It is one of my morbid habits I have followed with all my books, both nonfiction and fiction, that once I get a good chunk of the work done—enough that the project seems headed toward completion—I then ask someone if they would complete the work in the event I die before finishing it. For this volume, Gary Braunbeck graciously agreed to my morbid request, but it looks as though you'll have to settle for my more meager talents throughout.

Thanks to all my teachers and students over the years who have helped me better understand Dante's poem. Until recently, this novel would not have been the outcome I expected from all that reading and studying, but I hope it is a worthy tribute to all their work, as well as to Dante himself. Special thanks to my Iona colleague Dr. Goldstein, and our students in Humanities 101 during the spring of 2008, when I was working on this story

The quotations from *Inferno* at the beginning of each chapter are taken from the Longfellow translation, now public domain and available at such sites as everypoet.com.

Thanks again to the lads of Judas Priest for allowing their lyrics to grace the beginning of this book, as they have allowed their words to preface many of my nonfiction works. I don't think they were the main inspiration for my obsession with darkness and evil, but over the years they definitely have been one of my favorite purveyors of such imagery.

Kim Paffenroth
Cornwall on Hudson, NY
November 2009

Prologue

For the last nineteen years of his life, the Italian poet Dante Alighieri was exiled from his native city of Florence. In these years, he wrote his most famous poem, *The Divine Comedy*, which is still regarded as one of the greatest works of world literature and of Christian theological speculation. The poem is an enormous epic divided into three volumes, each of which describes one of the three realms of the Christian afterlife—*Inferno* (Hell), *Purgatorio* (Purgatory), and *Paradiso* (Paradise or Heaven). The *Inferno* is the most famous of the volumes, and is still read by many American undergraduates as part of a religion or literature course. Even those of purely secular tastes and background are fascinated and appalled by its graphic, ghastly, but hauntingly beautiful and unforgettable images. Also, I think, they pick up on the power the poem draws from being so intensely *personal.* Dante's simultaneous anger and love for his hometown, his nation, and his church can easily be heard throughout his writing, while Boniface, Beatrice, and many other real people in Dante's life—not to mention Dante himself—all appear as characters in the *Comedy.*

It's the intensely personal aspect of Dante's writing—easily observable by any first-time student and endlessly analyzed and praised by lifelong scholars—that started me down the path of reconstructing the events of this story. Dante fills all three volumes of his greatest poem with facts and images from his personal experiences—Beatrice's beautiful eyes, a baptismal font he had broken in a church, a bloody military battle in which he had fought, along with hundreds of other minute details—some beautiful, some horrible, some trivial. How else could he write so powerfully and convincingly? With that being verifiably the case, the conclusion seems almost unavoidable:

during his years of exile and wandering, when details of his whereabouts are lost and legends abound, Dante must have actually seen the horrors on which he would later base *Inferno*. He must have witnessed the very depths of human depravity and violence—hate, betrayal, sadism, dismemberment, torture, disease, unbelievable monsters, unquenchable fire, unendurable ice. Lest people think him mad, and building on his deeply-held religious convictions that God must have shown him these things for a reason, he wove these horrors into a supposedly "fictional" account of a journey through the afterlife, significantly changing the details, populating this world with what his contemporaries would have deemed more believable and acceptable characters—demons, angels, and mythological beasts. I finally saw clearly there really could be no other explanation for his poem.

As heady as my discovery was, I still didn't know exactly where and under what circumstances Dante could have seen these seemingly impossible sights, until I saw how this solved a further mystery of interpretation. With a chill as immobilizing, but far more invigorating, than the ice Dante describes gripping the innermost circle of hell, I remembered how one denizen of Dante's hell indulges in a particularly gruesome pastime: in the final circle of hell, there is a sinner vigorously engaged in cannibalism, even though he is not put there for that individual crime, and even though Dante does not assign a circle of hell to that sin. Here was the solution I had sought: Dante must have seen such a massive, horrifying outbreak of cannibalism that he couldn't bring himself to confine it to one circle of hell, but instead made it the state and situation of every sinner, the landscape or lifestyle of hell itself. Dante, based on some horror he had personally witnessed, came to regard cannibalism as not just one sin among many, but rather the epitome and model of all sin—self-destructive, self-devouring, never-ending hunger. And I knew, as you probably do, there is only one situation that causes cannibalism on such a massive scale, and which would cause a devout man to imagine all of hell must be populated by such cannibalistic monsters, or that hell itself was breaking loose upon the earth. I also saw with chilling clarity why, on the one occasion Dante does describe a cannibal in hell, he focuses on a rather unexpected part of the ghoulish feast: he describes the sinner devouring someone else's *brains*. Once again, there clearly was only one answer possible: Dante had witnessed what I had previously thought was a deadly plague only in our modern world—zombies, ghouls, the undead, the living dead.

What I have now laid down, as best as I could reconstruct it from passages in the *Inferno*, is the tale of how Dante survived that plague, and the lessons he learned there, making his ideas more accessible to many who might be put off by his overtly Christian language, and revealing the real-life situation on which such theological discourse was based. This is far more than an interpretation or adaptation of *Inferno*: this is the real story, of which *Inferno* is the interpretation.

Chapter 1

"Midway upon the journey of our life
I found myself within a forest dark,
For the straightforward pathway had been lost."
Dante, *Inferno*, 1.1-3

Dante was not lost in a dark forest. Far off to his left, league upon league of trees stretched out sullenly, until in the distance they crept up the sides of angular, defiant mountains. The road where Dante sat astride his grey horse was awash with sunlight on that spring afternoon, even though it was still fairly cold. The landscape around him might have seemed cheerful, were he given to such a mood that day—though like most of his days since being driven from Florence, he was not. But the rider's dour mood was not the only thing tainting the panorama around him. The whole countryside seemed to lack something: light abundantly overflowed, but there were no sounds beyond the horse's footfalls—and even these seemed small and muffled, though the horse was a big, plodding beast. No smells, and the air didn't carry to Dante's tongue any hint of budding life as it should at this time of year. He looked to the mountaintops and thought it right to withhold joy from a scene so unnatural, flat, and soulless.

Dante was also not midway through life's journey. He had been wandering Europe for several years already, and he had started his exile at age thirty-seven. Even with the rather generous biblical estimate that our lifespan was set at three-score and ten, he knew he had more years behind than ahead of him. But a life of exile had its own, special indignities that could age a soulful, sensitive man like Dante even quicker, making him more weary and despondent than a happy and content man would be at a far more advanced age. Most days, Dante felt very old indeed.

Dante had never been a handsome man. Though the arcs of his eyebrows were delicate and graceful, his brow overhung his eyes too much—eyes that were too small and set too deep. His chin was far too prominent, and his nose was too pointy, especially noticeable and unappealing since it bent slightly downward. But since leaving Italy, Dante sometimes wondered if his ugliness had been exacerbated and turned inward to fester and poison him in some more permanent, irreparable way. Often when he contemplated the afterlife—or even worse, the resurrection, with its more complete, perfected forms of retribution—this fear froze him, and all he could do was repeat the prayers of childhood, the mantras of innocence and hope corresponding so little to frightened, disappointed, cynical middle age.

It turned out that crawling to some petty potentate's frigid, ramshackle castle to beg for supper was the least embarrassing part of Dante's new lifestyle. Far more demeaning and debilitating was the dance of dependency and sycophancy that would ensue, the doggerel he'd have to write for the ruler and his court, celebrating all their munificence, bravery, and nobility. Given how meager their various accomplishments were, Dante had to take poetic license and embellishment all the way to outright, culpable lies in order to compose the verses they wanted, and for which they would tolerate and support him. God help him if they fell in "love" and required poetry to aid their pathetic quests to copulate like the beasts they mostly were.

There was humility, and then there was humiliation; worse, there was the humiliation one actively longed for, pursued, and embraced, like a dog returning to its own vomit. That was Dante's life, and he loathed himself for it.

If there had at least been the satisfaction of being able to produce something good, true, and beautiful, while whoring himself to these illiterate barbarians, it might almost have seemed worth it. Perhaps the value of his "real" art would outweigh and counterbalance all the sinful trash he was forced to produce in order to survive. Dante had thought like this at first, before the exact contours of his life in exile became clearer to him, but lately it seemed like a useless evasion. He doubted he could ever create something worthy of his beloved Beatrice, let alone anything acceptable to the God he had offended and betrayed. Better just to own up to the sinful wretch he had become and beg the Lord to forgive and heal him.

On that nondescript road on that featureless day, Dante burned with shame at the compromises, lies, and pandering he had willfully perpetrated in the name of survival. He now knew through painful experience these were far worse and more culpable than any of his wrath against the monster Boniface, or even his blinding arrogance at his own talent—talent for which he was often not sufficiently grateful to God. He prayed to God for punishment for all such affronts against Him—not with the hope of childish prayers, but with the steady, sober resignation of middle age.

Dante dragged the gaze of his hard eyes from the mountaintops to the road. Some distance ahead, he saw a small, four-legged form loping onto the roadway. It stayed there, as if waiting for him. As Dante approached, he could have sworn it was a lean, hopeless-looking wolf, though it hardly seemed possible. They usually traveled in packs, and one by itself would hardly lie in wait for a man on a horse—a victim too big for a lone animal to take down. Dante gripped the hilt of his sword, thinking perhaps the creature was sick or mad. Disease could make animals behave in unnatural ways. Whatever the animal was or whatever its condition, it remained there in the road, panting, its tongue hanging out, looking on as Dante drew closer. Each rib was visible on its taut, mangy side. And then, as though it really were just a phantom, it slinked noiselessly into the woods, leaving Dante blinking and shaking his head. Perhaps it had just been a large, starved dog.

Then, on that day without savor or sound, while sights deceived and confounded him, Dante finally smelled something. He smelled smoke. Not the pressing, earthy smell of burning wood, and not the heady, rich aroma of roasting meat. Those kinds of smoke would be black, and their odors would be alive. Up ahead to the right, the smoke was white, thin, and sickly, and its smell was dense but piercing, something raspy and malignant. Then suddenly the silent day filled with similarly harsh, disordered sounds—an explosion, shouts, and the high, long shriek of a woman. Though these were the punctuations in the din now assailing Dante, stranger and more chilling was the steady moan underlying all of the sounds around him. It was an animal drone both more and less alive than the other, frenzied sounds, for it was unbroken, unwavering, like the rush of wind or water. For all his harsh judgment of his own virtues, Dante was no coward. He automatically nudged his horse with his heels, urging it ahead faster.

The stench increased and the tumult rose as he rode forward, though the intensity and clarity of the sun's light did not change in any way at all.

Chapter 2

"All hope abandon, ye who enter in!"
Dante, *Inferno*, 3.9

Coming around a slight bend in the road, Dante could now see the cottages of a small village off to his right. They were the homes of simple people—farmers, woodsmen, and shepherds. Several of the buildings were in flames, and people were running around in panic, not attempting to extinguish the fire, but just trying to escape. Some were fighting savagely with one another among the buildings, using their bare hands or farm implements—axes, shovels, pitchforks.

Many years before, Dante had seen similarly-armed peasants fighting at the Battle of Campaldino. They had made up ninety-percent of the armies, in fact, while Dante had been part of the tiny but decisive cavalry force. This was far more ugly, graceless, and lethal. Men grappled and hacked at each other with a fury one would never see on a normal battlefield, where even ill-armed and poorly-trained soldiers could retreat or surrender. No, you only saw the limits of brutality on days like this, where men were forced to fight like beasts, in front of their homes, with their womenfolk and children screaming and running all around them in terror.

Dante switched the reins to his left hand and pulled back on them. He drew his weapon—a simple arming sword he could wield with one hand, useful on foot or mounted, and befitting his station and skill at arms. He had no idea how to intervene in the melee, who was fighting, or over what, but he hung back by the edge of the madness, unable to tear himself away.

Dante saw that even by the standards of bestial savagery, something was wrong with these people. When one man swinging a club was knocked down by three unarmed men, they fell upon him and tore his clothes off with their bare hands. From the screams and animal growls that followed, it seemed they were tearing into his flesh with their hands and teeth, dismembering him. Others who were knocked down were treated in an almost equally excessive, unbelievable manner. Men with axes or shovels would continue to hit their opponents in the head even after they'd fallen, as though they wanted not just to kill or incapacitate them, but to destroy their heads completely until their brains were spread out all over the blood-soaked ground.

A crackling sound tore through the air above them, and for an instant Dante glimpsed some smoking, orange object in the sky, before another house exploded in flames. Sparks and burning bits of wood and thatch flew out of the wrecked building, pelting people indiscriminately, some of whom caught on fire as well. The villagers were not just fighting hand-to-hand, but they were being bombarded by some other, unseen force, further off. That group must have been a real army, with real equipment, if they possessed incendiary projectiles like this. Another burning wall exploded as a man crashed through it, entirely engulfed in flames himself. He kept on walking for much longer than Dante would have thought possible for a person burning so intensely. But then, survival and pain frequently drove people beyond their expected or natural limits.

From out of the confusion, a young woman approached Dante. She pulled her long skirts up so she could run faster without tripping on them, and as she got closer, Dante could see she was flushed, bloody, and sooty. Her white blouse was torn in several places. She'd probably been hit in the face, as blood trickled from the corner of her mouth. She was a tiny wisp of a woman, thin and lithe everywhere except her huge, obviously pregnant belly. In her right hand she held a large cudgel—not really a formal weapon; it just looked like a piece of firewood that had been handy. Dante could see it was stained red.

He dismounted as she got closer, and although he didn't yet raise his sword, he held it ready, wary even of a woman in this strange place. She stopped a little distance away and eyed him, panting. She looked over her shoulder. Dante followed her gaze and saw one of the unarmed men had spotted them. He trudged toward them. He must have been injured, for he walked slowly and stiffly, as though it caused him pain.

The pregnant woman looked back to Dante. "We have to go, sir."

He had ridden for days in a generally southeast direction from Budapest, and he really had no idea what tribe or clan he was among at this point. But he knew he was nowhere near Italy or any other civilized race, so he was shocked to hear something he could decipher as a language somewhere between Latin and Italian. The vowel sounds she made were different than he was used to hearing, and the endings of the words were not quite like either Italian or Latin, but he could understand her. Even given their dire and violent situation, he couldn't help but ask, "You speak Italian?"

"What? No, sir." She again looked over her shoulder. "The horses are all gone. You have to take me, sir. I can't outrun them forever. Not like I am. And now the army has come, we'll all die."

She turned and moved closer to Dante, so they both stood facing the unarmed man who continued walking toward them. Still eyeing the woman's bloody piece of firewood, Dante turned his attention to the man. He could see his mouth hung open, and both his arms were bloody, together with much of his torso. He favored his one leg and all his movements seemed strained, forced, unnatural. Dante now realized the constant moaning he heard came from this man and some of the others. He was making an animal sound continuously, as he kept his vacant eyes fixed on the woman. Dante raised his sword. "Stop." His voice sounded small, polite, and impotent through the din of the moaning and battle. "Leave her alone."

The man showed no interest in him, no fear at his blade, no recognition even, but kept all his attention on the woman. He shuffled toward her and raised his arms, as if to grab her. Dante took a step and thrust his blade into the man's chest, then withdrew it. Although there was dried blood all over him, this new wound didn't bleed fresh.

The man didn't flinch. It had been a good attack, a stab in the region of the man's heart that had gone clean through to his back. He should have gone down immediately, dead or at least unable to breathe and on the brink of death, but he showed no signs of noticing the wound whatsoever.

"What are you doing?" the woman shouted. "Don't you know how to fight them?"

The man was nearly on her as she raised her club in both hands. With a shriek she brought it down on his head. He staggered back, his eyes rolling upward, his jaw dropping more. She pulled the club back over her right shoulder, still holding it with both hands, and delivered another blow, this one to the side of his head. It made him stagger, turn, and fall to the ground, facedown. She'd swung so hard it threw her off balance and spun her more than halfway around. The man didn't seem able to get up, but his left leg still twitched, and his hands clawed weakly at the ground, even though any of the three blows he just took from sword and club should have been enough to kill him. Then, like the men Dante had earlier seen savaging those who had fallen, the woman stood astride the man's back and brought the club down four more times on the back of his skull. Dante couldn't move or speak as he watched her reduce his head to a pile of hair, blood, brain, and bone that spread out in an irregular splotch on the ground. His leg and hands didn't move anymore.

The woman dropped her club next to the body as she stood up. Two more unarmed men were now approaching them. "Sir, now, we have to go," she said between ragged pants, breathing harder than before. "We can maybe fight off some of the *strigoi*, but if any of the men of the town see us, they'll kill us to get the horse and escape themselves." Dante didn't understand the word she'd used, *strigoi*. It was very close to the Italian word for "witches," but that made no sense. The woman stepped away from the corpse and toward Dante. "My husband and son are dead. You have to help me, sir. I can't do it alone."

He hesitated, as another projectile crashed into a house and erupted. The smoke and heat were building around them, stinging his eyes.

He looked from the approaching men, to the grisly pile of flesh on the ground nearby, to the panting, sweating woman right next to him. Dante was a worldly man and had seen his fair share of the weird, the violent, and the senseless, but he had no way of comprehending any of the horrors happening around him. As he looked down at the woman, he caught the rank smell of her sweat, and it was the first reassuring thing he had sensed since the silence of the day had been shattered minutes before. Of course, she smelled terrified and profane, like the animal she had just shown herself to be. But mostly she smelled alive—and more importantly, like something that was *supposed* to be alive, something with a purpose or reason to exist, unlike everything else around them, which seemed like random chaos existing only as the negation of everything true and real.

He stepped past her as he sheathed his sword. He put his right foot in the stirrup and swung up on to the horse's back, then leaned down to extend his hand to her.

"Come," he said.

With difficulty she climbed up behind him. Dante had seen women sitting astride a horse before, but it still surprised him when she swung her left leg to the other side of the horse. Proper women didn't ride that way, and especially not with their legs on either side of a strange man; but proper women didn't beat men to death, either, so there were other things to consider at the moment. He pulled the reins to the left, and started the horse trotting away.

As the sounds of panic and death receded, Dante asked her, "Which way?"

"Into the woods, sir," she said, pointing off toward the forest Dante had seen on the other side of the road before discovering her besieged village. "The army probably cut off the road in either direction to kill anyone trying to escape. In the woods we can head towards the mountains. Perhaps it'll be harder for the troops or the *strigoi* to follow us. Perhaps we might survive."

Dante still didn't know what she was talking about, either in terms of whose army this was, or what she meant by *strigoi*, but now was not the time to ask. He pulled the reins and pointed the horse toward the trees. As they moved under the canopy, it did feel safer in the shadows. The woman's arms around his waist tightened. As improper as it was, it definitely felt better and safer than anything he'd experienced in years.

"And what will we do when we reach the mountains?"

Her head rested on his shoulder. "Go over them, I suppose."

"And what's on the other side?"

"I have no idea."

"No idea, and yet you choose to go forward? You are a woman of great faith, then?"

"Sir, there are hundreds of men and monsters trying to kill me. Why would the unknown frighten me? I must either have faith, or else sit down, curse God, and die. I'm not ready to do that."

Her swollen belly was pressed up against his lower back. It did not feel soft, compliant, and sensual, the way a woman's body usually did, the way he thought a woman's body was supposed to feel. Instead, it was hard, insistent, resolute. And Dante felt sure that, like all women, she was much more aware of her body and the signals it was sending than a man ever could be.

"I understand," was all he could say to her as the horse picked its way between the trees and they went deeper into the silent shadows.

Chapter 3

"Her eyes were shining brighter than the Star;
And she began to say, gentle and low,
With voice angelical, in her own language . . ."
Dante, *Inferno*, 2.55-57

In a few hours they were far into the forest, embraced by its grim simplicity and, for the time being, insulated from all the madness of men and death. Before it got too dark, Dante stopped in a small clearing, tethering his horse and letting it graze on the grass. The woman helped him gather wood to build a fire. It was sure to be cold in the night, and the flames would keep wild animals at bay. She gathered mushrooms, some early berries, and nuts to help supplement their meager rations. There was a small stream nearby for water as well, its water icy, clear, and in some spots, deep.

While they were busy gathering wood, Dante studied her. Given their odd situation, he did so as discreetly as possible, out of respect. Even though she was of a much lower social class than he, Dante felt he had no right to judge or demean her. Dante's eye for detail—especially details related to beautiful, young women—was refined and acute enough that a few glances at her told him a great deal, put her into a context that related her both to this unknown, barbaric land into which he'd fallen, and compared her to things more familiar to him.

She was exceptionally thin and lithe—a small framed woman carrying no extra weight except what her pregnancy had put on her. Her arms were sinewy and, through the rips in her blouse, Dante could see the taut muscles of her back. He shivered when he remembered her savagery as she had killed the man. There was no doubt of her physical strength, or her determination to use it. Her face, on the other hand, was cherubic, probably from being pregnant, and with girlish features—small, dark brown eyes and long, thick, brown hair. She had dimples in her cheeks and her chin, an upturned nose, and a wide, thin-lipped mouth. She was clearly young, but Dante remembered she'd mentioned another son, so this wasn't her first child. She was probably in her late teens or early twenties.

Dante felt chilled then flushed when he realized she was about the same age as Beatrice was the second time he saw her in Florence, the time she had actually spoken to him and thoroughly enthralled him. He allowed himself a small, grateful smile for being granted such glimpses of feminine perfection. This woman seemed so much more physical and primal than Beatrice had been on the sunny streets of Florence, while Beatrice had seemed completely spiritual and sublime, compared to this sweating peasant in a dark forest. But at that moment it made no difference to him, filling him with awe at them both. As different as the two women clearly were, Dante knew there was something in both that made him want to serve them, earn their respect and affection, live up to his potential as a man. They had within themselves not merely the object of a man's desire, but the lure and hook that could draw him to desire something more, better, and higher than either them or himself, the same way the sun drew the tendrils of a plant upward, kept it alive, and filled it with the vital force to produce another of its kind.

The thought moved Dante from a small smile to a slight frown. He had never lived up to Beatrice, so why should today be any different? After seeing her a second time, he'd been inspired to write a poem about her. He'd called it *The New Life*, but his life had hardly been revived or improved by his writing it. In his mind he remained a weak, inconstant, and, most of all, petty and inconsequential man. The poem had only been a trifle, and he should have long ago exceeded it in beauty and depth, producing something worthy of Beatrice and the Lord she had served so much better and virtuously than he did. While he'd taken so long writing such a little, unimportant book, she had died, both of them already having married other, more suitable people. If in his comfortable, privileged, easy existence in Florence he had not been able to accomplish something great, beautiful, and heroic, how dare he think he might do something worthwhile for this poor woman here today, in this savage, deadly land? He could barely hope to save himself, let alone her.

Before they sat down by the fire they had built, Dante got a jacket out of the saddle bag and offered it to her. "Your blouse," he said, "it's torn. Put this on." The coarse, woolen, reddish-brown frock he always wore would be adequate for him, but modesty and practicality both called for something more for the woman, especially in her condition.

Without the danger and urgency of the deadly attack when they had first met, she now seemed acutely aware of the awkwardness of their situation, and the difference in their social standing. She blushed and looked down as she took the jacket from him. "Thank you, sir."

They sat down to eat the food she'd found, together with some bread and dried fruit he got out of the saddle bags. She didn't make eye contact, and sat on the opposite side of the fire.

Dante realized he still didn't know her name, so he asked her.

"Bogdana," she said, still looking down.

Dante nodded and restrained his grimace at such an ugly name, in case she did look his way. It was surely a further indication of the barbarity of this place—that anyone could even think to place such a discordant, three-syllable monstrosity on to such a beautiful creature. Back in Italy they gave better, more mellifluous names to types of pasta, or rodents, or even insects. "Beatrice" sounded exactly like what the person so named really was—a blessed person, a blessing to others. "Bogdana" sounded like some curse spat out when one stubbed one's toe or was gripped by an acute stomach cramp.

"What does this name mean?" he asked her.

"Gift of God, sir."

Dante continued to nod. Why quibble with the sounds and limitations of fleshly tongues and ears, if the meaning were so right and true?

After all, many blamed and mocked him for writing in Italian rather than Latin, for they thought his native language—even when it was the same as theirs!—was somehow low, vulgar, base. He would have to work on keeping that in mind when he spoke or thought of her.

"My name is Dante Alighieri."

"Yes, sir."

"Please, enough with the 'sir.' It's not necessary. We're here, trying to survive. There's no need to follow such rules. Is that all right?"

"Yes." She faltered and left it at that.

"I still don't understand what language you're speaking, why we can communicate, if you don't know Italian?"

She looked up and shrugged. "I don't know either. I speak what I've always spoken, what I learned as a child. I don't know why it's similar to your language."

"What is this place called?"

She finally met his gaze fully and again shrugged. "To the west is Hungary. Some say we belong to their kingdom. Some say we are Moldavians and should unite with other nearby people. We have always called ourselves Romani. I do not know what you would call us."

Dante thought perhaps "Romani" was a clue that the people here remembered, however inchoately and indistinctly, that they and their language were descended from Roman invaders, long ago. There was no way to check the theory. They would just have to accept that it made their present situation much easier, since they could communicate.

"But who is your king, your monarch? Who sent those troops that were attacking your village?"

"We have no king, if you mean someone who rules this whole land in all directions for many days' journey. Here there are just local rulers, *boyars*, who rule their little parts of the country. The *boyar* must've sent troops to destroy our village, or perhaps the plague is so widespread that several *boyars* banded together to attack us."

Just as Bogdana's name seemed oddly incongruent, Dante thought that word, *boyar*, sounded a good deal more gentle and peaceful than what he had witnessed the *boyar*'s men doing back at the village.

"Some people must have fled our village when the *strigoi* attacked.

They must've gone to the city and asked for help. But when the monsters attack, the only help is for troops to come in and wipe out the whole area. They should've known that and stayed with us to fight. We would've had a better chance than we do now, with both the army and the *strigoi* after us."

"You keep saying that word—*strigoi.* It must be different between our languages, because the only word I can think of in my language that sounds like that means 'witch,' a person who uses bad magic."

Bogdana smiled. "Yes, people used to think the *strigoi* were magic, some evil spirits or cursed, sinful people. But that's just superstition and nonsense. They are a disease, a plague. They are simply the dead, who rise up and kill the living." She lowered her voice. "And eat them." She raised her eyebrows. "You have never heard of this before?"

Dante shook his head. "No, never. I have never heard of such a thing anywhere else I have traveled."

She nodded. "Well, that is a good thing, I suppose. They are a curse only to us, and the rest of the world is spared. Well, good for you all. Not so good for us. And not so good for you and me today."

"So the man you killed back at the village, you're saying he was already dead?" Dante could not hide the relief in his voice. It was much more palpable than the shock and wonder at speaking of a dead man being killed a second time.

"Yes, he was my neighbor. I knew him. I could never do such a thing to a living man!" She lowered her eyebrows and a hint of a glare rose in her cheeks and eyes. "What kind of monster do you think I am?"

"Oh, no, I didn't mean anything like that," he stammered. "I'm sorry. I've never heard of walking dead people. I was just surprised."

Bogdana's eyebrows rose again and she looked less angry. "Well, I suppose, since you'd never seen the living dead before, you were confused. But, make no mistake, Romani are no different than you. We raise our children and tend our crops and, when we can, we bury our dead and mourn them. But when the plague strikes and the dead walk, we do the same as you would. We fight them any way we can in order to survive."

"I understand." He found himself saying that to her once more, and thought he did understand her, better than he had anyone for some time. She was simple and unadorned, unashamed and without guile. More than love or attraction, he felt mostly gratitude for being allowed to meet her. "You said your family was killed?"

She lowered her head. "My husband and son died. I am just grateful I did not have to take care of them when they passed, end their suffering. I don't think I could have done that." When she looked up, her gaze seemed more intense. "May I ask you something? A favor? It's quite important."

"Of course."

"If I die, before you kill me again, please try to get my baby out of me. I think I'm far enough along that it might live. I don't know. It's always hard, even in a normal birth. I know it'll be very messy and unpleasant, but someone needs to try. It's just not fair, otherwise. When adults die, that's one thing. It's to be expected. They've lived, they've sinned, they understand what life is. But a baby that's never seen the sun? That's something else. It deserves a chance."

Dante stared at her, as mesmerized and unblinking as when he'd watched her pound her neighbor's head into a greasy, grey stain on the ground, for what she was suggesting was nearly as incredible and unearthly as that act of violence. She was coldly, rationally making preparations for a nearly complete stranger to butcher her, reach into her still warm guts, and pull out her baby. Dante now saw what real survival and real love were, and how all the sacrifices he'd made were as empty and shallow as the survival they'd secured for him—small, ghostly imitations of life and love and beauty. He felt embarrassment for his meager existence. This tiny woman knew the real depths of life, while he had always played safely at the edges, not risking or suffering enough.

"I don't know if I'm able," he said, "but I'll do everything I can, as if he were another Caesar."

She smiled more broadly than he'd seen her do before. "Oh, nothing so grand as that. Just a baby, but one that is meant to live, I think. And thank you for agreeing to such a thing. If you've never known this plague, I know it must be difficult."

It was turning colder. Dante got a blanket from the horse. He and Bogdana sat at the base of a tree near the fire, leaning against the trunk and slightly against each other, with the blanket wrapped around them. Her breathing felt good to him, as her head and belly had earlier, when they rested against him with all their strength and reliability. Stealing a glance at her, then at the stars wheeling above, he fell into a strangely untroubled sleep.

Chapter 4

"A friend of mine, and not the friend of fortune,
Upon the desert slope is so impeded
Upon his way, that he has turned through terror,
And may, I fear, already be . . . lost."
Dante, *Inferno*, 2.61-64

Dante awoke to see Bogdana already up. She scattered the ashes of their fire about and tried to cover them with dirt, leaves, and pine needles. He stood and looked around. There were some muffled sounds of birds in the distance. Dante sniffed the air and discovered the faint smell of smoke—the same sickly kind as before. It seemed to be coming from the east, the direction from which they had come. They would have to keep heading west, further into the forest.

Bogdana noticed him. "Good morning," she said. Not friendly, exactly, but not wary or deferent, either, as she had been before. She just seemed comfortably familiar, and a little harried with her activities. Of course, Dante did not know the right tone for someone who'd asked him to rip her open like a fish, if it should become necessary. The tone of someone who'd slept peacefully through the night in physical contact with someone of the opposite sex, but without any talk of romance or guilt between them, was also unknown, disorienting territory. Things were not like this in Florence.

"Good morning," he returned her simple greeting.

"We shouldn't have slept at the same time." She focused on the purely practical. "The walking dead may be in the area. We don't know how far they've spread. They may have been pushed ahead of the army as it moves into the valley. The dead move around at night. They don't sleep."

"I'm sorry. I didn't know."

"No, it's my fault. I should've remembered, but I was just too exhausted to think of it. We're lucky they didn't get us. We should be grateful. Perhaps you are favored by God."

Dante smiled at her. "I don't know. The pope had me driven from my home. I can never go back to my family or he will have me killed—burned alive, in fact. I don't feel very favored."

"The pope? You mean, the anti-Christ?"

Dante hadn't reckoned with how far east he'd traveled in the last few days. He was now in lands beyond Roman Catholicism, where they were taught a quite different version of history, of who were the heroes or villains of Christendom, of who really held the keys entrusted to Peter. As with so much about this strange, beautiful woman, it put his problems in a different light. "I'm sure you call him that for a different reason than I do, but yes, that is the one."

"But if you are the enemy of God's enemy, some would say that makes you His friend."

"Let us hope so."

Bogdana brushed the ashes from her skirts. "I tried to hide what was left of our fire. I don't think the dead can track us. They're not very intelligent or observant about such things, but we shouldn't leave any unnecessary signs for the soldiers. They'll be looking to kill anyone they can find, so that the plague doesn't spread further."

Dante took some bread and fruit from the saddle bags, and Bogdana gathered some food from the forest. They shared these provisions before Dante mounted the horse and pulled Bogdana up behind him. He nudged the horse and they started off again.

"If we keep heading west, what will we come to, before the mountains?"

"It's a long valley that runs east-west. It narrows the further west you go. I have heard there are some villages and towns in the valley, but I've never been there. Perhaps we should find them, warn them of the approaching army, and ask if the dead are already in the area. Maybe they can help us, or plead with the army commander for mercy. Sometimes they only kill the dead people, and the ones who've been bitten by them and are dying."

Dante tried not to let naïve hope creep into his voice, but he couldn't help it. As bitter as he could be when alone, something wouldn't let him be as cynical and despairing in front of other people, and made him seem quite childishly optimistic sometimes.

"Really?"

He could feel her lean back, pulling her head away from him, though her stomach still pressed against him. "Well, not very often. Most of the time they're quite thorough. Usually the troops surround the city and destroy everything." Her belly was much more reassuring to him than her words.

"Oh."

"But maybe we can stay ahead of them. We'll see."

"Yes, I suppose we shall."

"So long as you remember your promise, there isn't much more we can do."

"I know. I won't forget."

The ground sloped upward slightly as they made their way deeper into the valley. The birds Dante had heard earlier sounded louder, and Bogdana leaned closer to him.

Chapter 5

These miscreants, who never were alive,
Were naked, and were stung exceedingly
By gadflies and by hornets that were there.
Dante, *Inferno*, 3.64-66

Dante kept as fast a pace as he could, but they never quite got free of the smell of smoke following them up the valley, though sometimes it seemed fainter. Looking around as he rode, he saw no other signs of danger from either the living or the dead. He only spied the trees and the occasional squirrel or, in the distance, a deer. The terrain was getting steeper and more difficult as they went. Dante thought now it was more imperative they find a settlement, so they could pick up whatever road went through the village and begin to follow it. It would help them make better time.

By late morning they had reached one of the towns in the valley. It was a decent sized settlement, with a vast expanse of the forest cleared away for their crops. Looking at the larger buildings, Dante thought the valley must offer some material wealth to the people there—probably from mining, quarrying, and timber. This early in the year, the fields they rode through were bare, as well as devoid of any people. But up ahead, coming from among the buildings of the town proper, Dante could hear loud, angry voices and the general rumbling of a crowd. Thankfully, however, he did not hear the moaning of the dead

Dante held the horse back, and looked over his shoulder at

Bogdana. "Do you still want to go there?" he asked. "We can skirt around the edge of the town. I'm sure we can find the road on the other side and get moving faster. It might be safer. There seems to be something going on there."

Bogdana looked past him, then around at the empty fields, and sniffed the air. Dante was quite sure she noticed the smoke, and evaluated its proximity and danger just as carefully as he had been doing all morning. "We have to," she concluded. "They may still not know the danger. We have to try."

Dante nodded and urged the horse forward. They passed between some two and three-storey buildings, as they entered the town on a street leading toward a central square. People looked down on them from some of the windows, and there were people on the street. All of them either headed toward the town square, or stood about, looking down the street to see what was going on there. All were on foot, and they made room for Dante's horse, but all eyed him suspiciously. He remembered how, years before, he had seen troops leaving the besieged castle of Caprona after a truce had been negotiated. The troops had to march between the ranks of the opposing army. Dante thought he now knew much better how they must have felt, surrounded and outnumbered.

The crowds became too thick for him to continue once they reached the edge of the square. At the corners of the square were four enormous oak trees. A white church occupied the middle of the area. To Dante, the church's architecture looked strange but graceful in its simplicity, with a low dome in the middle, and two steeples at the front of the building. The crowd gathered around the church was agitated, restless, seething with motion punctuated by shouts. Their attention was focused on a thick, wooden pole sticking up from the ground in front of the church. A woman was tied to it, with a pile of wood all around her. The wood looked wet, and even from this distance, Dante could smell the oil they had poured on it. His heart sank, knowing death and cruelty had arrived there in advance of the army, and the horror was going to begin even before the troops arrived to slaughter everyone. Dante tried to move forward to get a better look at what was happening, while still staying close to the street they had rode in on. He was relieved to see the crowd did not close in behind them.

Besides the doomed woman and the members of the crowd, there were two other figures there that seemed to have some special role. In front of the steps of the church, near a flagpole from which a colorful banner hung limply, there was a man in a floppy, burgundy hat and a dark, leather jacket of slightly better cut and quality than the rest of the citizenry. His clothes didn't look clerical or military, so he must have been some secular, civil authority. If not the mayor or judge of the town, he probably was at least some minor official, like a beadle or guild president or whatever equivalent these people had—one minor enough that he wouldn't have been warned to flee already by his superiors. Dante presumed he was nominally in charge of these proceedings.

The other figure he could pick out was the only other person there on horseback, a.young man, probably just a year or two older than Bogdana. He was powerfully built, with long blonde hair. He sat astride a brown horse and kept near the woman, trying to stay between her and the crowd, sometimes shouting back at them. From his clothing, he was clearly a soldier. His long sword was out, and he was strong enough to wield it with one hand, even though it was quite large. Dante had seen others with similar weapons training to use them with two hands.

Dante tried to make out what the people were shouting, but he could not understand their speech as clearly as he did Bogdana's. He did hear the word *strigoi* several times among their shouts and the crowd's general murmur. But the thrust of the exchange became clear quickly enough.

"She's possessed!"

"She's brought a curse on us! Her daughter died during the last plague, and now she's taking it out on us!"

"If we burn her, we'll be saved!"

"Leave her alone!" the young soldier shouted back at them, waving his sword menacingly and skillfully enough that they hung back. A rock bounced off his chest, but other than that, the crowd hadn't yet built up the recklessness for an attack. "She's done nothing wrong!

She's just an old woman! How can you people do this? Has the plague made you all go mad?"

Dante knew exactly how they could do this, and unfortunately, it had nothing to do with madness or any physical plague. Corpses getting up and walking around could easily qualify as "mad" in his estimation, and he'd never heard of such a thing happening ever before, except in the Holy Scriptures, where it had been a blessed miracle brought about by God and not the horror he had seen in this alien land. But people hurting those weaker than they were, in order to make themselves feel better or more secure? One could see that every day, in every city, in every land he'd ever visited or read about. He envied the young soldier his naiveté, thinking it would be nice to see such human evil as somehow inconceivable or aberrant.

Dante studied the woman tied to the stake. Her hair wreathed her head like a cloud exploding upward—wild, unkempt, and grey. There were twigs and ribbons in it, as though she collected these and decorated herself with them. Her clothes were similarly motley, made out of different scraps and layers, with nutshells, pinecones, and even animal bones hanging off of them. Like many who had sunk into madness and destitution, her age was impossible to determine. She was filthy and haggard, but there was no telling how much of it came from age, and how much was the result of no one taking care of her, including herself. Often people like her lived out of doors, and wherever Dante was at the moment, its climate seemed harsh enough that it would take a toll on someone living without shelter. Her frame still looked strong, and she didn't appear to be maimed or crippled. She could've been slightly younger than Dante, or many years older.

She didn't seem at all afraid of what was happening, though it wasn't because she was oblivious. On the contrary, she was very alert, looking all around and frequently breaking out into laughter or some incoherent song. Perhaps she was so far gone in madness she didn't understand she was going to die, in one of the worst ways people had devised for one another. Dante shivered; it was the same sentence placed on him in Florence, and he was about to see exactly what being burned alive was like. At least for this poor woman, death and pain were no longer objects of fear, if she could even understand what they were. He shook his head, wondering how such small graces from God found such enormous shoals of human wickedness on which to spend themselves in seeming impotence and humiliation.

"I've done nothing wrong?" the woman tied to the stake called out after the young soldier spoke up in her defense. "Silly boy! I've been bad! My whole family's been bad from the beginning!" Perhaps the townspeople had beaten or cajoled her into "confessing" before tying her to the stake. It was common enough in these situations. "I had two brothers! They both disappeared. I don't know where. Sometimes I go out in the field and the ground's wet, all wet. Nothing to be done about it." She laughed so shrilly even her tormentors quieted down, out of surprise and perhaps a little embarrassment at what they were doing to this obviously harmless, deranged creature. "The field's the thing, isn't it? Everything bad always happens in our field. There's mandrake and nightshade there and all manner of wicked, evil things. Perhaps you could bury me there, friends, and that'd be an end to all my family's wickedness."

Maybe she did still know, at some level, that she was going to die—but how then could she be so cheerful about it? Dante wondered if he could get through the crowd and save her from the flames with a quick and merciful death by his sword, though he was not sure whether such "mercy" would itself be culpable. He felt sick and dizzy, and he swayed slightly at the enormity of such mundane, reflexive evil.

"She admits it!" someone shouted. "See! She even admits it!"

"She doesn't know what she's saying!" the young soldier shouted back. More rocks hit him and, this time, the woman as well. She laughed.

"You there!" Dante heard someone shout, and he turned to see he was being addressed by the man near the church steps. "You, stranger, what are you doing here? Do you bring news? What is going on outside our town? Is the plague contained?"

"I come from far away," Dante answered. "But yesterday I found this woman," he gestured at Bogdana, "as her village was being destroyed by the army and by the walking dead. You have to leave, move west, or the army will kill you all. This woman you are tormenting has nothing to do with this plague. It's the army you need to worry about. Please just leave her and flee your town as quickly as possible."

"He's lying!" someone else shouted. "The army will leave us alone, once they know we've killed the evil one among us. They'll be glad we did it. Rid the land of her corruption! She admitted she and her kind have brought evil on us."

The crowd was now dividing its attentions between menacing the young soldier, the madwoman, and Dante. They also looked to the man by the church steps for some approval of their actions. Dante gripped his sword but didn't draw it yet. He didn't think he could intimidate the crowd as much as the soldier did, so he didn't want to draw on them till there was no choice. Some of them might finally figure out escape was a better plan than their superstitions of tribal scapegoating. Then they would see the usefulness of his horse, and the advisability of killing him and Bogdana in order to get it.

"Please, sir," he said as diplomatically as possible to the town official. "You seem like an educated, reasonable, godly man. Please explain to these good people that I'm right, and they need to leave as quickly as possible. Killing this wretched creature will accomplish nothing."

The man on the church steps shook his head and shrugged. "I'm sorry. I have no control over them. The mayor and the priest are gone. Perhaps they could have done something, but not me. The people have decided what they think is best to solve our town's problems. I am powerless over them."

"Then why are you here at all?" the soldier shouted to him. "You saw everything they did with her. They asked you if it was legal or not. How can you say now it's not under your control?"

"Well, I did advise them on matters of the law, but I know nothing of whether or not this will solve our problems with the living dead. But if the people think it will, they're entitled to that opinion and they may be right. Who knows what the truth is in this situation?"

"Yes! We are right. He said so." The crowd cheered at this, and this time Dante and Bogdana were hit by stones as well.

Bogdana leaned forward. "We need to get out of here," she whispered. "There's nothing you can do for her. You're just going to get us killed too."

His stomach turned over and he flushed crimson, but he knew she was right. The crowd was turning uglier and bolder by the moment, but so far their wrath was mostly directed at the woman and the soldier. Dante and Bogdana still had a good chance at escape, if they didn't invite more attention to themselves, or get drawn deeper into the crowded square. Dante pulled on the reins and his horse took a couple steps back. A few steps further from the square, and the crowd would be thin enough near them that Dante could yank the reins, turn the horse around, and be out of there.

The young soldier saw he was being left alone as the woman's only defense. "No!" he shouted to Dante. "You can't. You know this isn't right!"

"So do they," Dante shouted. The horse took another step back. They were almost in the clear. "It doesn't seem to be stopping them."

He heard the crackling he had heard at Bogdana's village, though louder this time. Dante looked up as another one of the flaming projectiles crashed into the top of one of the four, giant oak trees. Some dried, dead leaves left from last year were still on the tree, and these ignited immediately, as the main trunk bent from the impact, then the top part of it snapped off. A flaming mass of branches fell into the crowd near the stake, together with the burning bits of the exploded projectile. The people scattered and screamed, and Dante could see something more than just the flames was tormenting them. They were waving their arms over their heads as they ran, and as some of them crashed into the other onlookers nearer Dante, he saw they were being attacked by a swarm of hornets or wasps. There must have been a nest in the tree, and the creatures were released when it fell to the ground. Thankfully, the enraged insects seemed focused on those they had first attacked, and none of them broke off their pursuit to sting Dante and Bogdana.

Dante yanked the horse around and looked over his shoulder, back at the pandemonium of the square. The burning branches ignited the oil-soaked wood around the stake. The flames leaped all around the crazed woman, and her clothes were already burning, though oddly she seemed calmer than before. Dante could see the young soldier's horse was nearly uncontrollable, panicked by the fire and the screaming crowd, and it bucked and reared back, almost throwing him.

Dante heard the crackling sound again right before one of the church steeples exploded in fiery sparks and masonry dust. With a sound like some giant piece of pottery breaking, the tower fell forward. If the town official had been just a step closer to the church, or a few steps further away, he might have been safe. But he wasn't, and the top third of the tower fell right on him. Dante felt no inclination to contain a grim smile.

The madwoman screamed, though not in agony, but in something that chilled and disoriented Dante more, for it sounded like delight or even pleasure. "At night I see a dragon, too. It's only a small one, though. It lives east of the town." The flames climbed higher around her, sometimes completely obscuring Dante's view of her. "Now can I have some apples?" She laughed as she writhed against her bonds. For a moment, she looked right into Dante's eyes, and he was shocked to see her gaze was not filled with pain or terror, but with some manic, erotic excitement that seethed then burst forth from her—a frenzied glee as the cruelty of the crowd smashed into her innocence, like a hammer onto an anvil, and both these primal, unquenchable forces together savaged her fragile body and broken mind. Her eyes sparkled and her laughter rose above the flames and the screams from the crowd. "Don't go near the elderberry, Mother. Sometimes there's a pig that climbs its branches! He's a wily one, with red eyes and sharp tusks. But don't hurt him, Mother. He doesn't know any better. He thinks he can fly, like he used to. Wheeee!"

The soldier's horse reared up one more time, then he finally got control over it, pointing it right toward Dante and making it crash through the scattering remnants of the crowd. He pulled up next to Dante, panting and flushed. "Come!" he shouted. "We have to get out of here!"

The soldier rode off, but Dante couldn't tear himself away from the horror of the dying woman and the senseless, frenzied chaos of the people dashing all about the square, some of them on fire, some trampling others under foot, some swatting and screaming as the wasps stung them over and over. And beyond the flames, he now saw other people shuffling in to the square. These people did not seem panicked, but moved slowly, stiffly, and deliberately. Although the waves of heat coming off the flames made it hard to see clearly, it looked to him as though these people entering the square were covered in blood. The one closest seemed to be missing his left arm. Dante could hear their moaning, underneath and all around the other sounds of death and pain assailing him.

Bogdana tightened her grip around Dante's waist. "Go, go! You can't help her! They've all gone mad!"

Pulling back on the reins, he closed his eyes and could barely keep from sobbing. He kicked the animal hard to get them out of there. He could hear the woman's laughter a long time after they had left the town behind. Her eyes he would see in nightmares all his life.

Chapter 6

"These have no longer any hope of death;
And this blind life of theirs is so debased,
They envious are of every other fate."
Dante, *Inferno*, 3.46-48

Dante's horse galloped after the soldier. They veered to the right, circling around the town, back towards the west, away from the direction of the advancing army. There was no telling if they were already surrounded. Dante narrowed his eyes and scanned the nearest trees, expecting to be hit with an arrow or crossbow bolt at any moment, but for now nothing bad happened. He looked ahead and saw the soldier turn and glance over his shoulder at them, then the soldier kicked his horse to increase its speed. Dante tried to match him. His horse—more so than the soldier's—would not be able to keep this pace up for long, but they had to get as far from there as quickly as possible.

Crashing through a stand of fruit trees, they finally came to the road Dante had hoped to find when they reached the town. There were more fruit trees on the other side of the road, and looking back toward the town, Dante saw people running toward them. The way they moved, they obviously were not dead.

"Help us!" the man in the lead of the crowd approaching them shouted. He held a shovel in his right hand as he ran. "You must help us get out of here!"

A woman was close behind him. "Yes, help us! We didn't know the army was so close! We didn't know they would do this!" She looked better dressed than most of the townspeople Dante had seen, and he noticed she had something metal in her right hand. It looked like a brass candlestick.

The soldier still had his sword out. Dante now drew his. They looked at each other and hesitated.

"Get us out of here," Bogdana said to Dante. "They just want the horses. They'll tear us limb from limb quicker than the dead would, just to save themselves. You know they will."

"It doesn't seem right," the soldier said.

"None of this seems right," Dante said.

The townspeople were closing in on them, the closest maybe thirty feet away, when two dead men staggered out from among the fruit trees and attacked the people as they ran. One of them grabbed the man with the shovel. He screamed as the dead man bit into his left arm, then he brought the shovel down on the back of his attacker's skull. The dead man slumped to the ground, but the other one grabbed the man with the shovel and they fell to the ground, grappling, growling, and cursing.

The people further back in the crowd screamed and changed direction when they saw the dead, running back toward the burning town, even though that seemed a more certain death. The woman with the candlestick was still headed toward them when another dead man lunged from among the fruit trees and fell on her. She shrieked and pulled away from him, the sleeve of her blouse tearing off in his grip.

The soldier turned his horse toward her. "I can't stand and watch this. I don't care." He charged off toward the fighting in the road.

Dante tried to get off his horse. It was an awkward dismount with a second person, and he landed in a heap, still holding the reins. He scrambled to his feet, and handed the reins to Bogdana. "You—get to the edge of the forest and wait for us."

She looked down at him. "You're a fool, but I won't leave you. I'll stay right here. Hurry."

"All right."

The soldier was next to the woman and her dead assailant. The dead man had a hold of her arm, and she kept swinging the candlestick at his head, but he was warding off the blows with his other arm, so they continued to fight. The soldier raised his sword, but the way the pair kept moving around he couldn't strike without hitting the woman.

Dante circled around them, but he had the same problem trying to attack without hitting the woman. With a surprisingly dexterous move, the dead man got a hold of the candlestick and lunged for her forearm, sinking his teeth into it. Dante winced at the dark blood surging out of the wound, welling up around the man's teeth and lips, and at the woman's mortal howl of pain. He steeled himself, grabbed the dead man's hair with his free hand, and with an animal cry, he shoved his sword into the man's left eye. Dante was pressed up next to the injured woman and gripping the dead man's hair. For an instant, all three of them tensed and trembled in the terrible exchange between them—the woman with agony and the horrible surge of mortality, the man with the last, feeble ebb of life, and Dante with the thrill of killing, of feeling the life spasming out of something monstrous and deadly in his grip.

Dante let go of the man, withdrawing his blade and stepping back. The twice-dead corpse fell to the ground, as the woman slumped toward the other side, clutching her arm above the wound. Dante looked over to where the other man, the one with the shovel, was getting up. He was covered in blood, having just finished the messy job of pounding the dead man's head into the road with his shovel. His bitten left arm hung down at his side. He dragged the shovel behind him on the ground as he limped toward them. Where he wasn't smeared with blood, his skin was deathly white. "Please help me," he rasped. It was already starting to sound like the moan the dead made.

Dante thought he heard the woman weeping, but when he took a step toward her she looked up and snarled at him. Perhaps she had been crying, her eyes were red, but now they were full only of hatred and blame. "I asked you to help us," she growled. "You'd help that miserable beggarwoman, but you let me be eaten alive? What kind of man are you?" Dante had no answer for her.

Bogdana rode up, slipping off the horse next to him, offering the reins. The soldier turned his horse around, back toward the woods.

"They're bitten. There's no hope for them," she said quietly. "We have to go now."

"Yes, you'd say that, wouldn't you?" the woman snapped at her. "Go ahead! He defended that old whore. I guess you're his young one! It must be the kind of woman they like, where he's from. Leave me here alone to die. I don't care."

Dante sheathed his sword, mounted his horse, and pulled Bogdana up behind him. As he turned the horse toward the forest, the man with the shovel collapsed next to the woman in the road, while a projectile hit one of the buildings on this side of the town and exploded. As he rode away, Dante looked back. The two figures on the road faced away from each other, whether out of shame or pain, Dante would never know, though it seemed infinitely to increase their wretchedness in his eyes. Each of them looked completely alone, even though they were pressed up against one another.

Chapter 7

When some among them I had recognized,
I looked, and I beheld the shade of him
Who made through cowardice the great refusal.
Dante, *Inferno*, 3.58-60

Surging ahead through the forest, Dante thought they might have actually slipped through the army's lines surrounding the town, as there was no sign of anyone else, living or dead, on the road or anywhere near it. After a while, both horses slowed to a trot, and then to a walking gait they could maintain without exhausting themselves.

The soldier dropped back till they were riding alongside one another. "What are your names?"

"Dante."

"Bogdana."

"My name is Radovan." Dante thought that at least the men's names sounded as bad as the women's. "The army and the living dead destroyed your village?"

"Yes," Bogdana answered. "My family is dead. This man tried to help me."

"I am sorry. I was in the army that did this. I thought we had to, to get rid of the dead and free our land of plague. Killing the dead is one thing—it's bad enough, since they look just like regular people, some of them even children. But it has to be done. And I don't think they feel it so much, when you kill them. They seem numb, no longer really human. But the villagers, pleading for their lives—I just couldn't anymore. So I left during the night. I tried to help those people in the town, warn them, maybe have some of them escape into the mountains at least."

"What happened, then? Who was that poor woman?" Dante asked.

"You saw them, how crazed they were with all their ignorance and fear. I got to their town early this morning, and they were already dragging that poor, old, madwoman around, screaming how she was to blame. And that little dandy of a deputy, vice assistant, district councilman, or whatever the hell he claimed to be, strutted around like a peacock during all of it, but he was more of a gelding, is my guess." Dante smirked and Bogdana snickered at this. It was the closest any of them had come to laughter in some time.

Radovan continued. "They kept looking to him to validate everything, and he kept saying he had no authority, no jurisdiction. But then he'd tell them that *if* he were in authority, *this* is how he'd go about it, and then he'd wave them away and say no, no, he didn't mean for them to actually *do* it. I kept telling them to run, to give this all up, but they ignored me, except to occasionally ask some practical question, like how big was the army, or how far away it was. I'd tell them I didn't know, more troops were arriving every day, since the plague was so bad. They were close, but it was hard to estimate how long it would take them to move. The trebuchets take a long time to pack and reassemble, and sometimes they break and have to be fixed. Never mind if the army camp is attacked by the dead and they have to fight them off before moving on to the next village. So I kept trying to reason with them, until they were actually ready to light the fire around her. That's when I drew my sword and thought enough is enough. I'd rather fight them than let them do this. I left the army, and could be killed for it. How could I just let these people do worse than the army was doing? At least the soldiers just kill people. They don't torture anyone." He cast a sideways look at Dante. It was not quite as accusatory and condemning as that of the woman with the candlestick, but nearly so, and with more petulant, prideful hurt behind it. "That's when you showed up. You might have done more, you know."

Dante wondered how much more blame he would find in this

strange land, where so far he had done little else beside try to help people. "I know. I'm sorry. Really, I am."

"We'd all be dead if he had," Bogdana said coldly. "And we nearly died again, just now, because you had to try to do more than you can."

The petulance flared up into real vindictiveness now. "I wasn't talking to you, woman."

Dante pulled on the reins. "Don't use that tone with her. If you want to make up for destroying her village, fine, but stop insulting her." Even with women who rode astride a stranger's horse, and beat men to death like they were pounding the wash on a stone next to the river, there were still rules of what things a man was not to tolerate being done or said to them.

"Oh, enough!" Bogdana said. She slid off Dante's horse, landing awkwardly then falling. She got up and brushed herself off as she took a couple steps away from them, into the woods. "Stop it, both of you, or I'll take my chances by myself. I really don't need to hear which of you is more of a man, or who defends helpless women better! Stop with all your morality and honor and shame and guilt. We're way past those, all right? Can we just agree to work together to stay alive?"

Dante was much more taken aback that a woman would refuse an offer of protecting her honor than he was that a man might insult her. But, as usual, this half-wild woman made more sense in the given situation than the rules he had been raised to follow. He glanced back to Radovan, who gazed at Bogdana, looking just as shocked as Dante had been. The soldier looked warily at him.

"I want her to stay alive," Dante said. "If there are other people who aren't trying to kill us, I will try to help them too, but my first obligation is to her. I promised her."

Radovan nodded. "I will help you two survive. You have my word." He looked at Bogdana. "I am sorry, Miss. I have hurt you enough by what I did before. I will help you now in any way I can."

"Thank you," she said as she let Dante help her back up on to the horse. "You two seem like good men. Don't let all your rules get in the way of doing what's right."

They moved westward along the road. "I suppose we should keep heading west and try to stay ahead of the army," Radovan said. "Get to the mountains and try to get over them. Do you have any plan other than that?"

"No," Dante answered. "It was all we had come up with as well."

"Sometimes simple plans are the best," Radovan agreed. Dante thought optimism might come more naturally to him than it did to other people, and this seemed to him a good thing at the moment.

Chapter 8

And ready are they to pass o'er the river,
Because celestial Justice spurs them on,
So that their fear is turned into desire.
Dante, *Inferno*, 3.124-26

It was the middle of the afternoon when they reached the banks of a broad river. The road turned and they followed the river upstream. The water looked too deep, and the current too strong, for them to cross on their own. Dante wondered if they'd be able to follow it on this bank, or whether there was a bridge somewhere, when Radovan explained there was a ferry up ahead they could use to cross.

The ferry boat was a simple one, a large raft that, at the moment, was on the other side of the river. As they got closer, he could see there was a rope across the river. He couldn't see all the details of it this far away, but from having seen many small ferries that worked this way, he could guess the rope ran through hooks or eyelets on the boat, and by pulling on it, the ferryman could take the boat back and forth across the river. It was a simple and effective arrangement, so long as the river didn't have a lot of boats traveling on it to snag on the rope, and so long as the traffic needing to cross the river wasn't too great.

Radovan, Bogdana, and Dante arrived at the crossing. Looking across the river, Dante saw people on the ferry boat. They seemed to be milling around, but they were too far away for Dante to shout to them, or to see exactly what they were doing.

"What if they don't pull the boat over to our side?" he asked. "They might be afraid of the plague, and won't be letting more people across. Can we just follow the river up the valley without crossing it?"

"Not easily," Radovan said. "The terrain gets very rough on this side. It'd slow us down too much, and then we wouldn't be moving away from the army, but across its path. They're coming straight west, as we have been. We need to keep straight up the valley as far as we can, to stay ahead of them."

"Is there another place to cross the river?"

Radovan shook his head. "Not for a long ways. The river's swollen this time of year, from spring rains and the snow melting up in the mountains. You have to get up higher, near the side of the valley, before the river gets narrow enough to cross. Even then, we'd be risking the horses slipping in the rushing water, maybe hurting themselves. Then we'd be on foot, and that'd be the end of it."

Dante looked back at the people on the ferry boat. "Well, at least they seem to be pulling it toward us, so maybe we don't have to worry about that." He waved to the people on the boat. It seemed strange they didn't wave back, but they did keep pulling on the rope and working their way closer to their side of the river.

The three of them dismounted to wait. Dante smelled the air. It seemed free of the oppressive scent of smoke that had been following them since yesterday. As Dante looked around, he thought this spot along the river was the closest to peaceful and alive that he had seen so far in this land. All the sounds—the water, the wind in the trees, even the occasional bird—felt normal and right. "Your country is pretty," he said to both of his companions, trying to make small talk.

"Usually it is," Radovan agreed. "It is a strange fate, that we deserved to have the living dead infest our land so often, polluting it, making it into a desert."

Dante nodded and frowned. It was a strange fate, indeed. He could think of many places that deserved such horrors more. "Perhaps it is a test."

He looked at Bogdana. She had gone off just a ways and was gathering berries off a bush, most of which she was eating as she went. Dante thought how hungry she must be. They hadn't stopped since leaving the town, and they probably wouldn't stop again until nightfall, but she needed to eat and rest often in her condition. She caught his eye and took a few steps over to offer some of the berries to him and Radovan.

"A test?" she said. "I don't know if we will pass. And I'd rather not have such a test, even if I did pass it."

"I don't suppose any of us want such things," Dante said as he ate some of the berries. They were the same kind she'd given him the night before. It seemed quite early in the year for berries, and to be honest, they were so tart as to be barely edible. "But we are tested, nonetheless, all the time."

She gave him just a hint of a smile as she stepped past him to get more berries from another nearby bush. "What were you, in your country, before you were driven out?"

"I joined the apothecaries' guild, mostly because the men in my city were required to belong to a guild, if they wanted to hold public office. In a way, I wanted to be a politician." He looked down. "Then I tried to write books, but couldn't." He didn't know what was more embarrassing: his life, explaining it to some peasant girl, or the wholly inappropriate and mostly unpleasant feeling of being instinctively attracted to her and craving her approval. He watched her without looking up.

"I think you wanted to be a monk once," she said between mouthfuls of berries.

Dante scowled, but almost smiled in spite of it. She was right; he had thought of joining the Franciscans, to be exact. Again, there was something mostly unpleasant yet somewhat exhilarating about a woman knowing too much about him. "Well, yes, I did, once."

"I think you did, too," she said to Radovan.

Dante looked at the younger man, who also discreetly stole glances at the woman, though he mainly watched the approaching ferry boat. "Well, yes, I had thought of it, since I'm not the firstborn. It's practical, sometimes, even though I suppose it's funny to say that about that kind of life."

"Always testing yourselves." She almost laughed. "Or seeing life as a test. But maybe you're right. Maybe this is our test. But I think it upsets you, because you didn't choose it. You think the ones you chose are noble or heroic, but you think this one is evil and dirty and unfair, since you didn't. Why not pretend you did choose it, if it makes you feel better? Or pretend all the other tests were thrust on you?" Dante thought he heard her laugh at this point.

He heard a loud snap from her direction. He quickly looked up and turned toward her. She was walking toward him, a thick section of a tree branch in her hand. Her snapping it off must have been the sound he'd heard. Her gaze was fixed on a point over his shoulder, then she lifted her chin, indicating for him to turn and look where she was looking.

Dante turned. The ferry was about two-thirds of the way across the river. Though the people on the boat were pulling the rope, Dante could now see their motions were uncoordinated and frenzied, and they were constantly bumping into each other, knocking each other down as they staggered about the raft. He could again hear the low moaning of the dead.

Chapter 9

But all those souls who weary were and naked
Their color changed and gnashed their teeth together,
As soon as they had heard those cruel words.
Dante, *Inferno*, 3.100-102

Radovan drew his sword. "We'll have to fight them. We need the ferry to cross the river." He turned to Bogdana and offered his horse's reins to her. "You should take the horses off a ways and stay with them until it's done."

Bogdana looked to the raft, then to the two men. "No."

Dante drew his own sword. "You should, really. We can't be having the horses or you hurt."

She scowled. "I'm not a horse. And I'm not helpless." She narrowed her eyes and watched the ferry. "How many of them are there?"

"I'd say maybe six or seven," Radovan said after briefly surveying the boat.

Dante looked closely at the raft's passengers. "It's hard to say. They keep moving around and flailing about. I think I count eight." One of the dead people lurched to one side, thrown off balance by the pushing and shoving of the others, tottered a moment, then fell into the water. He kicked his legs a few times, trying to stay afloat. His head and arms remained above the surface of the water for a few seconds, before he sank out of sight. "Well, maybe only seven."

"Either way, that's too many for just the two of you," Bogdana said. She ignored Dante and Radovan's commands, and busied herself with snapping the smaller twigs off the large branch she'd broken off for her weapon. It was about as thick as her arm, and slightly longer.

"She has a point," Dante offered.

Radovan frowned. "They tell us in the army not to fight more than two at a time, or they'll grab a hold of you, drag you down, and overwhelm you. Seven would be a lot, I suppose."

Bogdana finished stripping the thick branch, and she swung it at a tree trunk to make sure it wouldn't break. It made a loud crack, and some bits of bark flew from the tree, but the stick itself remained intact. Dante thought it an odd skill she had, to be able to pick very effective, deadly clubs from among random firewood or branches. "And you two won't do me any good if you're dead," she said. "I'd just have to kill you as well, and I might not be able to, if there were still some of them left standing."

Dante thought she probably underestimated herself.

Radovan looked to Dante, who nodded. They led their horses a ways off and tied them to trees, then returned to where the ferry would pull up. Dante could hear the young man mutter something. Probably a prayer. Dante was not particularly in the mood, so he simply said, "Let the girl live, Lord, if it is your will." He added quietly, "And let me do something worthy of her."

The ferry was quite close. The dead people's moaning had turned to growls and snarls. Their progress slowed somewhat, as their focus shifted from pulling on the rope to watching and reaching for the live people on the bank. "My armor gives me some protection from the bites," Radovan said. "Try to keep me in front. Keep her in between us."

The raft was close enough that some of the dead people tried wading the rest of the way. Two young men near the front tumbled into the river, falling forward then rising up to stand waist deep in the water. Dante and Radovan stepped into the water as the two corpses staggered toward them. Dante was glad Bogdana was still hanging back.

Radovan's sword was heavy enough that he took the head off the one closest to him. The torso and head made two separate splashes as they hit the water. Dante shivered to think of the head rolling around on the bottom, jaws still snapping, and he wanted to do nothing more than turn and run. Bogdana was at the edge of his field of vision, just to his right, and the other dead man was making for her. She had her club raised and looked much more ready to fight and kill than Dante felt at that moment. He was fairly sure he couldn't take the thing's head off the way Radovan had done, and he didn't know if a deep cut in the neck was enough to stop one of the monsters, so he thrust upward, under its chin to the top of its head. Dante withdrew his sword and the dead man fell face first into the water and started to drift a little until he brushed up against Dante's shins. He grimaced and kicked the corpse further out into the stream.

Now all the remaining dead people were clambering off the raft, splashing into the water, which was just over their knees, and setting up a howl as they attacked their would-be prey. Dante could see a dead man and woman were on Radovan, swiping at him as he backed up. A slash from his sword hadn't connected with them, and had thrown him off balance. Now he was struggling to stay out of their grip and bring his sword back up. A dead woman had gotten too close to Bogdana, and with a shriek, she had brought her club down on the woman's head, hard enough to crack the dead bone and send the corpse face down into the pink, muddy runoff swirling about their feet.

Dante, meanwhile, was approached by two dead children. The last to stumble off the raft, they had waded through the water slowly, since it was nearly up to their waists. They had been a boy and a girl. The girl was the smaller of the two. The boy was larger, strong, maybe about twelve. They looked similar, with the same dark hair and eyes, their skin slightly ruddier than Bogdana's. Perhaps they had been brother and sister. They were old enough to be betrothed, as Dante had been when he was twelve, but that was more the custom among the aristocracy, and those who hoped for their children or grandchildren to ascend to that class. These people probably never had such aspirations, and now they were dead, they aspired to nothing, other than to kill.

The boy was on him first. Looking into its big, brown eyes, Dante couldn't help but hesitate. Its gaze registered nothing but an inhuman, animal need, with no recognition of danger or sympathy. But it was still childlike enough to make any normal man pause. Tears welled up and blurred Dante's vision, the way pity was blurring his cold, rational judgment. The moment allowed the boy-thing to get close enough that Dante's delayed slash was awkward and had less force, striking the side of its head, driving the thing down, but neither breaking its skull nor cutting through its neck. It and the girl were now both on Dante. The girl tugged at the hem of his frock, while the boy got a hold of his right arm. He grabbed the girl's long hair with his left hand, pulling her away before she could bite into his thigh or stomach. He tried to pull his right arm away from the boy, but the dead grip was powerful and tenacious. The two children were dragging him down, and for a moment he felt fairly sure he'd be dead soon, too.

Bogdana's club came down on the boy's head with a loud crack. His soulless eyes rolled back and somehow looked even more dead. His grip still held Dante's arm, though now the body felt so much lighter than before. Perhaps the water was buoying him up. Bogdana nudged him with the stick, so he slipped off of Dante, splashed in the water, and floated away.

Dante was left holding the girl's hair as the thing struggled and growled. He gritted his teeth and pulled her upward as he raised his sword. Radovan walked up next to him. Apparently he had killed the two dead people who had been attacking him. "Go ahead," he said to Dante quietly. "You have to."

"No one ever *has* to do anything," Dante whispered. He could hear the catch in his voice, hear the sniffling in his nose, as he breathed in after saying this. It was embarrassing, and it stung him that his emotions felt more embarrassing than killing children did.

Dante could feel Bogdana move around behind him. She kept her hand on his shoulder and back as she moved, perhaps so he'd know she was there and feel reassured by it. He heard her say something to Radovan, though he couldn't quite make it out, then he heard the other man splash out of the river. He couldn't see him, as he kept looking at the girl-thing. Bogdana came around on his left side and drew his dagger.

"It's all right," she whispered to him. "You're right. No one has to do anything. But sometimes things have to happen. We don't know why. Just look away for a moment. Please."

Dante glanced from the girl to the dagger. It was a practical, rugged weapon, not a dainty or decorative piece, but Dante had never before thought it looked so ugly and evil. It caught the afternoon sun and he thought it looked like a sliver of cold hate. He wished, for a moment, it would be going into his brain and not the girl's.

Bogdana gently put her hand on his face, over his eyes. Her hand was every bit as rough and calloused as he would have expected, but the touch was as maternal, loving, and reassuring as any he could remember ever feeling. She gave the slightest push, turning his head to the right. "Hold on to her hair tightly, please." Dante tightened his grip. "It's for her good, too. The soldiers will be much less gentle, or she'll kill others, and cause more evil."

The growling turned into a kind of high pitched wailing, and Dante could feel the girl thrashing about so hard he didn't think he could hold on to her. Then the wailing eased down to a wheezing gasp, at the same time as the thrashing dissolved into one, slight, convulsing twitch. Like the boy, she felt strangely light now.

Bogdana's hand slid down from his face, along his arm, and rested on his hand. "All right," she whispered. "Let her go now." Dante didn't just release his grip, but slowly lowered the girl by the hair into the water. That way there wasn't a loud splash this time, but more like a wet, accepting embrace, as the water closed over her head and over his hand. Held up now by the water, she felt even lighter still. Then he finally let go, and looked down at the girl's body as it floated away from them. The water all around them was red and fouled, but where she was floating now it looked clean.

Once this nearly sacramental act was done, Bogdana turned to the physical and practical, bending down to the water to wash off the dagger's blade. She handed it to Dante, as she put her hand on his. "I've done this before," she said. "So has Radovan. It's all right to be sad the first time. It's not just all right, it's the only right way to be. I could never look at you again if you didn't feel this way."

The two of them walked over to where Radovan was untying their horses. Dante thought Bogdana picked words about as well as she picked clubs. He was glad of it, though, as usual, chastened that he was not better with speech.

Chapter 10

We came unto a noble castle's foot,
Seven times encompassed with lofty walls,
Defended round by a fair rivulet.
Dante, *Inferno*, 4.106-108

No one spoke as they got the horses on the raft and pulled themselves across the river. It felt good to Dante—the repetitive, monotonous, physical exertion of putting one hand over the other to pull the rope. It wasn't like the frenzied rush of battle, nor the quiet calm of riding, nor the sedentary thrills of reading and writing, but it was soothing and exhilarating simultaneously. Most of all, such work never made him feel guilty, as fighting, resting, or writing always threatened to, with their confusing and complicating connections to violence, rage, pride, or sloth. This felt more like what one was supposed to be doing—hard work, with a simple goal that didn't include hurting anyone or anything, or acquiring any substantive object. Even speech would taint the balm of this guiltless, selfless interlude. The silence of the other two seemed to confirm they felt this too. But a glance to the left, where several of the bodies could still be seen drifting, reconnected Dante quickly to the horror they had just witnessed, and in which they had participated. The corpses were far enough downstream they could barely be distinguished from other objects in the water, but it was still enough to make Dante's stomach contract and his head feel light and useless.

They got off on the other bank and Radovan cut the rope that ran across the river. The ferry slowly eased out into the stream and picked up speed, as the rope slipped into the water. "The army has sections of bridge already built, to put across the river here when they arrive," he explained. "But they would have sent a boy across on the rope to get the raft, and get troops across that way until the pontoon bridge was built. So perhaps this will slow them down just a bit, at least the forward scouts who would have caught up with us first."

They mounted their horses and followed the road into the forest. It was late afternoon. This time of year it stayed light fairly late, but they would need to stop before too long.

"Is there another town on this side of the river?" Dante asked. "Is there any place safe to stop tonight?"

"I don't know if anywhere is safe," Radovan said. "There are more villages further up the valley. And there are individual houses and logging camps scattered all over. But up ahead there is another road that leads to a monastery. Perhaps we should try asking for shelter there. I have only heard of it. The brothers there are hermits and are seldom seen out among the people."

"Perhaps they would be more likely to help us—more helpful than the villagers were," Bogdana said.

"Or the army," Radovan said.

"Or the clergy," Dante added.

The sun was poised above the mountains ahead of them, as they turned down a road that forked to the right. Since he had no better plan, Dante did not object to going to the monastery, but he was not completely confident they would receive sympathy and hospitality from men who had retreated from human society. It would probably come as no surprise to the brothers that their neighbors were now physically as well as spiritually diseased. Dante looked at Radovan, then down at his own arms. They'd washed their hands in the river, but their sleeves and shirts still looked like they had just come from slaughtering cattle, and the monks would surely guess the truth was much worse. And as reassuring as Bogdana's large, taut belly felt to Dante, he knew that men who had devoted themselves to the perfect, pristine God, and withdrawn from the presence of their sinful, polluted neighbors—especially those neighbors who were female—might find it much more disconcerting than comforting. Dante remembered the story of the Good

Samaritan, of how a priest and a Levite had left the man to die, because they believed him less clean than themselves. But he also remembered how years ago he had heard a sermon preached on this same gospel story, about how the Samaritan had done something especially virtuous and admirable, because he had helped someone so unlike himself, someone from a different, hostile tribe. The story started to give Dante hope on that spring afternoon, as the shadows lengthened and they rode on into the deepening darkness.

He knew he had been unable to commit to the monastic vows because of his own weakness, together with the ambition of his father for a socially advantageous marriage, and he tried to hope these men were better monks than he would have been.

The road ascended for some time, switching back on itself to make the slope climbable, until they came to a break in the trees and emerged into a large, open area. It was a striking vista, with the sun just touching the tops of the mountains to the west. Spreading out before them was a bowl-like indentation in the land, with a lake in the middle of it. In the lake was an island, at the far end of which was a stone building, several stories tall. The water of the lake was an especially brilliant blue, and the pine trees on the island were a particularly deep green. All the colors in this part of the valley seemed to take on a special vibrancy and vitality. The air seemed completely clear and fresh for the first time since Dante had entered this land.

They followed the road down through the field that stretched from the edge of the forest to the shore of the lake. As they got closer, they could see that a narrow, wooden bridge ran from the large island to a much smaller one that was only about thirty feet from the shore. On the smaller island was a mechanism for raising and lowering a drawbridge that connected it to the mainland. The bridge was in the up position, and there were two robed figures on the small island.

Before they got all the way to the shore, Radovan turned to Dante and Bogdana. "I don't know who should address them," he said quietly. He looked at Dante. "Your strange accent might put them off, but they would probably suspect I'm in the army, and I don't know how they feel about the army coming here, or how they feel about deserters." He looked at Bogdana. "They might have more sympathy for a woman, or they might have rules about not letting you anywhere near the place. I don't know what to do."

"You, go ahead," Bogdana said to Dante. "The accent might make them less suspicious than the sword and armor, I think, and less suspicious than they would be of a woman."

They had reached the point where the road ended by the lake. As Dante waved to the two figures, he felt a sick dread at the thought they might be dead like the people on the ferry. But they weren't moving about in frenzied hunger, the way the dead always seemed to. They just stood there. One finally waved back. "The plague is abroad," he shouted to Dante. "Are any of you bitten?"

"No," Dante replied. "We can come across one at a time and you can inspect us, if you like."

"We shall. But what do you want here? We are hermits and we don't usually accept visitors, except in extreme situations, and they are never allowed to stay long."

"We are traveling west. The army is coming this way and we fear they will kill us. The undead are in the woods. We need shelter for the night. We will move on in the morning."

The two figures conferred, then they turned the wheel to lower the drawbridge across the water. When it was in the down position, the one who had spoken before did so again. "Dismount, all of you. You, the one we spoke to, lead your horse across. You other two, stay on the shore."

Dante did as he was told. When he was on the other side of the drawbridge with the two figures, he was shocked to see that the one who had not spoken was in fact a woman. A young one at that, about Bogdana's age, though her hair was cut short, nearly bald, as was the hair of the young man with her. She noticed his surprise. "I will turn around if you like," she said. "And my brother monk will do the same when your woman comes across."

"He can turn around for her if she likes, but no, you needn't do anything special for me. I just didn't expect to see women here," Dante said.

The man had been looking Dante over and poking him with a staff. "Lift up your frock," he said, "all the way to your armpits."

Dante reconsidered having the woman turn around, but everything was so weird and outside of normal decency here, he just went ahead and lifted his frock. "Roll your pants up past the knees."

He followed the directions, then he was waved on to cross the narrow bridge to the island and wait there. Bogdana was the second across, and although he didn't see her ask the male monk to turn around, Dante did look away when she was inspected. She joined him on the island, and a few moments later the man and the woman in robes came over with Radovan, after they had raised the drawbridge.

"Please, follow the trail," the man said. "Our monastery is on the other side of the island."

They did so, leading their tired horses. It was twilight, but nothing here seemed as threatening and unnatural as everything else they had encountered. In a short while, they heard clacking sounds and shouts. Even these, though unexpected, did not have the sound of panic and alarm, but seemed orderly and normal. The three travelers and their escorts emerged from among the trees into an open area in front of the monastery building. Here there were a couple dozen people in grey robes, practicing at fighting each other with wooden staves. They were all ages, from teens to the elderly, and like the pair who had met them at the bridge, there were both men and women among them. They stopped their practicing when they saw the newcomers, and one of the older men approached them.

The young man who had accompanied them from the bridge explained who they were to the older man, who was bald, with a closely-trimmed beard, and an exceptionally short and wiry build. "Thank you, Brother Jonas and Sister Genya. Please return to the bridge and keep watch there and do not let anyone else across. But you were right to let these in, I think." He turned to Dante, Bogdana, and Radovan. "Welcome. I am Brother Adam. We are just finishing our evening's exercises, before dinner and our final prayers. You may make our home your sanctuary for tonight, if you wish it."

Dante still did not know if these people were better monks than he would have been, but he could definitely tell they were very different from the Franciscans.

Chapter 11

Thus we went on as far as to the light,
Things saying 'tis becoming to keep silent,
As was the saying of them where I was.
Dante, *Inferno*, 4.103-105

After washing at a fountain in front of the stone building, and giving their horses to attendants, they were led inside. The main doors opened into a large central room, under a domed ceiling. The vault of the dome was decorated with constellations of the night sky. The paint used must have had metal flecks in it, or else the pictures were inlaid with bits of glass, because the stars on the ceiling sparkled in the torchlight and the final rays of the sun coming through thin windows in the dome. The capstone at the very top of the dome was decorated with a golden, stylized star, like a compass rose.

Painted around the bottom edge of the dome were mythological creatures: centaurs, harpies, and minotaurs, as well as stranger ones Dante did not have names for. One looked like a giant snake with wings, another like a plume of smoke with a woman's face. The artist who had painted these had done them in such a way one could imagine they were supporting the vault above them. At the same time, they looked like they were assailing it, either to ascend or destroy it. As beautiful a room as it was, Dante wondered about its appropriateness as the central hall of a monastery, nearly as much as he wondered about the presence of women in their group. The capstone should have been a depiction of God on His throne, the stars should have been accompanied or replaced by angels, and the mythological creatures should haven been angels. Or demons, so long as the painting made it clear they were being cast down and imprisoned by God and the angels. Nothing about these people quite made sense. Yet here in the monastery the feeling given by such incongruity was a sense of wonder and bemusement, rather than one of dread and confusion.

Under the dome, the room was full of round, wooden tables with chairs set around them. Dante, Bogdana, and Radovan were directed to sit at one with Adam. Although there were two other chairs at the table, these remained empty.

"I'm sorry," Adam explained. "Although we do not have the same rules as other monasteries regarding proximity to the opposite sex, we do keep our members away from strangers in general. I will be your host tonight, while my brothers and sisters will keep their distance. I hope you understand it is not disrespect."

"Of course," Dante said, though he was still baffled and curious about their arrangements here.

"I've lived just outside the valley all my life," Bogdana said, "and I never knew this monastery was here. And I certainly wouldn't have thought there were women here. I don't think I understand your group."

Adam smiled. "Our female members seldom leave the island openly, except in emergencies, as during a plague."

"But what order are you that allows this?" Dante asked. "This is not done, where I come from."

"I have never heard of this, either," Radovan said.

The food arrived. As to diet, these strange recluses followed the norms Dante was used to, at least. The food was hearty and abundant, but there was nothing unnecessary or extra beyond the minimum to nourish the body. They were each presented with a large bowl of vegetable soup, and in the middle of the table was a loaf of black bread. Dante saw Bogdana could barely keep herself from it, she was so hungry, but manners dictated they wait. Dante could only imagine how ravenous she was in her condition, with only a few berries since the morning.

"Please," Adam said, "pray as is your custom. There is no need to follow any special prayer of ours." He and the other monks bowed their heads to silently give whatever blessing it was they were used to giving. Dante could only follow their lead. He saw Radovan and Bogdana were equally surprised by their customs.

The prayer being done, Bogdana immediately began eating, though she was still attentive to what was being said by the men.

"Yes. I'm sure our order does not quite fit your expectations," Adam continued. "But there is some precedent, from the time of the apostles, of men and women saints living or traveling together in chastity, as they spread the good news and served the Lord. We believe the flesh is not so weak it cannot withstand temptation, and we do not believe it so strong it can lead the soul and mind into temptation against their will."

"I see. This is not how it is done elsewhere," Dante said.

"Well, we do have some… reinforcements to strengthen our resolve. All members are raised here in the monastery from childhood. They are taught to look upon one another as brothers and sisters, so any feelings of a more carnal, disorderly sort would seem like incest to them. And if, God forbid, someone were to act on such incestuous urgings, they would be punished according to the harshest laws of the Bible—with public execution." Dante thought that part of their order sounded more like the kind of harsh, earthly justice he was used to hearing preached, if only selectively practiced. "Thankfully, this has not been necessary for hundreds of years in our monastery."

To have brutality applied so infrequently was also outside Dante's experience, and he marveled at it. "But what is your order, exactly?"

Adam pointed back at the main door they had entered. Dante turned and saw there was a large crest on the wall above it. The symbol consisted of angry, orange flames pointing down from the top. They were reaching down to something that looked like an iceberg, within which was encased the outline of a small, blue heart. Like the dome, the crest was strikingly incongruous for a religious order—there was no cross, or crown of thorns, or lamb, or dove, or any other Christian symbol on it.

"We are the Order of the Blessed Death," Adam explained. "We are neither of the eastern nor western churches, but have existed since long before the two split." He gestured back at the crest above the door. "Our crest tells much of our beliefs and practices. There is a legend that the next time God grows weary of humanity's wickedness and madness, and regrets having made us, He will use fire instead of water to destroy the earth. But we believe that before His fire turns to destruction, it is intended to melt the frozen human heart that seals itself off from God's love, and that such healing flames rain down on us all the time, if we were but aware."

"But when was this order founded?" Dante asked.

"Legend has it Cain was the founder of our order. Out of penance for his wickedness and lack of love, he spent all the rest of his life wandering, pleading with others to live a life of love, and to pursue a blessed death."

Dante exchanged looks with Bogdana and Radovan at this strange revelation. Bogdana's spoon was poised in midair for a moment, before she gave a shrug, emptied the spoon in her mouth, then set it down to reach over and tear off another hunk of bread.

"That is a most unusual founder, Brother Adam," Dante said. "And what is this 'blessed death' your order is named for?"

"Why, that you must surely know, if you are good and godly people, as you appear to be. It is the opposite of a cursed life, of course. What life could be more cursed than one lived out of selfishness and hate and burning, never-ending desire? And what death is more blessed than that died by Jesus, giving himself to death out of love and selflessness, with no desires for his own needs, but only for the needs and healing of others? Where did you say you were from?"

"Italy."

"Ah." Adam nodded. "I think you'll agree that those who follow the cursed life have put down deep roots of corruption in your land."

Dante nodded. At least there was something coming closer to orthodoxy in this part of the description, as odd as the rest had been. "Is your order spread far abroad, in Italy and beyond?"

"We believe all men and women of good will are members of our order in their hearts, even if they do not know to call themselves such.

But as for actual members who wear the grey robe and follow our life in community—yes, we are all across the world. In lands you don't even know of yet, lands beyond what you call the Pillars of Hercules, lands to the east of Persia and India, lands where men and women have never heard of Jesus, there are those who follow the blessed death as He did, and spurn the cursed life as He taught."

The description had turned odd once more, to say the least. "I see. And all these people in your communities—if you keep yourselves so secret that none of us have ever heard of you—where do your new members come from? How do you recruit them? If you believe every good person is a member, what is the special mission of those who join? Are you warriors? Penitents? Do you care for the sick rejected from their societies?"

"We perform all those functions, as required by the times. Our unique calling is to combat the special kind of cursed life that afflicts those with the plague of undeath. Their affliction simply makes literal, in their flesh, the cursed kind of life embraced by so many. A life of mindless hunger and violence, with no concern for others. So our members patrol the countryside secretly, usually at night, tending to the final rites of any who have succumbed to this abominable, hateful kind of living death. Usually, we can keep the plague under control this way, and only a very few die in each generation. But we are not God or His holy angels. Sometimes our vigilance is not enough, and the plague grows too strong and spreads too fast. Then we can only withdraw within our walls and let the army and the civil authorities deal with it their way. When they are done, our surviving members move into the devastated areas and find any children orphaned by the plague. Usually there are many, whose parents' last act was to lift them on to a tree branch, or stuff them into some animal's den, or cram them into a garret, while they fought and died at the monsters' hands. We take these children and raise them, and they become the next generation of our community."

"But the army is coming this way. Won't they destroy your monastery, as they have the towns and villages in the area?" Radovan asked.

"This has never happened in the history of our monastery. The stones of this building were laid down before Caesar, and it will outlast any petty tyrant in our land. But we must respect our agreement with them, if we are to receive their special protection. We have agreed never to take in and harbor people from the plague-ridden area once the army has been called in. We must submit to their authority. As long as we do, they will bypass the monastery. That is why you cannot stay with us after tonight. My brothers and sisters out on patrol have told me that the army will not be here before tomorrow afternoon. In the morning you must leave, so the community can be safe. I assume you are trying to move west, to the end of the valley?"

"Yes, and then over the mountains, we hope," Dante said.

Adam nodded. "It is another job of our monks to guide people over the mountains when they try to escape. There is a little-known pass that every brother and sister knows well. Those from the outside seldom find it, or if they do, they forget the way and cannot find it a second time when they come looking for it. It is dangerous for the monk who serves as a guide, since once outside the monastery he can be killed by the troops, just like the villagers are. But it must be done for charity's sake. It is part of the blessed death, to show others the way."

Adam turned to Bogdana, Dante, and Radovan, and addressed each of them in turn. "My daughter, you are great with child. And you, from Italy, you seem marked in a special way, for some special purpose, the details of which I cannot intuit, but I feel it strongly, nonetheless. And you, a soldier come to us from the army, you seem pure of heart, a pentitent who fights for the weak, sometimes even for the unworthy. You are not three random refugees, I think, so I will accompany you myself. I had a premonition some special group would come before I grew too old to make the trip, so I must welcome the task as a special honor from God."

Adam stood, along with the three of them. He called over two young monks—one man and one woman. "My young brother and sister here will show you to your rooms. I must go now and prepare for the journey. This will require much prayer and clarity of mind. The dead, and those who would exterminate them, are more powerful and relentless than ever. Good night to you all."

Dante and Radovan bowed slightly to him, while Bogdana gave a surprisingly graceful curtsy. Just as her gentleness and grace had been apparent, even in the calloused hands she had placed on his eyes, so too this woman's beauty could always shine through her rough exterior, Dante thought.

Dante felt a strange elation over Brother Adam's belief he might have some important work yet to produce. There might be some heroic deed yet to do, whether for the memory of Beatrice, or—he blushed to think it—for the roughhewn beauty whom he had now sworn allegiance to, and whom he knew he was growing to love. His blush turned into a bracing, shivering chill when he thought he might even do this great thing—whatever it was—for the God of this "blessed death." What a morbid but uplifting concept adopted by these strange, seemingly heretical monks, hidden deep in the woods of this bizarre backwater of the world. He looked up at the stars depicted on the ceiling, and wondered if Brother Adam's estimate of the monastery's age was anywhere near accurate. If it were—and stranger things had been known to happen—then those jewels had glinted down on someone standing in this spot when Christ was alive, just as they now sparkled above him. Dante smiled, thinking how their artist had achieved such unexpected immortality.

Chapter 12

The infernal hurricane that never rests
Hurtles the spirits onward in its rapine;
Whirling them round, and smiting, it molests them.
Dante, *Inferno*, 5.31-33

The four of them left the monastery early, before the sun was even up. The monks gave them back their two horses, along with two of their own—a black one for Bogdana and a white one for Adam—so Bogdana no longer rode behind Dante. As unfamiliar and disconcerting as her sitting behind him had been at first, he stole glances at her now, and felt less sure of himself without her being so near.

They rode over the drawbridge and back on to the road leading up the valley. As the sun rose behind them, the wind came up suddenly, plunging the temperature from that of a cool spring morning to the first blast of winter in late November. Dante looked ahead and saw a flock of starlings shoot up in front of them, wheeling first to the right then to the left, increasing their speed to flee from the rising windstorm. The wind started picking things up off the forest floor, even tearing branches off trees. Their faces stung as the flying leaves and sticks pelted and cut them. Their progress slowed to a near halt, as the horses bucked and snorted, terrified by the sudden, violent change. Dante looked back to see the sun pressed between the jagged line of the horizon and a black, roiling ceiling of clouds that seemed intent on pressing it back down.

"What's happening?" Dante asked.

"Storms come up quickly in the spring," Radovan shouted.

"Yes, but not usually like this," Adam said. "This seems quite out of the ordinary. It's so dark, and the wind so powerful, overwhelming us and our animals. We should find some shelter, quickly."

Dante looked about, trying to see anything between the swaying trees and swirling debris. One tree snapped and fell over right by them. "There!" he said, pointing off to the right. "I think I see a light!"

"Yes," Radovan said. "Let's go."

With difficulty, they worked to get their horses through the woods. After a few steps, they could see there was a small cottage among the trees. The constant raging and howling of the storm was now punctuated by an irregular, slamming sound, as the door of the cottage swung open all the way, smashing into the wall of the building, then swung back when the wind shifted in its frenzied assault. The door didn't slam shut, but stopped three-quarters of the way closed, as though it were hitting against something keeping it from closing all the way, then a second later it would swing back and slam into the wall.

They dismounted and dragged the animals closer. Near the cottage there was a simple lean-to built between a large boulder and a tree. It was open on one side, and whatever animals it was meant to house were not there. Just some typical farm implements—shovels, spades, wooden buckets—within. The structure was not quite big enough for their four horses, but they would have to try to tie the animals in there and hope they didn't escape. Dante's horse was on the end, with its side pressed up against the boulder. Sticks continued to hit the wall and roof of the structure, and the wind's howling was fierce and unnaturally high-pitched, but Dante thought the animal might stay, now that it was at least partly protected from the storm's fury. He'd had it some time, and like many such animals it was more trustworthy than most people. Dante patted its head before backing out between it and the large, white horse Adam had been riding. "Easy, friend," he said. "I need you to stay here. I'll be back soon."

Leaving the makeshift stable, the four of them approached the cottage. Dante noticed Bogdana had picked up a short-handled shovel from the shed. Through the flying debris, he could see the light coming from the cottage's window and partly open door. As they got closer, Radovan raised his left hand to stop them. He drew his sword.

Dante drew his weapon as well. He looked closer, squinting and raising his left hand to try and protect his eyes. The door couldn't close all the way because two motionless, human legs were sticking out through the doorway. He heard the familiar moaning. It rose in volume and pitch, cutting above the sound of the storm, as it grew into a howl of hunger and rage—and this time, Dante thought, of infinite, sleepless sadness.

Chapter 13

I understood that unto such a torment
The carnal malefactors were condemned,
Who reason subjugate to appetite.
Dante, *Inferno*, 5.37-39

They hung there for a moment, as another tree was uprooted and crashed down nearby. Then, though it hardly seemed possible, the wind increased to the point that they were swaying, and had to lean into it in order to remain standing. Tears streamed down Dante's face as the wind stung him, worse than anything he'd ever felt before. Even his tears seemed to scald unnaturally, mixing with the windblown debris into rivulets that burned and tore more than they cleansed. He squinted, and thought that even fighting the dead was preferable to this relentless, remorseless assault, against which their bodies seemed insubstantial and wholly inadequate.

Radovan looked to Adam, who nodded. They moved closer to the cottage with faltering steps, planting each foot then pausing before moving the other one. Dante was behind them, with Bogdana slightly ahead of him. He could still see only the bottom half of the body, though now he could see there was a good deal of blood splattered on it, and on the doorframe as well. He saw Radovan survey whatever was inside the cottage, then turn back to them and motion to follow him.

Dante entered the cottage last, stepping over the dead man. The handle of a knife stuck out of his left eye. His right eye was eternally open; it still seemed filled with hate for whoever had done this to him. His mouth and beard were covered with gore. He had been a broad man, dressed in the furs of a hunter or trapper.

Inside the cottage, Dante found himself in a fairly large room, by the standards of such a building, though the ceiling was low. He wondered how the man had been able to live there and move about comfortably. There was a fireplace to the left and a rough table made of dark wood in the middle of the room. To the right was another door, presumably to a second room. It had a chest, a chair, and another table pushed up against it. A fire was dying in the hearth, while a candle burned with more vigor on the table.

The candle cast its light up into the face of a young woman seated at the table. She was wrapped in a coarse, brown blanket, which had several darker splotches on it. From the way she held it wrapped tightly about herself, and the glimpses of her legs and shoulders when she moved, it looked as though she were naked underneath it. Her face had no color, not even her lips, though her eyes were red with blood around the dark, brown irises, and even darker pupils. Her black hair was matted to her face and streaked with more dried blood. Dante saw her hand was bloody, too, when she reached up to brush her hair out of her face, before she pulled it back under the cover of the blanket. She was not as taut and compact as Bogdana, but her features looked finer, more elegant, if somewhat fuller. She had probably been quite beautiful before all this.

She watched them, then blinked slowly and wetly. Her breathing was a labored wheezing that could be heard over the moaning, which came from the other room.

"You're hurt," Dante said. "Can we help you?"

As soon as he spoke, the door to the other room shook violently, as a storm of blows pounded it from the other side. The moaning increased to a roar of hate Dante imagined almost sounded like jealousy.

The woman at the table drew herself up slightly, though the movement seemed to cause her pain. "Pavel!" she said in a hoarse shout. "Stop! Be still!" Given what he had seen so far of the dead, and their general incomprehension, Dante thought it quite remarkable the pounding did stop at this command, and the roar diminished to a steady and slightly wounded-sounding moan.

The woman turned her attention back to him. "I've been bitten badly," she said. "I'm afraid there's nothing you can do for me."

"Is that your husband in the other room?" Radovan asked.

"Oh, no," she said, tilting her head down to indicate the body in the doorway. "That's my husband."

"Then who's in the other room?" Dante asked.

"My sister's husband," she said, watching them steadily and wheezing between her short answers.

"And where's your sister?" Dante continued.

She frowned. "How should I know? They live… lived way on the other side of the valley, by the river. He had a mill there. Only one nearby. Very successful. Quite wealthy."

Dante looked at his companions, then back at the woman. He tried to understand the situation. "You had to kill your husband and brother-in-law when they got the plague and attacked you?"

She shook her head. "No, no. It was a bit more complicated than that. My sister's husband was still alive when he visited yesterday."

"He came to warn you of the plague?"

Her bloodless lips curled. "Please, stranger, I don't think I have much longer. Don't make me waste what breath I have explaining the obvious. He was here because my husband was not." Her sickly smile turned into a wet, bubbling sort of chuckle. "Though I suppose he did have my well-being in mind, so long as it meant making him feel good as well."

The chuckle changed into full-on laughter, then hideously transformed into deep, barking coughs and retching. The heaving bent her over the table. She repeatedly banged her head on it as the spasms wracked her whole body. She lurched forward, then drew up slightly, as her body tried to expel its diseased fluids one moment, then the next it tried desperately to get breath and life back into her drained, broken frame. When the convulsions finally stopped, she remained facedown on the table. Dante thought she might be dead already. He was bothered by the fact he didn't know whether that would make him feel sad or relieved. When she finally lifted herself up, there was a puddle of bloody spit and bile left on the table, and for a second, a long, pink thread stretched from the table to her glistening mouth, before she licked her lips, spat, and then wiped her face on the blanket.

Her eyes shined darkly, like holes filled with ink. They were so wet and red Dante could barely look at them, for fear they would ooze out all over her cheeks, draining what was left of her into a pool of mortality and sadness. At the same time, he knew he couldn't take his gaze from them.

"I didn't know I'd think that was all so funny, now, at the end," she continued. "But I suppose it is. My husband walked in on us. And he most definitely was not alive when he did. It's funny. The dead usually make so much noise, you can hear them coming. Well, it's probably my fault. I was making a good bit of noise, too." She started to laugh again, but managed to hold it in check this time, lest the convulsions finish her completely.

She pulled herself up and shrugged. "Well, even if he had been alive and snuck up on us, Pavel and I would still both be dead now, I suppose. My husband was a big man—a hunter. Very strong, very angry, very violent. Pavel was on top, so he got him first. Got him from behind. Tore his neck open with his teeth. Blood all over me." She ran her fingers through her long hair, pausing and tugging when they caught on the knots of dried blood. "I'm sure most of this is his. It gave me a chance to get away. I got a knife, but he was on me before I could stab him. Bit me twice. Horrible, burning pain, into my heart, down to my stomach. My big, disgusting, dead husband tearing my breast off with his teeth, making me as dead and loathsome as he was."

Her eyes had dried a little, and she sighed. "I finally stuck the knife in his eye. I barricaded poor Pavel in the bedroom. I sat down here to die. And then you showed up. I suppose you should go now."

Bogdana moved slightly away from the men. "Did you have children?" she asked quietly, looking up and around, as though trying to figure out if there were an attic or loft, or possibly some of the orphans Brother Adam had described.

"What? Oh, no, I didn't. He blamed me for it, of course." She shrugged. "He was probably right. I never got pregnant, even when my Pavel started visiting me, so I suppose it was me. But it's not like it was my fault. I would've borne children, if that was what was meant to be. But it wasn't. If God wanted me to be a different way, He could've made me a different way, couldn't He?"

"But some things were your fault, weren't they?" Adam said.

Dante thought he had an odd tone, accusing and soothing in equal measure, but it seemed to have no calming effect on the woman, nor to make her aware of any guilt. She spat on the table. Dante thought it looked more black than red this time.

"I very much doubt it," she said. "I was alone all the time. It made me feel good not to be alone. It made me feel good to be desired, wanted, needed more than food or wine or honor. It made me feel good to be told how beautiful I was, how much more beautiful than my sister, after she'd been so high and mighty about marrying the wealthy miller. The wealthy miller who'd rather be with me than with her, who'd sneak from her bed to mine and tell me how much better I was. All that made me feel good, so what was I to do? Feel bad all the time? No. I feel bad now, but that's just the fault of this hellish plague. It'll probably get you too, and I doubt you'll feel guilty when it does."

Dante noticed the wind was no longer howling. He turned to look toward the window and door, and saw a sick, yellowish daylight seeping in.

"The storm has passed," Radovan said. "We should finish her and be on our way."

The woman turned to him. "Is that what you want?" She leaned back, looking up at the ceiling and baring her neck to them. "Go ahead. It hardly matters to me." She closed her eyes. "There—will that make it easier? Though I've known few men who needed my eyes closed before they hit me, perhaps you're better than they were."

Adam raised his hand. "No, I don't think so." He turned to Dante. "What do you think?"

Dante looked at the woman's neck, still so beautiful. He listened to her pitiable wheezing, and needed no time to consider further. "She is unrepentant. Killing her would be no mercy, but a terrible crime against someone who's done us no harm. So long as she draws breath, we can pray she will use it to utter just one word of remorse and be saved. There is always hope, and we would be the worse sinners if we took that away."

Adam nodded slowly. "You know much of the blessed death, brother, for one from such a sinful land."

"I wish there were another way to learn of it," Dante said.

"So do we all, but the method of learning is not our choice—only that we learn."

"Well, we can't wait here for her to have a change of heart," Radovan said, sheathing his sword. "Let's go."

Adam turned toward the door. "Yes, that is true, too, unfortunately. We shall go."

The woman opened her eyes and tilted her head to look at Dante. She gave him a slight nod, then leaned forward, placing her left arm on the table and resting her forehead on it.

As Radovan and Adam walked out the door to retrieve the horses, Dante sheathed his sword and watched Bogdana. The mysterious woman put down the shovel, leaning it next to the fireplace, and inexplicably walked up to the nearly-dead woman sitting at the table. Dante opened his mouth to say something of a warning to Bogdana, fearing how contagious the dead and dying were. But as he drew in a breath, he noiselessly closed his mouth, feeling somehow it would be impertinent, perhaps nearly blasphemous, to give voice to the deadly, numbing cancer of fear and mistrust during this woman's final moments with another, live human being.

He watched Bogdana put her hand on the other woman's shoulder and bend down close to her. She cast a sideways glance at Dante, then turned all her attention to the woman, bending even closer, till her mouth was right by her ear. Dante saw her lips move, but he couldn't quite hear the words. Her full, brown hair was hanging down, making it hard to see. He didn't hear her whisper, and it seemed to him as though she ever so slightly pursed her lips and lightly kissed the woman's ear. Then Bogdana partly straightened up and took a step back, her hands out in front of herself as she backed away, the way one would retreat from a wounded animal—or, Dante had the oddest fancy, from a statue or altar.

She finally turned toward him. She walked past him, then stepped over the dead body in the doorway. Dante followed her out, his gaze lingering just a moment on the swaying of her skirt, before the bright, unforgiving sunlight drew his focus upward and dazzled him.

Chapter 14

In the third circle am I of the rain
Eternal, maledict, and cold, and heavy;
Its law and quality are never new.
Dante, *Inferno*, 6.7-9

They rode deeper into the valley, though the bright sunlight did not last long. The day turned overcast almost as soon as they left the dying woman's house. It was not the violent storm of earlier in the morning, but just a solid, even blanket of clouds that hung over them, lifeless and still. The sun was now only an indistinct area of lighter grey in the oppressive mass.

After the four of them had been riding for some time, the trees gave way to another area that had been cleared for human cultivation and toil. There were no signs of people in the fields this morning. Dante noticed the ground was quite wet here, almost swampy, with puddles here and there, both in the road and fields. The water in the puddles looked oddly dark, as did the mud here. Perhaps such dark soil was good for the crops, Dante thought, more fertile—though he had trouble imagining this place full of plants and life. He gazed up at the lighter spot in the clouds, where he knew the sun was. Everything was still. Even the stagnant clouds didn't seem to move. No birds, no sounds, no motion besides the miserable creeping of the four of them. The storm was preferable to the silent dread of this place.

Ahead, a wall stretched across their path for quite some distance to either side. It looked to be masonry, about the height of two men.

"What's that?" Dante asked.

"The settlement furthest up the valley," Radovan replied. "It's fairly big. The mining and lumber here are quite valuable and attract lots of people."

"Why do they have a wall?" Dante asked. "The last town didn't."

"These people live far from civilization," Adam said. "We have our lake to protect the monastery, but they need a wall, for beyond this town there are only wild things and savage men, even in the best of times."

Dante considered the situation. "Will we have to ride around it? It would slow us down a lot."

"We might," Adam said. "There will be no choice if they've locked the gate and refuse us entry. But let us see if the gate is open, and perhaps we can go straight through. Of course, if the gate is open, then they must not be aware of the danger. We should warn them."

They went a bit further before Radovan raised his hand and they stopped. He pointed ahead to some reeds growing along the side of the road in the swampy ground. They rustled, though there was no wind. Dante strained to hear something more, voices or the braying of animals or the moan of the dead, but there was nothing.

Dante followed Radovan and Adam in dismounting. This time Bogdana agreed to stay with the horses while they moved forward on foot to investigate. The three men had gotten quite close to the stand of reeds before they saw the source of the rustling. The tall stalks had been concealing four shapes: one human figure lying on the ground, with three others kneeling around it. The prone figure was a big man. He had been torn open in several places. The three kneeling figures were two boys and a woman. There was blood all over the four of them, spattered on the reeds, and more of it flew off their hands as they tore pieces from the man's body.

The boys were even younger than the two children Bogdana and Dante had killed at the river crossing. The woman had her back to Dante. She was kneeling near the man's midsection, and from the motions and sounds she was making, it was clear she was pulling the man's organs out and eating them. The two children growled at her, apparently displeased she was getting the better share of the food. She snarled back and swatted at the one boy who was struggling with the tough sinews of the man's thigh, trying to claw out a piece of it with his fingernails. Dante watched as the other boy, near the man's head, bent down further, placing his hands on the ground and leaning down to tear into the dead man's neck with his teeth. As the child rose back up to a kneeling posture, he held one end of a long strip of flesh in his bloody mouth. The other end was still attached to the dead man, and the undead boy thrashed his head around like a dog would, till the morsel snapped and he sucked it into his mouth like pasta. As he did so, he looked right at Dante with red, rat-like eyes, though he made no move to get up or attack, but slowly chewed the ghoulish mouthful with something like a half smile.

Dante could feel his head going light and feared he might faint. He lowered his gaze, breathing deep and feeling himself shake slightly. He longed not only for the fury of the storm, but for the previous silence, because the slurping and smacking sounds from the three undead people assailed him like cudgels hammering his head. Not just the outside of his skull, but the sounds rattled around inside, giving wet, slapping blows to his brain. He looked up to see Adam and Radovan right by him, apparently watching him to see if he were going to fall over.

"Now we really are in hell, aren't we?" Dante asked in a soft, dry whisper.

Adam shook his head, though he kept an eye on the three kneeling figures. "We live our whole lives right on the edge of infernal places, right where we can see, hear, and touch them at any moment. And, more importantly, where they can touch us. You should know that. There are foretastes of blessedness, and there are foretastes of damnation. Today you will see a great many of the latter in a very short time. You would take God's blessings, and then refuse to look upon evil? Or perhaps even resent that it exists? Are you like Job's wife? I didn't think you so ungrateful, brother."

Dante slowly took in the small, spritely man, dragging his gaze up and down him. Adam had an irrepressible liveliness about him, the bright spark of reason and intellect, but at times like this it seemed to Dante it burned with a cold and comfortless brilliance. Nonetheless his words made Dante look up at the featureless sky, as he tried in this forsaken hell to think of any foretastes of blessedness.

He thought of the warmth of Beatrice's smile, and also of the beauty of her eyes, remembering they too could at times burn as brightly, coldly, and distantly as Adam's wisdom. He thought of the babbling laughter of his two daughters, who could make him smile more easily and comfortably than the intimidating Beatrice ever could. His children held the promise of the future, full of unquestioning love, rather than the threat of rejection or reprimand. He reached farther back in his memory than he had in a long time, retrieving an image of his mother at his bedside when he was very young and sick nearly to death. Although he knew intellectually he had been in great pain during the time he was now recollecting, all that remained now for him to contemplate was the love and devotion shining from her face, the compassion pouring from her gaze even more tangibly than the tears she shed.

He brought his gaze down and glanced over at Bogdana, who carried within herself another blessing, though it chilled Dante to recall his horrible promise to her to preserve and protect that blessing, no matter what horrors were necessary in order to do so. He nodded, and although it still made no sense that blessing and suffering should be so intertwined, he felt a little calmer and less despairing at their strange confluence.

He looked past Adam at the three dead people still feeding, still oblivious to the three living men, gorging their apparently limitless bellies and empty minds with as much blood and flesh as they could rend and tear from either the body or from each other's greedy hands.

"Why don't they attack us?" he asked.

Adam seemed to hear Dante's voice was more resolute and less pained. "Why do you think?"

Dante considered them in as detached and objective a manner as he could. Although he could keep himself from shaking or weeping or running away, the nausea was unavoidable at the sight of what they were doing to another human being's body. "They don't realize we're a danger, so they go on eating. They only kill in order to feed, so they won't attack us until they're done with their present victim."

Adam nodded. "Exactly. They are both more and less human than we are, more and less evil. They cannot kill for pleasure, or honor, or even hate. If only all men were as they are, in this one respect. But they are so full of hunger, so completely full of emptiness, they cannot think of anything else—not even self-preservation. And their emptiness will never be full. They will never stop on their own."

"I understand," Dante said. "But if it would not be considered a kind of ingratitude, I would ask not to have to kill a child again, since I already helped kill two yesterday."

"That is not ingratitude, my son. That is decency," Adam said, and he and Radovan moved to either side, to stand behind the two children as Dante stepped forward and stood behind the woman.

They left the woman and the two boys slumped forward on the body they had been desecrating, though Dante knew the three who had been eating were far more tainted and defiled than the one they had eaten. But now at least all four of them were finally and truly dead, and death was sometimes a blessing, as Brother Adam's strange theology would have it.

After Dante got on his horse and they moved forward, Bogdana leaned over and touched his shoulder. He could not bear to look at her, to sully her beauty by gazing on it with the same eyes that had just beheld such monstrous, revolting things. He only let himself feel her presence and sympathy through her light touch, as he looked down at the ugly, nearly black mud sucking at the horses' hooves.

Chapter 15

Howl the rain maketh them like unto dogs;
One side they make a shelter for the other;
Oft turn themselves the wretched reprobates.
Dante, *Inferno,* 6.19-21

As they approached the town walls, they could see that the gates were open. Not only open, they also seemed to be abandoned. The entrance to the town was as desolate as the fields through which they had been riding. They stopped just outside the gates to survey the situation.

"Go through?" Radovan asked.

"It'd save us time," Adam said. "Perhaps the people have left already." Just then, from somewhere inside the town they heard a cheer, followed by what sounded like singing, though it was too far away to make out clearly. "Well, then there are still people here. We need to warn them. Clearly if they're singing, with their gate open and unguarded, they must not know what's going on."

They proceeded through the gate, past deserted houses and shops. Everything was in a violent disarray, with carts spilled over in the street, and various items—tools, implements, broken pottery, and glass—scattered on the ground. There were some dark brown splotches and burn marks on the ground and on many of the walls. Some of the windows were smashed, but most were boarded up. Dante caught the metallic scent of blood, and the heavy, stinging, malignant smell of smoldering embers that had been left to fester. He saw nothing move, however, and no fires raging or blood flowing, so they kept moving forward.

The cheering sound returned, followed by laughter, then the indistinct murmuring of a crowd. All of them flinched and bristled at the sound of an animal roaring in pain or rage, but this was drowned out by laughter, so they kept going.

They came out into a more open area, where they finally saw the crowd they had heard. Several dozen men were there, gathered around long tables. There were no women or children in sight. Most of the men were standing, though several were lolling on the ground; some of the prone figures appeared immobile. There were many barrels on the tables, along with various foods, and nearby three boars were spitted over low fires. Here the smells were slightly more savory than what had greeted Dante so far in this town. Although it was still impossible for him to consider food after what he'd just seen, even he could appreciate the sweet but heavy aroma coming from the roasting meat. It was an irresistible kind of pull to anyone's senses, even if their minds rebelled unnaturally against it.

But the pleasant smell was more than offset by the other, animalistic scents that came with several days of debauchery—spilled beer and wine, wasted food left to rot, and even men's urine and vomit. Such animal detritus lay all over the ground, pounded into the dark, wet mud by hundreds of feet until all of it was mixed together into a sickening, grey slop. Those men still conscious waded through such filth carelessly, as they grabbed up more food or guzzled down more drink, while those who were groggy or passed out wallowed in it without shame.

Beyond the men and tables, the ground sloped down into a large indentation, like a pit. In it there were two poles erected. They were much thicker than the stake Dante had seen the woman tied to the other day. Two bears were tied to one of these. Both of them were fairly small, but one was obviously still a cub. The other was probably its mother, judging by how it stayed close to the smaller animal and seemed to be shielding it. The rope holding the cub was tied to the one holding the mother, and the mother's rope was tied to the pole. To the other pole a large dog was tied; it strained against its bonds, sometimes moving close to the bears to bark at them, sometimes running to the other side to menace those of the crowd who stood close to the bear pit, shouting and laughing at the tormented animals. All three animals were bloodied, with gashes on the faces and sides, and patches of fur torn from their abused bodies. The bodies of several dead dogs were scattered around the pit as well, some bent in such a way that their backs were clearly broken, some with their throats ripped out, some with their entrails hanging out, victims of the cruelty of man and the savage power of beasts.

Some of the men closer to Dante and his companions had now noticed them. "Eh, what have we here?" one drawled, as the group of drunks staggered toward them. He was bigger than the others, with a thick, black beard and hair, and perhaps slightly less drunk than most of his companions. He leered at Bogdana. "Oooh, you brought us a lovely little mother bird, I see. I like the way you wrap your legs around that horse, darling. Care to spread them for me, before we all die? Can't do any harm."

"She's so big, I'm afraid something would grab me if I stuck it to her!" shouted another drunk, causing the crowd to roar with laughter.

The laughter died down as Bogdana pulled back on the reins and her horse reared up, then it took two steps back. "Pigs!" she shouted. "Why do you have no sense?"

Dante and Radovan both pulled their horses to one side to get between her and the crowd, which gave way before them. Both men also drew their swords. "What is wrong with you?" Radovan shouted at them. "This isn't the time for such foolishness."

"There's never a time for acting like beasts, but that won't stop them," Dante muttered.

The crowd backed up at the threat of harm. "Easy, strangers," said the man who had first spoken. "No need to spoil our fun, is there? Like I said, no harm in some fun before we all die. Isn't that what the Good Book tells us? 'Eat, drink, and be merry, for tomorrow we die.' We were just offering to make merry with this fine lady." The crowd chuckled, though much more restrained than before. "And it's not very Christian of you not to share, I'm thinking." The crowd grumbled some agreement, but despite their numbers, the way they tottered and laughed and retched, Dante hardly felt threatened by them, just disgusted.

Adam still seemed to think common sense and self-interest would work, though Dante doubted it would have any more effect than trying to argue biblical interpretation or Christian morality with such men. "Friends," Adam began. "The dead have obviously been here. Perhaps you fought them off the first time, but there will be more, and the army right behind them, to destroy you all. Surely you can see that. Please, flee—either to escape the army or to beg their mercy. Please do it and give up this madness."

The crowd was already losing interest in them, going back to the barrels and bottles and platters that held more reliable and less contentious distractions. "Ah, some bookish, churchly, old fop and a couple of loons with pig stickers. Begone!" Black beard waved them off as he turned away. "Not worth getting my nose bloodied for a knocked up skirt like her anyway. Better just to drink away the memory of skirts, and children, and work, and dead people walking around. Right boys?" The crowd cheered at this. Black beard raised a tankard. "Here's to dulling the pain. The only thing fit for a day like today! Or any other!" The crowd roared even louder, then Dante heard a flute from somewhere in the crowd, and they broke out into song again. This time Dante was close enough to make out the words:

Oh Fiddler's Green is a lovely place,
Where no scolds stop you from stuffing your face!
The weather's always fine, there's never a storm.
And everything's beautiful—no rust and no worm!
And work? What work? There's nothing to do!
Except eat fine dainties and drink the best brew!
There's a river of wine, and trees that drip brandy.
And under each tree—a wench with a fig sweet as candy!
So if I've been laid low by Jehovah or some spirit unclean,
Then just look for me, friends, on Fiddler's Green!

The song degenerated into random laughter and shouted obscenities, accompanied by the sound of smashing tables and glasses, as the newcomers were forgotten completely and the men returned to what they did best and most cheerfully with their lives.

As Dante pulled the reins to the left to get his horse moving forward, he looked over to Bogdana. He was aghast to see her off her horse, leading it by the reins and making her way toward the crowd.

"What the hell are you doing?" he said, pulling his horse back the other way to get closer to her.

She'd taken another step. Now Dante noticed an unconscious man on the ground not far from her, a generous shank of roasted pig held across his chest. Bogdana nimbly lunged for the food, snatched it out of the man's hands, then turned and swung herself back on to her horse, before any of the semi-conscious members of the crowd took a renewed interest in her. She turned her horse and came up next to Dante, biting into the meat as she went, pink juices welling up out of it and on to her lips.

"What were you thinking?" he scolded her. Seeing her ripping off the glistening, greasy meat with her teeth nearly made him gag. "How the hell can you eat now?"

She chewed as she eyed him, tilting her head down a little and cocking an eyebrow. "You are an exceptionally kind man," she said. "And I think a very smart one, too. But I know for certain you have never been pregnant, and you can have no idea what roasting meat smells like to me right now, and how it makes me feel. So please, just look away if it bothers you, and let me eat."

Dante looked at her eyes, which were as stern and as beautiful as Beatrice's, but much more simple and direct. They filled him with a different kind of strength. Not the strength of wonder and awe, but of appreciation and a kind of freedom, so long as he could look into them without noticing the animal leg, which she was so savagely tearing into. He could just manage this trick, if he held his head up and squinted a bit, which he gladly did, so as not to retch or lose courage.

Over to Dante's left, Radovan said, "Let's go," just before several long, high-pitched screams of fear and pain assailed them from the far side of the crowd.

Chapter 16

Cerberus, monster cruel and uncouth,
With his three gullets like a dog is barking
Over the people that are there submerged.
Dante, *Inferno*, 6.13-15

At first Dante couldn't tell what was happening. Then he looked where the crowd was parting, men running and screaming in all directions, and he could see the enormous dog they had been using for sport had broken free from its tether and was now running amok. The animal bit and tore at the men, and when it caught one and took him down with a crippling bite, it didn't stay on him, but immediately got up to attack another man. Its rampage was doing the most damage to the greatest number of men. Dante thought if several of the men stood together, they might be able to get the animal back under control. Instead, every man scurried randomly around the area, crashing into others, sometimes knocking one another down, where they were even more helpless against the dog's attacks. Some dashed into the buildings nearby, or ran down the streets. Then Dante heard another roar and looked to where the two bears were. The mother bear had also torn free from her bonds. The cub was still attached to her by the rope, and they were tearing a swath through the crowd, driving some of the drunken, panicked men back toward the dog.

Dante thought perhaps they should do something to help, or at least make a move to get away from there, but the whole scene of pandemonium held him mesmerized. It didn't include just the vicarious, indulgent cruelty of a public execution or flogging. What they were watching now was even more enjoyable, because there was more going on, like some terrible, violent, random dance put on for them. It was, for Dante, a consciously guilty pleasure, but he nonetheless sat there with the others, dumbstruck and enthralled. He could see out of the corner of his eye that Bogdana kept on eating, steadily gnawing the shank down to the bone as the men dispersed or fell screaming and bleeding to the ground.

After just a few seconds of furious animal violence, the three marauding creatures cleared the area and now stood before Dante and his friends. Oddly, the bears and the dog barely seemed to notice one another now, but stood there with all their attention focused on the four people on horseback. Dante's attention moved between the three wild animals, even more captivating now in their still and savage beauty than they had been in their frantic orgy of destruction. The cub was the least bloodied of the trio, its mother the most injured. So many teeth and claws must have raked her flesh for the sake of her young. Both of them seemed more bent and diminished from the ordeal than the dog, but all three animals looked powerfully in control, their large knots of muscle tensing slightly as they shifted their weight, their fur sleek and surprisingly clean. They did not growl or roar, nor did they blink. Their eyes were tranquil in their blankness, like polished obsidian. For what seemed to Dante a very long time, the only sounds were the moans of the wounded men, the ragged, wet panting of the three beasts, and the occasional neighing of their horses, nervous to be so near such wild, dangerous animals.

"They're only animals," Adam observed. "They know how to behave."

"Well, I'd still like them to get out of the way, so we can move on," Radovan said.

"Hey, doggie," Bogdana said, leaning to the right and dangling the bone she had cleaned of most all its flesh. Dante's eyes went wide at the sight of her small hand holding the greasy bone. He thought despite how nimble she was, the giant dog could probably lunge and bite through her wrist before she could pull it back. She was smiling and making clicking sounds, however, as she shook the bone at it. The dog crouched, still not growling, but coiled, ready to spring, its eyes now fixed on the prize she held. "No trick, just treat! Now find the way out of this mess! Hyah!"

Bogdana flung the bone back down the street they had come in on, and the dog tore after it, the two bears following right behind. It only took the dog a second to snatch the morsel up, and when it did, it looked back at them, though it made no move to return to them. The bears went shambling by the dog as it gnawed on its prize, then it too followed them down the street, back toward the town gate.

The three men stared at Bogdana, eyebrows raised, mouths slightly open.

"What?" she said, looking from the fleeing animals back to the men. "It was only a dog. You yourself said it behaved well."

Adam smiled and shook his head. "I didn't know you trusted my judgments so completely."

She shrugged. "Well, not really, but I've seen a lot of dogs before. It wasn't acting like it was going to attack. Bears are harder to judge, of course, especially a mother with its young, but they didn't look like they'd harm us, either. They just needed an excuse to run away, a prize, something to make them think they were choosing to do so and not just being told to—sort of a way to save face." She moved her gaze between the three of them. "What, you don't think animals need to save face too, feel proud of themselves and not ashamed?" She shook her head and rolled her eyes. "Oh, please. They're not so hard to understand, if you'd just pay attention. Now, let's get out of here." She nudged her horse's flanks with her heels. Dante and the others followed her away from there. Dante constantly looked over his shoulder, though he saw nothing other than the empty buildings, the overturned tables, the spilled food, and the moaning, writhing bodies scattered on the corrupted ground.

Chapter 17

**"For all the gold that is beneath the moon,
Or ever has been, of these weary souls
Could never make a single one repose."
Dante, *Inferno*, 7.64-66**

They kept moving further into the town, past more deserted buildings. As before, there were no signs of the living or dead. Dante looked up and saw the sky remained featureless and still, the clouds unmoving and oddly dry looking, like a dusty shroud over them. He thought how refreshing some rain would feel on his face, but also thought it might impede their progress, muddying the roads and making it harder to see. For the time being they were moving ahead steadily, making for the other side of the town, where he hoped they could exit through another gate and continue on their way, perhaps making better time once they were out in the wilderness again.

From somewhere up ahead, they heard a commotion. It wasn't as loud as the drunken party had been, but it also didn't sound as cheerful, consisting of the sound of breaking glass, some crashes—like the sound of boxes being dropped and smashed—and men cursing.

They came around a bend in the street to find the source of the noise—four men trying to load a large cart, which was attached to two sturdy looking horses. One of the men was well-dressed, as was a woman who sat atop the cart, holding the reins to the horses. The other men were dressed in coarser, simpler clothes. The cart was already loaded to the point where it was difficult to imagine how the men intended to climb aboard it themselves, yet they continued to cram crates and bundles on to it, tying them to the other contents in an attempt to keep them from falling off. Two crates lay broken on the street next to the cart, and one man was scooping up their contents—clothes and some metal objects, like candlesticks and pots and pans—and tossing them into the nooks and crannies between other packages on the cart.

"You there," Adam addressed them. "You're preparing to escape? You know the dead are nearby?"

The well-dressed man stopped to answer, as the other men kept loading the impossibly-full cart. "Yes, of course."

"Good," Adam continued. "But really, shouldn't you hurry? It'd be better just to leave all this stuff behind."

The man waved him off, turning his attention back to directing the other men loading the cart, who took his orders as though they were his servants. "No, no, of course we can't just leave everything! That's ridiculous! Don't be silly! It's bad enough we have to leave all the furniture and big items, not to mention the house! We can't leave all the smaller valuables as well!"

Adam looked to Dante and shook his head. "I see," he said. "Well, could you tell us where the gate is on this side of town?"

The man gestured down the street they were on. "Just follow this street. It's not far from here."

"And is that gate open, would you happen to know?" Dante asked. The idea of having to backtrack through this town, with its strange, unpredictable inhabitants, was extremely unappealing to him right now. Not to mention all the time they'd lose if they had to double back. Indeed, he felt sure either the delay or the inhabitants could prove fatal to them at this point.

"How should I know?" the man said in a huff. "Now can you please just leave us alone? We need to finish here!" He was acting frustrated, probably because it was becoming clear even to him that all the bundles and crates they had piled up on the street were simply not going to go on the cart, no matter what they did, how hard they tried, or how much he wanted them to fit. Indeed, as he yelled at his servants to be careful with some package of goods, and gave directions on how better to stack the things, one of the ropes snapped and several more crates hit the pavement with the sound of splitting wood and shattering crockery.

"Really, perhaps you should go now," Adam suggested. "We could go with you to the gate, and we'd all make it out of here."

"Curse you!" the man yelled. "Stop distracting these useless dolts! Just begone! We can't fit the cart through that gate anyway. It's too small! We'll go to the main gate!"

Adam still tried to reason. "But the army is coming that way. They'll be here very soon."

"Just leave, damn your hide!"

Dante watched, with the same sick fascination as he had watched the animals attacking the drunken men before, as the man began kicking at two of the servants, who were scrambling on the ground to pick up some of the unbroken items. Then Dante caught another motion out of the corner of his eye and heard a sickly groan, savage and unrestrained, but at the same time dry, hoarse, and pathetic. He turned to see a dead man clutching at Radovan, who reeled from the loathsome touch, lost his balance, and tumbled off his horse on the other side. Dante saw two more dead people, a man and a woman, slightly behind the first attacker.

Bogdana gave a shriek of surprise. She was off her horse before anyone else could react. She didn't bother with an improvised weapon this time, but snatched a hatchet from her saddlebag. The way she had it in her hand so quickly, she must have deliberately packed it so it would be easy to bring forth as a weapon. Dante hadn't noticed that particular precaution on her part, and although he thought how he should be used to it by now, he could not help again wondering at her preparedness and savagery.

Adam dismounted as well, while Dante stayed in the saddle and drew his sword as he wheeled his horse around. Fortunately for Radovan, falling as he did put his horse between himself and his attackers.

"God's blood!" he cursed as he drew his own sword.

The dead man was clawing at the horse, still trying to get at

Radovan, and that made the animal neigh and jump forward. As it did, Radovan raised his sword, and as soon as the animal was clear, he smashed the blade on to the dead man's head. But this walking corpse was wearing a helmet. The blow threw him to the side and off balance, but it didn't crush or penetrate his skull. His arms clawed out in front of himself as he came back to a standing posture and his groan rose in pitch to a howl of rage.

Radovan drew back his sword for a thrust, then shoved the point up through his attacker's neck and on through to the back of his head. The dead man clutched at the blade, the sharp edges digging into his palms as he thrashed about, yanking the blade around, thereby widening the wound in his neck and further shredding the base of his brain with the sword tip. But this last spasm prevented Radovan from pulling back his sword, and the other two dead people were almost on him as well. Before they could attack, Bogdana had closed with the other dead man, drawing the hatchet back across her left shoulder as she ran, and then she brought it down diagonally on to his head. The blow buried the iron blade two inches into the dead man's skull. She kicked him in the stomach as she pulled back on the hatchet, sending him to the ground, where he lay still.

At the same time, Dante had come up on the other side of Radovan and raised his sword against the dead woman. She turned her attention from Radovan to look at the blade raised above her head. Whatever had killed her, it had left her face uninjured, and she had clearly been a young and pretty woman, perhaps no older than Bogdana. Her hair was blonde and curly, her figure more voluptuous than Bogdana's; her clothes were finely sewn, with lace around the neck, and she still had on some jewelry. She looked, in short, much more like the kind of woman Dante was used to—pampered, feminine, fragile, demure. At least until she bared her bloody teeth and snarled with all the rage and hunger a human mouth could spit forth at the uncaring world, and the cruel blade held above her. But even then, Dante held his hand, shaking slightly with a terrible fear at the perverted beauty in front of him, and with a sickly disgust at his own impotence and confusion.

As he stayed there, the woman's snarl turned to a wheeze, her jaw dropped more, and she fell to her knees, then on to her face. The back of her head was split, and some blood and brains slipped out on to her blonde locks. Bogdana stood over her, holding the bloody hatchet. She looked up at Dante as she bent down to clean the blade on the dead woman's skirts.

"As much as I admire your kindness," she said softly, "this is not the place for mercy."

Dante could only nod and sheathe his sword. "I know," he said. "Thank you."

Dante now noticed how Bogdana held the hatchet close to the axe head. It would give her more control and keep her from being thrown off balance by a wild swing, even though it would bring her closer to her adversary and lose some of the force of the blow. He marveled at her controlled, calculated violence, and again could not understand how a woman knew such things or behaved in such ways. Everything she did was always so direct and practical, without subtlety or guile. Women in Florence were not like this.

Radovan finally disengaged his sword from the dead man, whose body fell on its side and continued to twitch. His useless, gutted head flopped around every which way, the way a fish did when it's pulled out on a hook and dropped on to the ground. His paroxysms kept clanging the helmet into the cobblestones over and over, as his tongue lolled out and he gurgled in the most sickening way. Then his legs danced around, propelling his body around like a spoke on a wheel, with his shoulder as the center point of the axle.

"Oh, this is just the end," Radovan muttered as he sheathed his sword and drew his dagger. "You two, hold his legs. Keep him from spinning around like that or he might knock me over."

Bogdana and Adam grabbed the dead man's feet as Radovan knelt down and sawed through the helmet's chin strap with his dagger. He pulled the helmet off, raised it up, and smashed it back down into the side of the man's head. The whole body finally went slack with a low, dry moan.

Radovan sent the helmet clattering across the paving stones as he stood up. They all looked to see the people by the cart had stayed right where they were, watching them, and now the four men returned to their futile attempts at loading the vehicle. Radovan pointed to them.

"You!" he shouted. "I was almost killed because we were busy arguing with you over your madness, and you keep loading your silly cart?"

The well dressed man shrugged and heaved a bundle up to one of his men who was perched atop the heap of possessions. "I didn't ask you to argue. I didn't ask you to stay. I wouldn't have said anything to you, if it were up to me. So go."

Radovan shook with anger as he stomped to his horse and pulled himself up. Adam helped Bogdana on to her horse, then he got on his. "Please," he tried one last time, "you see the dead are already here. Won't you come with us? Just leave these things and come with us."

"I said we would not!" His voice had risen to a shriek. "Why can't you just go? Are you crazy?"

"No," Adam said as he pulled the reins and they started forward. "We are not."

Dante heard cursing and crashing as they rode away, but he did not look back. He half-expected the sounds to turn to screams as more of the dead attacked the cart-fillers, but the sounds did not change until they were out of earshot. Dante felt some relief at this, though he could not help but feel that the blonde, dead woman, snarling like an animal in a trap, and the dead man spinning on the pavement like a bird with a broken wing, were both much fitter objects for his concern and pity.

Chapter 18

And I, who stood intent upon beholding,
Saw people mud-besprent in that lagoon,
All of them naked and with angry look.
Dante, *Inferno*, 7.109-111

They came within sight of the wall. The gate, as the man at the cart had said, looked small—wide enough for a horse and rider, perhaps for two animals or people, if they were pushed right up against one another. They saw no one near it, but before they got too close to it, they heard voices from one of the houses.

Many of the larger houses in the town were built in a way Dante was familiar with, having two or three storeys surrounding a central courtyard. A sort of tunnel passed through the ground floor, under the upper storeys, thereby connecting the courtyard directly to the street. The voices seemed to be coming from the courtyard of one of these buildings. The door to the tunnel was open, and inside it was dark, though they could see the grey light of the courtyard beyond it.

Radovan looked into the tunnel. "It's too narrow and low for the horses," he said. "And we can't leave them alone out here. Maybe we should just keep going."

"There are people in there," Adam said. "Bogdana and I can stay here. You two go in and warn them and come right back out. Unless one of you wants to stay out here and I'll go in."

Radovan and Dante looked at each other. Dante was not at all sure which was really the more dangerous assignment: staying out here in the street, visible and exposed to attack from any direction, or going in to greet more citizens of this town, when all they had met so far were less than welcoming. But he was sure, from the way the offer had been presented, to refuse or modify it would seem craven, dishonorable, and unworthy. He climbed down from his horse at the same time Radovan did.

The two of them proceeded to the door, and Radovan shouted down the tunnel. "Hello? Do you need help?"

The voices stopped for a second, then one replied, "Help? No, but come in, if you want. It's safe."

Radovan and Dante looked at each other, drew their swords, and proceeded down the tunnel. The tunnel was short enough that it was not too dark inside it, so they could see where they were stepping. As dank and frightening as it was there, nothing menaced them as they walked through to the courtyard.

In the courtyard were six big men, standing around two large tables in the middle of the area. A ladder leaned against one of the walls, thereby connecting the courtyard to a window on the second floor. The men were all dressed in the coarse clothes of those who worked with their hands—laborers, smiths, miners, masons. The inside of the courtyard—both the walls and ground—were spattered everywhere with blood, as were the men. The place reeked of blood, with a tinge of alcohol rising above the metallic, slightly sweet smell of mortality. In one corner was a pile of motionless bodies. In several other places, indistinct to Dante at first, other bodies writhed and moaned. They appeared to be chained to the walls or ground. Dante kept his focus on these more than on the men, as he and Radovan approached the tables.

The tables were not set for the kind of debauchery Dante had just seen, but for more simmering, malignant entertainment. What food there was set on it was simple—large loaves of dark bread mostly, with a few scraps of cheese. There were wine skins and bottles too, but the smell was not of wine or beer, but of distilled liquor. It was the strange, smoky, bracing smell of brandy or the like, not the acidic and cloying smell of wine, nor the stale and yeasty smell of beer. Scattered among these provisions of animal necessities there were tools and weapons—knives, hatchets, pliers, awls, hammers. Most all of these had blood on them.

Dante looked at the men. They were not the red-faced, wide-eyed drunks he had seen at the bear-baiting spectacle. The faces here were dark and grizzled, with dirt, soot, and blood filling every crease, and their eyes squinted slightly. These men didn't loll about and laugh like drunks. They stood there as erect and solid as tombstones, their huge fists waiting at their sides. These were not the kind of men who drank to forget and to lose control. These men drank just enough to gain control and direct their fury more potently and destructively. These were the kind of men who could come home every night and beat their wives nearly to death, or who could come home and pummel the neighbor to death, because he had been beating his wife or children. Or because his dog was barking. Or because it was Tuesday. Or they might go their whole lives without ever striking anyone in anger, though the thought had been with them every waking moment of their lives, as well as filling their every dream, and they had restrained such violence with an inhuman denial and discipline, never vanquishing or exorcising it. These men were not dissipated. Instead, their animal essence was too tightly packed within their huge frames. They were not brash and loud, but that made them all the more dangerous.

The six men seemed to sense their visitors' unease. They stayed on the other side of the table and did not make any moves to approach Dante and Radovan, which was just fine with Dante.

One of the men, with a bushy, red beard and hair, addressed the two newcomers. "You are right, strangers, to be on your guard. But please, we mean you no harm. We have everything we need here to vent our anger and keep ourselves content with our lot. Perhaps you would join us for a moment? Surely you too are sick at what is happening all around us, and need the blessed release that comes from roaring out your anger against all this madness and pain?"

With this strange speech, Dante began to rethink his estimate of how much the men drank. "What do you mean?" he asked. "What are you doing here? Are those people dead?" He gestured with his free hand at the chained bodies, writhing in various postures around the courtyard.

"Of course," the man responded. "We only chain them up if they are. What do you take us for?"

"Men who have lost much," Dante said.

"Then you are right." The man gestured to his friends. "You all stay here, by the tables. Take a rest, while I explain to our visitors. Will that be all right?"

"All right," Dante said.

The man led them to where a dead man was chained to the wall by a thick collar around his neck. His mouth was gagged with cloths and a leather belt, and his hands were tied behind his back. He was bloody all over his face and torso. The dead man grew more agitated as they came closer, straining at the end of his chain and roaring into the gag, though all that came out was a sort of huffing, snorting sound. His eyes went wide with rage at them, with seething jealousy that they were alive, and overwhelming frustration that he could not make them dead.

Dante and Radovan stopped about ten feet from the furthest reach of the dead man's tether, but their guide took another couple steps, raised his gigantic right fist, and smashed it into the dead man's left eye. The blow turned the dead man slightly and drove him down to one knee, but he was almost immediately back up, still huffing into his gag, and looking more at Dante than at his attacker. The undead creature appeared almost plaintive now, it seemed to Dante, though he might have imagined it in the toxic swirl of emotions in the dead man's eyes.

"Good afternoon, Filip," his attacker said then punched him in the stomach, and then in the face again. The one blow bent him down, while the other straightened him back up.

The big man stepped back to where Dante and Radovan watched silently, mouths slightly open. "This is Filip," he said. "He was my neighbor. He must've turned into one of them while I was away from my home, working at the forge. He killed my wife. She's locked up, down in the basement. I found him eating her heart. He might as well have eaten mine, since I stopped feeling anything at that moment." He held up his two enormous, calloused hands. "Perhaps I should've crushed his head at once, but I had this better idea: to keep him here, so my anger and grief would never have to go away." He gestured to the other men, in the center of the courtyard around the tables. "I found some of my friends, and they liked the idea, too. It would give us something to do. It would give us some relief. So we brought some of these things here, the ones we didn't kill outright, the ones who'd caused us some special pain and loss, and now we know they'll always suffer. Our revenge against them never needs to end. Never."

Radovan shook his head. "Where is the honor in that?" he asked in a hoarse voice. "He's chained up. He can't fight back. He's not even alive or responsible anymore. It's over. End it."

The man smiled. His teeth seemed larger than normal, and they looked exceptionally white against his dirty face. "Honor? Oh, I know there's no honor here. But where is there any honor anymore? Men say they kill other men for honor, but I don't believe them. They kill animals for food, I suppose. But this is better than honor or food. These things aren't even human anymore. That's what makes it right! I can hit these things over and over and never kill them. I can spit on them, piss on them if I want to, and no one will dare stop me or tell me I'm doing something wrong, exactly because these things aren't human, and because they hurt all of us so badly. I can do anything I want, just for spite and revenge. Come, let me show you another."

"No, really, that's not necessary," Dante stammered.

The man was not smiling now. "I will show you another," he said slowly. "And then you can go."

Dante tried to keep himself from looking at the man's fists, so as not to show fear, but it was all he could do to stop from shaking, either at the idea of this giant losing his temper, or at the prospect of what further torture and inhumanity they were going to be forced to witness.

"Another," he said quietly. "And then we'll go."

The man led them to where a thin man was chained to the wall by his wrists, his arms straight out from his sides, parallel to the ground, his body leaning forward slightly, bending his arms behind himself. The man was older, with a long, grey beard almost down to his waist. He wore a robe, and both it and his beard were soaked in blood. He wore no muzzle, and his lips fell inward to his mouth, the way someone's lips do when they have no teeth. If he only imagined the other dead man looked plaintive, Dante could not say the same about this one. Both his moan and his wet, exhausted-looking eyes could only be described as mournful and pathetic, like a beaten dog's.

"This is my favorite," the man said. "This is our dear priest. This is the all-licensed fool who told us every week about peace and brotherhood and a kind, loving, sky Daddy who'd make everything all right! A Father? My real father never brought me much joy, and you promised me yet another one to punish me? But this one would be even more powerful, more terrible? Is this your Kingdom of God? This is hell on earth. It's not heaven, but I can enjoy it in my own way." He bent down to pick up a pair of pliers off the ground. It was then Dante noticed all the teeth scattered around. The old priest hadn't been toothless when they bound him to the wall. "'If your eye offends you, pluck it out!' Didn't I hear you preach that shit once? But eyes come later. I want you to see what I'm doing, see what's coming, a little longer, I think. So we'll go with, 'If your hand offends you, cut it off, and cast it from you.'"

With the pliers he grabbed the pinkie of the dead man's left hand. Dante was still not sure if the dead felt pain. He had seen them receive crippling wounds without flinching, but he didn't know if this was because they didn't feel them, or had the willpower to ignore them. But as the dead man's moan rose to a piercing wail, and his whole body went rigid as he strained against his bonds, it seemed all too likely he was feeling the abuse, as well as the burning hate and rage that guided the torturer's hand. There was a sick snapping sound, then the digit and the tool were flung to the ground.

"Well, at least part of a hand. We need to save some of it for tomorrow, and the next day, and the day after that."

Dante watched the dead man go slack. His attention was drawn away by some clattering, moaning, and shrieking nearby. He looked to where there was some kind of animal pen that was built next to the wall of the courtyard, which formed one side of the enclosure. The gate at the front of it had been reinforced with metal bars, and there was a lattice work of metal bars across the top of it as well. This lattice work on top was rattling violently, and Dante could see small fingers poking up through it. Almost involuntarily, he took two steps towards the enclosure.

"I know I promised only one more thing to show you," the man said. "But perhaps you'd look at these as well?"

Dante took another step and peered closer at the metal grate. He saw lips pressed up to it, along with mad, wild eyes. Some tongues snaked up through the gaps between the bars. The sounds subsided to grunts and growls.

"These are the children. We keep them safe here. They like being out in the fresh air, I think."

"But why?" Radovan asked. "You keep the others to torture them, because you're so angry at them. But what do you do with the children, if you say you're keeping them safe?"

"Well, we don't punish or hurt them!" The big man actually looked taken aback by the insinuation, if that were possible. "We're not animals."

"No, you are not animals," Dante said quietly, still looking at the hungry eyes staring at him from behind the metal bars, the tongues licking the air like they could taste blood and fear.

"Sometimes, before we go to pay a visit to Filip or the good reverend or one of the others, we like to look at the children first, in case we need a reminder of how angry we are. We look at their poor, innocent faces, turned into ravening beasts, at their bloody necks and broken limbs, and then we can spend a much more satisfying few minutes with one of the monsters that made them this way. Sometimes our grief and rage subside, just a little. We find the children do a fine job of renewing it."

Dante looked at the man. "We have seen what you wanted to show us. We will go now."

"Of course."

"You won't come with us?"

"No, why would we? We have everything we need right here." He gestured around the courtyard. "We will find more of the monsters to satisfy our wrath. And if there get to be too many of them, we can climb up to the second floor." He pointed to the ladder. "We have a couple chained up there, too, in case."

Dante nodded, then he and Radovan walked back to where Adam and Bogdana were waiting for them.

"We heard screaming," Adam said. "We were about to come in and see if you needed help. Are you all right?"

"We're fine," Dante said. "Physically, we are fine."

"Are there people in there? Did you warn them?"

"Yes," Radovan answered, as he and Dante got back on their horses.

"Are they coming out?" Adam continued.

"No," Radovan said.

"Why not?"

"They say they already have everything they want," Dante said.

"That's funny," Bogdana said.

As usual, she had caught and interpreted his tone much more fully than Adam, as wise as he was. Dante lowered and turned his head away from her. He couldn't stand for her to see his eyes filling with tears—both because of the shame it caused him at his own weakness, and out of fear it might cause her to lose courage. "In a way, I suppose it is," he said very softly, so only she could hear it.

She leaned closer to him, till her shoulder touched his. "But you are not laughing." Then even more softly she said, "I know when you are hurt, Dante. When what you've seen is almost too much for you." It was the first time she'd said his name, and he felt quite certain she knew the power that would have over him. All women did. "And I know you are stronger than you think. I need you. I trust you."

He wiped his eyes on his upper sleeve as briefly and discreetly as he could, so that he could turn back to her. Her face was serene—not happy or sad, not even concerned exactly, but placid, as he needed it to be at that moment. He dared to touch her cheek with the back of his hand, and she let him, briefly, before she withdrew just a little. She gave him the barest hint of a smile before she lightly kicked her horse's flanks and moved on ahead of him.

Chapter 19

"Fixed in the mire they say, 'We sullen were
In the sweet air, which by the sun is gladdened,
Bearing within ourselves the sluggish reek . . . '"
Dante, *Inferno*, 7.121-123

Crossing an open area where various items were strewn, they arrived at the smaller gate. The wall itself was masonry, about fifteen feet high, the gate in it about nine. The doors across it were metal grates, hinged at the two sides and meeting in the middle. A chain with a padlock was looped around the metal bars. They dismounted to investigate it. It was locked.

"Damn," Radovan muttered.

"I'm supposed to keep the gate closed," a voice came down to them from above.

They looked up to see a man poking his head over the parapet at the top of the wall. He wore a helmet, but they couldn't see any more of him. After the statement, he withdrew and they didn't even see that anymore.

"We need to get out," Adam explained. "The dead are already in the town. Most of the living seem to be gone already. Could you please open the gate? Do you have the key?"

"Of course I have the key," the voice came from behind the parapet. "But I'm not supposed to. I could get in trouble."

"I ought to climb up there and give you trouble," Radovan said, clenching his fists.

"You're welcome to try. The ladder's in pieces down there. I made sure it was before I dropped it on the ground."

They saw two long poles on the ground nearby. About half the rungs that connected them were broken, like someone had chopped through a few at one end, then yanked the two uprights apart to split it in two.

"Why can't you just throw down the key?" Adam said. "You should get out too. It's best."

"Why? I don't know you. I don't owe you anything. I have orders. What good would come of it? If I came down and ran, I'd just die out in the woods tonight or tomorrow. I'm perfectly safe up here for now, and you have no more problems because of me than you'd have if I weren't up here, so I'm not doing you any harm. Go away and leave me alone."

Adam turned away from the futile conversation and back to the lock. "What strange people," he said. "Can you break the lock?"

"The lock?" Radovan said. "No. The links of the chain are thinner. Find a metal bar or pole and we might be able to pry one open."

They heard moaning and shuffling from nearby, and looked over to see two dead people approaching them. "You two—work on the chain," Adam said, gesturing to Dante and Radovan. "We need to distract them." He reached into his saddle bag and pulled a flat, black stone from it.

Bogdana had her hatchet out. She followed Adam to a wooden handcart full of hay that lay in the open area, between them and the two dead people. Dante looked around and saw two more dead people had also picked up the alarm, shuffling out of another door and heading toward them. Adam overturned the cart and knelt in the hay spilled on the ground. He struck a knife against the piece of flint he had gotten from his saddle bag, sending sparks on to the tinder, which he kept blowing on till it smoked and a small flame started to take hold of the dried grass.

"Get more wood to throw on," he said to Bogdana as he took out his staff. "They're afraid of fire, but only if it's burning very intensely."

Dante and Radovan, meanwhile, rummaged around among the things scattered on the ground, trying to find a piece of metal big enough to pry at the chain.

"Here," Radovan came up with a chisel. "This probably isn't long enough, but it's thick enough."

A second before, Dante had seen a wooden maul, its head covered with dried blood, but he'd ignored it since it wasn't what they were looking for. Now he snatched it up and showed it to Radovan.

"Can you use it with this? To smash the link open?"

Radovan took the hammer and handed Dante the chisel. "All right, but you'll have to hold the chisel in place. Unless you want to swing the hammer?"

Dante shook his head. He had felt how heavy the maul was and knew he couldn't swing it effectively, even if the prospect of holding the chisel while the other man swung the bloody tool right at him didn't sound appealing. Dante placed the tip of the chisel on a link of the chain, wedging the link between the chisel and the metal bars of the gate. He turned his head away.

His whole body shook as the hammer hit the chisel. He looked at where the chisel's tip had dug into the metal of the link, and he placed the tip back on that exact spot. As he waited for the next blow, he looked to Bogdana, who was smashing the ladder into bits. She had already smashed an empty barrel into pieces and thrown it on the fire. She and Adam had a fairly large blaze burning in the middle of the open area, with a lot of smoke and bright flames. The four dead people stayed at some distance from the fire, cowering and moaning. Just before the second blow struck, Dante noticed their moans had attracted two more of the dead, who were further back, but shambling in their direction. Dante knew they'd be overwhelmed soon enough, even if the fire kept the dead away for a while.

The second blow slammed into the chisel. This time it cut almost all the way through the link. Radovan threw the maul on the ground and took the chisel from Dante. He forced it into the broken link.

"Hold the chain taut," he said as he twisted the chisel back and forth, trying to widen the gap they'd broken in the link. Both were sweating and looking nervously at the growing crowd of the dead.

"I wish we had one of those giant, angry men to do this," Dante panted as they struggled with the metal.

Radovan grunted. "I fear they'd be more interested in smashing in the heads of the dead, but they'd be helpful for that at least, unlike that lout up there."

"Lout, shmout," came the reply from above. "I'm safe. You're not. That's all I know."

"All right, I've almost got it," Radovan said. "Hold it in place one more second." He strained with both hands, trying to torque the chisel around and wrench the gap open wider. "There!" He dropped the chisel as Dante let the chain go slack. Radovan slipped the adjacent link out of the broken one.

The two of them quickly unlaced the chains from the gate, as they looked over their shoulders at Adam, Bogdana, and the still-advancing dead. The chain clattered to the ground and the two men shoved the gate open.

"Now, come on!" Radovan shouted as he and Dante got back on their horses.

Adam and Bogdana retreated from the pyre and remounted. All four of them urged their horses forward and went through the gate, one at a time. Once outside, Radovan moved his horse in front of Bogdana's, with Dante and Adam in the rear, next to each other. Dante looked back through the gate, to where he could now see the dark silhouettes of the dead, slowly working their way closer to the fire, even as they held their hands up to their bloody, disfigured faces, moaning louder, terrified of the flames.

"Their desire is stronger than their fear or pain," he said softly.

Adam raised his eyebrows. "Stronger than their fear, surely. But their pain?"

Dante considered this. "Their desire *is* their pain."

Adam nodded. "Yes. Now you have it right."

"And it will last forever?"

"Yes. That is how horrible the cursed life is, and why we must pursue the blessed death."

The sky remained the same grey. There was still no breeze. To Dante, it seemed to have gotten slightly warmer—the kind of heat that comes not from the sun, or even from fire, but from diseased blood flowing too swiftly in channels too narrow for its overwhelming, animal vitality.

Chapter 20

Soon as I was within, cast round my eye,
And see on every hand an ample plain,
Full of distress and torment terrible.
Dante, *Inferno*, 9.109-111

Dante turned away from the dying town and examined the fields through which they now passed. In better times they would've been surrounded by crops, but now everything around them was dry and barren. It seemed unusually warm for this time of year, especially considering it was overcast. He scanned the open area around them and relaxed a bit. As strange as their surroundings were, it felt good finally to be outside the town, in a place that seemed deserted, without any immediate threats from either the living or the dead.

"What was your life like when you lived in Italy? Why did you journey so far, to come to our insignificant land?" Adam asked him as they rode along slowly.

"He wanted to be a monk." Bogdana looked over her shoulder as she said this. Dante could not help but notice her dark eyes sparkle just a tiny bit, and the hint of a smile on the one side of her mouth. Radovan snorted a laugh at her playful remark, and she turned back forward. "You did too," she chided him.

"Yes, I did once want to be a monk," Dante said. "Instead I joined the apothecaries' guild. I wanted to change the politics of my city, and guild membership was required to hold public office. But I didn't change much. Instead I was exiled by those in power, who had help from the leader of my church. I wanted to stay in my city, but I will never see it again. And I wanted to write poems, to create something beautiful, but I never have. I wanted many things that did not happen."

"You desired much, friend, but you just saw how strong and dangerous desire is," Adam said. "Perhaps that was your problem."

Dante looked over at the older, smaller man; everything seemed compact about him. His body, his desires, even his mind—all were compact, focused, efficient, never wasteful or dissipated. And though it was all very admirable, it could never be beautiful, Dante thought. He remembered Beatrice's refined, fragile beauty, and even glanced at Bogdana, with her rough sensuality and awesome simplicity. Such beauties and complexities were never commensurate with the sharp, compact analysis of Adam. It would be like trying to get life-giving water to one's mouth using a knife.

Dante had spent plenty of time alone in the past few years—more than most people spent in a lifetime, more than he would've liked, more than he would've wished upon anyone, even an enemy. He had spent much of that time dissecting his own beliefs, so he knew his perspective was closer to Adam's than it was to the kind of feminine luxuriousness and ambiguity he had seen in Beatrice, and which now so confused and fascinated him in Bogdana.

"No," he replied. "In our lives, everything is desire. We must learn to desire good things. Not all of my desires were directed toward bad things. I believe most were not, in all truth."

"Toward what then? Did you desire wealth?"

"No, not in the least. I have never understood men's fascination with money or possessions."

"That is good. I suspected that when I met you. What about honor? Respect? Did you crave these from other men?"

Dante frowned. "When I was active in politics, I know it was mostly because I wanted people's lives improved. I didn't want them to live in a cesspool of corruption and violence. But I'll admit that, sometimes, I did want honor, at least a little, and that made me proud and boastful. So those desires were mixed, I'll grant you."

Adam nodded. "All right. What about women?"

Dante turned his gaze from Adam and let it rest on Bogdana's back. "Yes. I loved a woman, but she died. And I was never worthy of her anyway."

"Then why was this desire good, my friend, if it only made you feel disappointed, frustrated, and sad?"

"Because she made me want to be worthy of her. She made me long for it more than anything. And not just so I could have her and possess her. Why then would the longing continue after she died, when I could not possibly have her? I wanted to be a better man, just for her." Dante shook his head and gripped the reins tighter. He hated how he couldn't put his thoughts and feelings into words. "No, not for her, really. For her goodness. I wanted to be better, so I could be worthy of the goodness I saw in her." His stare fixed on the nape of Bogdana's neck, where her long hair had parted slightly to reveal a triangle of skin above the collar of the jacket he'd loaned her. He was glad she could not see him blush at this point. "And I have seen such goodness in a few other women since she died, and it has had the same effect on me."

Adam followed Dante's gaze and smiled. "I see. Did you ever marry one of these women who had this wondrous effect on you?"

Dante shot a glance at Adam, then looked down at the ground. "I married a woman. We had been betrothed when we were still quite young. She has been an excellent mother to our children. I am very grateful to her for that."

Dante had chosen his words with great precision. Adam nodded, apparently at the careful choice of words, and at what had been left unsaid. "Then I am not sure I quite understand your desire for women, my friend, or how it is a desire for something good, if its fulfillment has been postponed for your entire life."

"Our love of God is never completely fulfilled in this life. We live on in hope, always striving to be worthy of Him. The love of another person's beauty and goodness is like that. It is like practicing with a weapon or a musical instrument, so one can improve at it for the real performance."

Adam raised an eyebrow. "Yes, the love you describe is like the love of God in this respect. I am not sure of the practicing part, however. It seems a bit farfetched, and too optimistic about the things of this world."

"You said when we first met you thought perhaps I was destined for some special, noble purpose?"

"Yes, I did, and I still think that is so."

"If you are right, and if I prove worthy and capable of achieving such a goal, it will be because of such love, one that draws me beyond myself and beyond the person who sparks such a love in me. It is a love not for the person, but for the Source of all love."

"I hope you are right. I cannot judge you, if you tell me this kind of love has such a benefit to you, and you have such a goal in mind when you experience it."

Dante looked back at Bogdana, then at the desolate lands around them "I think perhaps I know now why I have come to your country: to see all the strange, terrible things created by love and hate, desire and attraction, so I may better understand them, and tell others of them."

"That would be a great accomplishment indeed, my friend. Many do not know the risks and rewards of their lives. And deaths."

Ahead of them, on the right side of the road, the rectangular monuments of a graveyard came into view.

Chapter 21

"Their cemetery have upon this side
With Epicurus all his followers,
Who with the body mortal make the soul."
Dante, *Inferno*, 10.13-15

Most of the monuments in the cemetery were small markers of weathered, grey stone, though there were a few larger, more elaborate sepulchers among them. As they rode by, Dante thought of the much more extensive cemeteries at Arles and Pola, and how all such places always had the same effect, regardless of their size or location. It was a salutary but chilling reminder of death, of the limits of life and the depressing, inescapable sameness that caught up to every member of the human tribe. No matter how different or glamorous, good or evil they all might be when alive—an Achilles or an Aeneas, even a Paul or an Augustine—every one would be reduced to a pile of dust under a nondescript block of stone, until the centuries wore the stone down to an unidentifiable nub that could be a mile marker on a forgotten highway, or a paving stone on the floor of a slaughterhouse.

All is vanity. Look on my works, you mighty, and forget them. Turn your mind from them in embarrassment and contempt. Look elsewhere. Nothing to see here, and there never was.

Of course, in their present circumstances, Dante couldn't help but have other associations with such a city of the dead. He found himself imagining hordes of shrieking, cackling ghouls, bounding over the tombstones, leaping from the tops of the mausoleums, as bony, grasping claws thrust upward out of the cursed earth. But in reality, there was nothing but the smooth stones and the dry grass around them, undisturbed by the dead, untouched even by wind or sun, as Dante and his procession slowly went by. After a few seconds, the quiet cemetery even seemed to him one of the more peaceful, wholesome places he'd seen in the last couple days. Perhaps death was a blessing, as Adam had said.

On the other side of the road from the graveyard, and slightly further from the town, Dante saw a barn or storage building. It looked like a sturdy one, with stout wooden walls and a high, thatched roof. As he studied it, he saw some of the thatch move, followed by two hands thrusting upward through the roofing. Dante gripped his sword, thinking perhaps his morbid, fatalistic reveries were about to materialize. The hands made the hole in the roof bigger, then a man climbed through the opening to stand on the roof. The way he moved, with coordination and purpose, he was clearly alive and not dead. By now, Dante saw that the others had also noticed the man. As they got closer, Dante also noticed the low moaning of the dead coming from inside the building.

The man on the roof now saw the four of them approaching on horseback and waved to them. "You there!" he called. "You'll ruin everything. They'll come out after you. We have to close the door. Quick!" Dante looked at the side of the building perpendicular to the road, facing back toward the town, and saw two large, wooden doors there. They were open.

The man slid down the thatch to the edge of the roof, turned, and nimbly dropped down to the ground. He ran to the open doors and quickly closed them, securing them with a bar that he laid in two brackets on the door frame. He also barricaded the doors with some boxes and barrels that were nearby. Dante noticed the moaning inside the building had increased during this process, and the sound of fists hammering on wood was soon added to the chorus.

"There, that should do it," the man said as he turned from his work to address them again. "Who might you be? I don't recognize you from around here. Visitors? Someone important?"

"Well, I'm not important, sir," Adam said. "We are just travelling up the valley as fast as we can, trying to escape from the dead and the invading army."

"I see. Well, good luck to you then. As you can see, I am taking care of some of my serfs and a few of my neighbors. Lured them into the barn, then I climbed up to the loft. Now I can be rid of them all in one shot. A little ingenuity always fixes a bad situation."

"Often it does, yes," Adam responded.

As the man turned back to his work, Dante examined him carefully. He was about Dante's age or slightly older, with a full head of black hair, a slightly dark complexion, broad shoulders and chest. He carried himself confidently, almost imperiously, as he busied himself. Dante watched him take a small barrel and pull the plug out of it. The man started splashing its contents on the barricade he had built. "The roof will go up just fine, I think," he said as he worked. "It hasn't rained in so long. But this could use some oil."

Dante considered the plan. "It must be awful for any creature to die in flames," he said. "But it is good to release them from their torment, to free their tortured souls from their wretched, diseased bodies."

The man grunted as he tossed the empty barrel on top of the barricade. "That's one way to look at it, I suppose. But souls in torment? Really, stranger. Who believes that anymore?" He raised his eyebrows as he looked Dante up and down, then turned to give Bogdana a more lingering examination — one that was both more and less appreciative than the one he had given Dante. "I mean, consider such a lovely but simple peasant girl as we have here." He smiled and gestured toward Bogdana, lifting his right hand palm down, then lowering it palm up, in a motion that was as gallant and dismissive as his words. "From one with so fetching a body and so dull a mind, I would surely expect such old-time religion, such quaint drollery. Such people are ever credulous and easily manipulated."

He leered. Not enough to be blatantly offensive, but with the merely casual, offhand derision of a man used to authority and privilege, a man with enough intellect to be arrogant, and not enough to be humble. "And who really would have it otherwise? I know when I lay my weary eyes on such a captivating body, I almost long to hear the inane, superstitious ramblings of the inferior mind that goes along with it. For when I hear about her boundless, childlike faith; her undying love for her kind, heavenly Father; the value she puts on her chastity; the contempt in which she holds the flesh; all the hopes she has for the world to come ... Then I know how easy it will be to mold her malleable will and feeble reason to my ends. I realize how quickly I'll have her dainty feet on my shoulders, sharing the untold delights of her sweet, soft flesh." His leer was now as blatantly offensive as his words. "Is that how it was with you, dear? Did you find yourself in the bed of some nobleman, such as myself, who was smart enough to see through the pathetic hypocrisy and emptiness of your uncouth religion, and crafty enough to use it to his own advantage? Did you bring home his sterner, hardier seed in your belly? Maybe even to a gullible husband, who thanked God he'd been blessed with a child?" He snickered.

The way Dante was grinding his teeth, he thought he'd pulverize them into a mouthful of bitter, poisonous dust, even if they had been made of stone. He could see out of the corner of his eye that Radovan—though he had earlier allowed himself to disrespect the same woman—had reacted to this vulgar display, drawing his sword halfway out of its sheath, as Dante gripped the hilt of his own. But he could see, at the same time, Bogdana took the abuse neither with anger nor embarrassment but with cold disdain. "You know nothing of my mind or faith," she said calmly. "And an arrogant fool such as you will never know my body."

The man rolled his eyes. "Oh, fine. You're the most virtuous woman in the whole damned valley, I suppose. More chaste than all the strumpets, young and old, that I now have locked in this barn, now they're of no use to me or themselves or anyone else. I had more than half of them in exactly the way I just described. You think you're more virtuous than all of them? And you call me the arrogant one?" He shook his head and laughed. "Fine. I won't begrudge you your high opinion of yourself. I already said it was only your body I found interesting. I couldn't care less what you think of me, or of yourself."

The man finally turned his attention back to Dante. "Ah, is this the suitor who's so in love with your mind, my pet? No need to get all in a huff, stranger. We'll all be dead soon enough. As I said, I've had more than my share of peasant sexing, so I don't need to fight you over the silly, proud girl you have chosen to spend your final moments with. Did she get you to swear to protect her and her child, if she'd but glance your way, bat her eyes, perhaps touch your hand? Is that part of the bargain?"

Dante blushed more violently than he could ever remember doing so—past a flushed, warm pink and all the way to a burning crimson, overflowing with rage and shame. He could feel the sweat pour from his forehead, and his ears felt like they'd caught fire. None of it was lost on the vile but perceptive stranger.

"Oh my God. She did, didn't she? And I was only bluffing! Don't be embarrassed. I'm sure you go in for that sort of thing. I don't even accuse you of lying to her, just to get up under her skirt. That would be more my taste, simple and direct, but I imagine you enjoy all the gallantry and oaths and high-mindedness. That is some people's tastes, I know, even among more intelligent, enlightened people. So, in a way, you're exactly like me. You've gotten the pleasure you want out of her, and she out of you, so no one's to blame. No one need blush! But I also know that delectable body of hers—and her elevated mind you claim to prefer—will be reduced to nothingness in a few short hours, or days at most." He stepped back and looked serious, less lecherous or mocking. "You're clearly not from around here. And not, I think, from such low, basic stock as this pretty, young thing. Yet you prattle on about the souls of my dearly-departed neighbors and servants? That mystifies me. It truly does. You look intelligent. Intelligent enough that such absurdity coming from you could almost trouble me, could almost make me rethink or regret what I believe. Almost."

"I do not say I'm intelligent," Dante said softly. "But I do say your neighbors' souls are in torment, and you are doing them a kindness by releasing them, whatever ugly opinion you hold of them, or whatever selfish, misguided beliefs motivate you."

Again the man grunted dismissively. "Oh, the arrogance! Such blinding, overweening self-assurance! You two really do deserve one another! It's truly a match worthy of Greek poetry, of high tragedy, rather than the low comedy of my more honest, less refined life! You say you know my neighbors have souls, even my starving, wretched serfs have souls, yet I know that I have none! Are you asking me to believe all these dirty, misbegotten creatures have this God-given gift, this amazing faculty of immortality, this indestructible spark of Divinity, which I know I do not possess myself? They are immortal, and I am not? Are they more beloved, more blessed by this non-existent God of yours? If so, what poor and ridiculous taste He has!"

Dante shook his head, his gaze fixed on the man. The blood drained from his face, leaving him cold and distant. "No, you were as blessed with life and existence as they were. You were, it seems, more blessed with wealth and intellect and perhaps other gifts. But what you do with all that is entirely up to you."

The man waved them off as he started pulling handfuls of thatch down from the edge of the roof, making them into a pile by the barricade at the barn doors. "Fine. On that point, at least, we can agree. What I do is entirely up to me. And I choose not to believe in all your foolishness, and to seek what pleasures I can find in this life." He knelt down by the pile of thatch he'd made and began sending sparks into it with flint and a knife. He laughed as he worked. "There used to be a lot more of those simple pleasures, as I just described to you, and which so offended your delicate morals. But now? Just some grim satisfaction in destroying the monsters in this world." He laughed louder, as the thatch began to smoke and take light. "It just occurred to me how funny that is! These monsters are an inconvenience to me—more so than fleas or mold, to be sure—but still, just another inconvenience that makes life more difficult and threatens to diminish my pleasure. But to you they must be absolutely maddening and disheartening! Tell me, in your tidy universe of a just, loving God, who made these abominations, these creatures of evil, malice, and destruction?"

"God made them so we may overcome them and grow stronger," Radovan said.

"They make no difference to us, since this life is unimportant," Adam said. "We care only for the soul and eternal life."

"They are just people left to their own sinful ways," Dante said. "They are what we have made of ourselves."

The man had taken a burning piece of wood from the barricade and was now lighting the roof. "Oh, my," he said. "I did underestimate you. I thought you'd have no answer, but instead you have too many." He pulled back his arm and tossed the brand high up to the top of the roof, apparently satisfied the barn was burning vigorously enough. He turned once more to Bogdana. "And nothing from you, my little plum? I thought you were known for your mind?"

Dante watched Bogdana's eyes reflect the flames. "They are here for us to pity." Her eyes did not look as disdainful as before. "As are you."

The man laughed, though it seemed more rueful this time. "Ah, more of that arrogance! I suppose it's only fair, isn't it? I look down on your faith, and you look down on me. I pity your ignorance, and you pity my hopelessness." He gave Dante a playful, slightly mocking glance. "Looking back on all those godly wenches I had in my bed, I still think I got the better end of the bargain, but to each his own, I suppose. Again, I do wish you luck. Perhaps you'll still find some pleasure in the short time remaining of your life. There. That can be my 'prayer' for you: I hope you find pleasure. Now, do you have a prayer for me? I know you all are into that sort of thing, and I need to be going now."

The barn was ablaze now. The moaning from inside increased in intensity, turning into more of a pained, terrified wailing.

"I hope you find there is something more than pleasure," Dante said.

The man nodded. "Something more than pleasure would be a very great thing indeed. Would that there were such a thing, but I know there is not."

Dante watched him turn and run away, back toward the town, presumably to find more of his neighbors to kill, or whatever else he had planned for what he believed were his last moments of existence. Dante pulled back on the reins, drawing his horse away from the flames, turning it back down the road away from the town. The others had also fallen in line.

He looked over at Adam, as erect and compact as ever. The man's words did not seem to have shaken him at all. Then Dante gazed at Bogdana's long hair and her thin yet sturdy frame, not seeing her face, but certain that she too felt unmoved, either by the man's theology or his insults. Radovan was further ahead, and Dante very much doubted the young soldier, with his simplicity and virtue, would be perturbed by the conversation they had just had. The four rode on in silence, Dante quite convinced that only his faith was weak, for he could feel neither outrage, condemnation, nor pity for the stranger. Dante felt his stomach twist and his head lighten, because he knew he could only feel envy. Not for the women the man claimed to have bedded, of course—Dante could never be so crass as that—but for the certitude and inflexibility of his unbelief, the utter unassailability of negation, the numbing comfort of oblivion. These were things that could never be loved or admired, but they could certainly be envied, in all the anguish and doubt gripping Dante that day — feelings that had taken hold of him on many other days before, and would on many thereafter.

Chapter 22

And when he us beheld, he bit himself,
Even as one whom anger racks within.
Dante, *Inferno*, 12.14-15

As they slowly rode on, Dante heard the roaring crash of the barn's roof collapsing behind them. For some time before that, he had no longer heard the moaning of the doomed creatures inside, though after this final explosion, he imagined a faint wheeze, like an exhalation of breath or a light wind playing over dry grass. He did not look back at the ruin. Whether out of dread or respect, he did not know.

Up ahead, he noticed two dark figures in a field with a decrepit wooden fence around it. Dante could not tell what they were at first, but they moved, so they weren't trees or stones. Then he could see the figure closer to them was a man. From the way he was moving he was clearly not alive, holding his arms out in front of himself as he lurched toward them. The figure farther from the road was an enormous, black bull, its head down, tugging at what grass was there, oblivious either to them or to its undead neighbor.

Dante had not considered whether animals were susceptible to the plague of undeath. "Do the dead attack animals?" he asked. "Do the animals here become undead as well?"

Radovan was in front, and turned back toward Dante to answer. "I've heard the dead will eat carrion, if they've been unable to kill and eat any living humans for a long time and have grown hungry enough," he replied. "But live animals never interest them. Not that I've heard."

"No, they don't bother animals," Adam agreed as he rode alongside Dante. "And animals cannot become undead. It is our curse alone."

Dante couldn't help but ask: "Why?"

Adam turned to him. "Humans receive many more blessings, and many more curses, from God than animals do. It is always thus, and usually pointless to ask why. But in this case, I believe it is because this plague is a disease of the mind, of the soul. The animals lack these essences, so they cannot be afflicted. Only their bodies hunger, while people desire with their souls as well, and desire so much more than just food. They desire so intensely their hunger can outlive even the death of their bodies. That is the cursed life we see all around us, threatening everything, even the sanctity of death."

They were right next to the field with the dead man and the bull in it, when Dante saw the bull raise its huge head and shake it, snorting as it glared at them. The dead man never took his eyes off them to look at the bull behind him, but just kept shuffling forward. The bull lowered its head and charged, impaling the man with its right horn, then thrashing its head to toss him off to the right. The corpse landed in a ball, its knees crammed up under its chin, before it started to unfold itself, getting up to its knees and planting its one foot as it tried to rise. The bull charged again before the man could completely stand. This time the remorseless, unyielding wall of its forehead smashed into the man's skull, sending him to the ground, where he remained, unmoving.

They had stopped their horses to watch the attack. Now the bull moved away from the motionless corpse, walking parallel to the road, its stare fixed on them.

"Why did it do that?" Dante asked quietly, mesmerized by the massive animal.

Adam looked to Bogdana. "I'm afraid you've shown more knowledge of animals than I have."

She shrugged. "You might as well ask why didn't it do that before? There's no telling. You can walk by the same bull every day and it never takes a step toward you, then suddenly one afternoon it charges you.

Walk behind the same mule every morning and it never moves, then one day it kicks you. You always have to respect animals and what they can do. But the dead don't know to do that." She pointed. "I do think it wants out of that field now."

The bull turned to face the fence by the road, and it charged. The barrier was just a rickety collection of sticks, and the giant beast crashed through it easily. The animal stepped out into the road and turned its head toward them. Radovan was the closest to it.

"If you're going to throw it a bone or something, I wish you'd do it now," he said over his shoulder, keeping an eye on the bull.

"Just stay still and let it go," Bogdana said. "It's outside your control. Just let it do what it's going to do. All you can do is react."

The animal's black-eyed stare remained fixed on them, and a muscle in its massive shoulder twitched, but still it didn't move. It gave a huff, turned, and walked slowly off into the field to the right, only stopping to look back at them when it was some distance away. Then it lowered its head and returned to its task of trying to find some edible grass among all the dead stalks.

"See," Bogdana said. "Now it might stay still and eat for hours. Or it might charge us in the next moment."

"Let's go," Adam said as they started moving forward. Up ahead, the road led back into the forest. "We have to get much farther before nightfall."

Dante looked back at the bull, which raised its proud head to return the gaze. As it did, the clouds parted slightly, and a shaft of sickly sunlight fell on the beast, making it look more erect and noble. It seemed to lend some of its strength to the thin, weak illumination. The clouds closed back in, and the bull lowered its head to return to its meager supper.

Chapter 23

"Of every malice that wins hate in Heaven,
Injury is the end; and all such end
Either by force or fraud afflicteth others."
Dante, *Inferno*, 11.22-24

The road sloped more steeply upward, once they passed from the fields and were back under the cover of the forest. At this point the road was little more than a dirt track, impassable to carts or wagons, forcing them to ride single file with Radovan in front, followed by Bogdana, Dante, and then Adam. The trees were less dense than they had been farther down the valley, which was probably good, since it gave them more visibility, in case the living or dead were lurking.

Looking all around, Dante couldn't tell if he felt more uneasy out in the open, constantly exposed to the lifeless, unchanging grey sky, or if he felt more oppressed in this thin, desiccated forest, whose shadows were barely distinguishable in the weak light. He supposed it didn't much matter. As most everyone they met seemed intent on reminding them, they'd be dead soon enough. Though Dante never fancied himself an especially virtuous or religious man, he did believe God would grant him an eternal existence somewhere better than this netherworld of dull heat, dim shadows, and occasional terrors.

They continued to climb. To the right of the trail the ground dropped off into a steep ravine running parallel to their path. If there was water at the bottom of it, it was too deep for Dante to see. All he could discern at the bottom were jagged rocks. At least the dead couldn't jump out at them from that side of the road. He leaned away from the precipice and thought it was just like everything else he'd seen in this valley—another way to die.

Radovan pulled back on the reins and stopped, pointing to the left. Dante had to peer a moment, but finally he too saw the movement among the trees, almost at the same time as he heard the low moaning. The sound held so much less dread for him than it had just the day before, and Dante thought how one could eventually get used to anything, no matter how horrible it was at first. Not just get used to it but expect it, even long for it, as though familiar things were always comforting and desirable in some way, just because they were familiar. Once people grew used to something, even if it were something harmful and ugly, it would always be what they craved, what they would return to over and over, no matter how much pain it might cause them.

As Dante's eyes focused, he could distinguish three dead people moving toward them between the trees. His stomach and the back of his neck turned cold and he shivered in fear—not because of the approaching dead, but because he had gotten used to them.

"Forgive me," he whispered as he drew his sword.

Dante asked his silent God for forgiveness, not for the violence he knew would soon follow, and which he knew was as necessary as it was unavoidable. Dante asked to be forgiven for the terrible, chilling realization he had just come to: if the familiar was always craved, then the unknown was always feared and avoided—even, or especially, if the unknown object were God. And although Dante knew that one might disguise this embarrassing truth by using other words like "awe" or "reverence," he felt quite certain that his God, unknown though He may be, would not be particularly impressed or appeased by such obfuscation. So all Dante could do was ask forgiveness for this desperate, fatal flaw of his race.

All four of them turned their horses to face the attackers, and urged the animals forward a bit, so they weren't so close to the edge of the ravine. The three dead people were two men and a woman. All were middle aged, all bloody and torn in various places, and all had slack jaws and blank, uncomprehending stares. Dante remembered asking to be excused from killing a child earlier, yet it now seemed like it was a memory from his own childhood, something distant, irrelevant, and quaint. Now it didn't bother him at all that it was the woman who was heading toward him, and it'd be her he'd have to kill. He wondered if it would make a difference if she were a little girl. The chill spread from his neck and stomach to his back and chest, when he realized it might not matter in the least to him. He could even calculate with great speed, based on his experiences so far, how he would have to alter his attack to cope with a smaller target. Dante was cold all over when he realized that, in his diseased mind, childhood innocence now only meant the height of his victim. He gripped his sword tighter and raised it.

Dante heard shouting on either side, and then saw more people moving among the trees. There was a group of men, perhaps a dozen, closing in on the three dead people from both sides and from behind. They must've been lying in wait, or tracking the dead at some distance, and chose now to attack. The dead people were confused, turning back and forth between their original targets and these new people. Dante observed the newcomers as they gathered around the dead, not yet attacking, but circling and taunting them. He thought it odd they were all armed with long sticks; not as long as Adam's staff, but bigger than a club, maybe three or four feet long. He would have thought at least some of them would have swords, or if they were using impromptu weapons such as tools, it would make sense for some of them to have shovels, axes, or picks, as all these seemed sturdier and better able to deliver a fatal blow to the head.

With a whooping cry, the men finally fell on the dead, and their tactics made even less sense to Dante than their weapons. They pummeled the three dead people all over their bodies, rather than giving them a solid rap on the head, so as to end their suffering. Some even poked and prodded at their opponents, forcing them to stagger back under the barrage of blows. The three dead people growled in frustration and rage, raising their hands to try to defend themselves, but they were too slow and clumsy to stop many of the non-lethal blows that rained down on them from all sides. The men seemed quite practiced at their brutality, for in a few moments they had the three dead people bunched together, and were backing them toward the edge of the ravine.

The men never stopped shouting during the whole attack. Some of them even laughed and threw insults at the dead, which Dante increasingly saw more as victims, rather than their attackers or opponents. Dante acknowledged that a moment before he was ready to kill the dead woman, ready to do so without feeling guilt or remorse or even sadness. But it was something else entirely to do so while laughing the whole time. It was one thing to cease hating violence. It was quite another to love it, enjoy it, and even seek it out. And unlike his previous uncertainties, Dante was convinced the display he now saw was something he could never do himself.

The three dead people had been driven to the edge of the cliff, where they stood, snarling and trying to lash out at their attackers, who kept them tottering right on the brink. One of the men, a tall man with long, brown hair and a mustache, took his stick and finally hit one of the dead men hard on the top of his head, enough to stun him and make him sway, waving his arms uselessly. The tall man then kicked him in the midsection and sent him over the cliff. He did much the same to the other dead man. The crowd cheered and guffawed at all of this. For the woman, the man put down his stick, then pulled off his leather jacket and threw it over her head. He stepped toward her, grabbing her by the shoulders and spinning her around three times. He stood at her side and clamped his hands around her throat, thereby holding the jacket so that it was tightly covering her head. Kicking her feet out from under her, he forced her down to her knees, as he knelt down with her and pressed her head into the ground. Her arms clawed weakly, but she couldn't get any leverage. Her large backside, covered with filthy, torn skirts, stuck up in the air, the sight of which sent peals of laughter up from the crowd. Dante noticed her one shoe was missing, the bare foot black with dirt and blood.

The man who had forced this degradation on the dead woman smiled and shouted to the others. "Why, I do believe it's this old whore's birthday!" He bent down next to her. "How old are you, love?" Tilting his head, he raised his eyebrows and nodded, as though she were giving a response, then he turned back to his audience. "She says a lady doesn't tell her age, and a gentleman doesn't ask! Oh, that'll get you some extra smacks for implying you're a lady, or that I'm a *gentle* man!" The crowd roared with laughter. "So let's just call it an even fifty, eh? Though God knows I'm probably being generous, by the looks of her! Go ahead boys, have at her!"

The men started in on her, taking turns slapping her raised buttocks. Some did so with their open hands, some with their sticks, some lightly like it was a game, some as hard as they could—so hard that the man holding her down had to struggle to keep her from being battered off the edge of the cliff. They began to chant, counting as each blow fell on her. When they reached fifty, they broke down into laughter so hysterical they were nearly incapacitated, doubled up, slapping their thighs, almost unable to catch their breath. The man who had been holding the dead woman down stood up and pulled his jacket off her. He moved around behind her as she kneeled, still facing the ravine. Dante focused on the woman's bloody foot; he was glad he could not see her face. She stuck her arms straight out as she leaned her head back and gave a roar of the purest outrage, despair, and loneliness. Dante had seen criminals executed back in the "real" world, the normal world. No matter what their final words, there was always a tinge of regret, a hint that at some level they blamed themselves, if not for what they did then at least for being caught. Dante did not hear anything like that on this afternoon.

"Happy birthday!" the man howled. "Time to be born again!"

He took a step back then rushed forward to kick the woman between her shoulders. The blow was strong enough to send her tumbling forward over the edge. Though it hardly seemed possible, given how loudly they'd been carrying on, the laughter increased.

The man who had led the abuse picked up his stick and turned his attention to Dante and his companions. "Well, then," he said, "you're welcome!"

"They needed to be killed," Adam said. "But I don't think that was necessary."

The man frowned. "Necessary? No, of course not. I try not to do things because they're *necessary*. I do things because I like to! Don't you do that?"

"Of course," Adam answered. "But a man should like to do what is necessary, and no one should like to do what you just did."

"Really? Well, I never liked doing necessary things, and I liked messing with those three a lot! How about the rest of you?" A cheer went up from the crowd. "It's always fun to hit someone, but now it's even better because you don't get in trouble!"

"I can see where you would find that to be an advantage."

"Good! Now where are you off to?"

"We're going up the valley. We hope to escape over the pass to the other side."

"Leave the valley? Strange. I never heard of a pass up there. Besides, what's the point? Who would want to leave? There's no law here. No one to tell you what to do or where to go. Just killing those things all day and having a bit of fun doing it. I like it!" He shrugged. "But, if you don't like it here, I suppose it's up to you. The trail continues on, and you'll get to the top of a waterfall, at the head of the ravine. The water's shallow there and you can cross over and continue on up the valley, though it gets steep from here on. But you shouldn't see many more of those things around here. We've been killing a lot of them!"

"I'm sure you have."

"All right, then. Let's go find some more of them!" the man said, and he and his group faded back into the woods almost as suddenly as they had appeared.

The horses picked their way forward again, as Dante looked over the side of the cliff. This must have been a favorite spot for the men to throw dead people into the canyon. Dante could now see there were many broken bodies on the rocks down there. He still could not see any water, but there had to be plenty of blood spattered and seeping among the cruel stones.

"It is why God used a flood last time," Adam said, noticing where Dante was gazing and apparently guessing what he was thinking. "To wash away all the blood men spilled. So much blood spilled for sport, for greed, for malice, or sometimes for nothing at all."

Dante turned in his saddle. "And the fire you believe is coming?"

Adam nodded. "Sometimes the flames of desire cannot be extinguished with purifying water. They have raged so long and so out of control. And their lack of control means they can never return to the true source of all heat and desire. Instead they flicker and sputter here and there—dissipated, wasted, wretched. Such flames of merely human desire are still eternal, like the sun, but are such puny, infantile stars next to the real source of light. They are exactly like the dead we see walking in this terrible valley—lost, empty, hopeless."

Dante did not know whether anyone could feel more lost and empty than he did at that moment; he was not entirely sure he even had any hope. "How much farther do we have to go?"

"You will be out of the valley tomorrow, friend. I know this is true."

Dante turned to face forward, knowing he could not share Adam's certainty. But did he even have hope, he wondered? He knew he had none for himself, but he did think he might still be holding on to a shred of it for the sake of the woman and child in front of him. In such a world any man could lose hope, but no man could refuse to hold on to hope for the sake of another's beauty and goodness. It calmed and strengthened Dante considerably, when he realized his hope did not rely on his own ability or capacity to feel it, but rather on her power to elicit it from him, a power which was, to him, utterly irresistible and undeniable. If it were a source of overwhelming pain and confusion to Dante that God had suspended the rules of death, it was also a source of invincible strength and certainty that He had not suspended the laws of love.

Chapter 24

Not foliage green, but of a dusky colour,
Not branches smooth, but gnarled and intertangled,
Not apple-trees were there, but thorns with poison.
Dante, *Inferno*, 13.4-6

They hadn't gone far before Dante heard the sound of falling water, and soon after, they came to the waterfall the man had described. To their right was a trickle of water, which fell over a cliff and down into the ravine they'd been following up the valley. The stones at the top of the falls were a rusty red. Dante thought they must contain iron, or the leavings of a mine had been dumped into the stream. The water itself looked a foul pink near the banks, with a thin border of yellowish slime. The stream was small enough they easily forded it and climbed the trail on the other side.

The forest on the other side of the stream continued to get thinner as they went. They were up high enough that most of the trees were pines, and most of these appeared diseased and twisted, many of them dead. The forest floor was covered in what Dante imagined to be a millennium's accumulation of needles, filling the whole space with a caustic, smothering scent. Both the needles on the trees and those on the ground were the color of slate. Once the sound of the waterfall had disappeared behind them, there was silence and stillness, without any breeze, without the call or movement of birds or any other animals. The whole place stung the senses in every way, either by starving, overwhelming, or seeming to deceive them.

The trail bent more or less north, so Dante looked to his left to see where the sun weakly illuminated the blanket of grey clouds filling the sky. The brighter spot in the cloud cover moved closer to the mountains in the west.

Adam must have noticed where Dante was looking, and seemed to guess his thoughts. "We will stop soon," he said. "We should try to make it as far as we can. There are two steep ascents before the final, hidden trail to the pass. It is too late in the day to make it up the first of those, but we should get as far as we can in this forest and find a clearing to make camp. We will need to rest if we are to have the strength to overcome the final obstacles of this valley."

Dante saw movement in the trees above them, and looked up to see dozens of vultures perched there. He did not remember such birds being as large as the ones he now saw, spreading then refolding their enormous wings. The motion set the branches swaying up and down, making the whole canopy above them an undulating mass of dark shapes. Dante could make out some of the birds' faces, and they were horrible to behold, especially for a man with an imagination like his. In the birds' tiny, shining eyes, he fancied he saw an inhuman intelligence to match their bestial hunger, as though the animals did not just crave dead flesh, but also understood something about death that they would never divulge to mere humans, some piece of knowledge as simple and terrible as their black eyes. Dante could even imagine such birds laughing at their eternal secret with their croaking, tortured call. The sound appeared so vividly to him he did not jump like the others when the creatures screeched.. More and more of the birds joined in, the sound rising till it was a frenzied cacophony of choked, grating sounds, as though something were strangling all the birds at once. As the four of them passed under the noisy, seething mass of feathers, Dante thought perhaps the former silence was preferable after all.

When they'd gotten some distance from the hideous birds, they stopped and looked back at them.

"Do you believe in omens?" Adam asked.

"Yes," Radovan said. "Though they change nothing. We must go on anyway in life, even if we know we are doomed."

"That's true," Dante answered. "Even if the signs are real, we still have free will, and our responsibilities are not changed at all. But often I wonder if the signs are true, or if they're just superstition and they come from ignorance. Other times I'm not so sure, and I wonder if they could be a kind of revelation."

"I don't think superstition always comes from ignorance," Bogdana said quietly. "Sometimes it's a kind of knowledge, like a kind of respect. People call it 'superstition' when they're arrogant and don't want to obey, when they don't want to have respect or follow tradition. People think they're so smart, but they almost never are."

Dante glanced sideways at her face. In profile, with her full cheeks and upturned nose, she looked especially girlish. Most of her hair was pulled behind her ear, but one long curl hung down next to her eye, spiraling below her jaw to end just above her right breast. Such unadorned, youthful beauty made her sober words all the more captivating to him, even if they contained a gentle reprimand.

"I think you're right. But what does this omen mean?" he asked as he gestured at the birds.

Her smile looked a little sly to Dante, perhaps mocking, though he knew even if it were it wouldn't bother him in the least. "You strive to know so much, and it hurts you so, whether you get an answer or not. If I said I knew what this sign means that would be more arrogant than saying it's only superstition."

"Just knowing it means something—without knowing what that something is—is enough for you, daughter?" Adam asked.

"Yes," she said simply, as Radovan moved forward, and she pulled her horse in line behind his.

Adam watched her, then turned to Dante. He lowered his voice. "I see now what you meant about how women could affect you, friend. There is the clearest spark of the divine wisdom in her, like I have seen in our students who have trained at the monastery for years. Another thing I have noticed is how the wicked often see something that others do not, although they cannot understand or appreciate it. That man back at the barn, the one who mocked you, he was like that. He knew of your love for her as soon as he saw you, but I was too busy and distracted by other things to notice."

"Yes, I suppose he did," Dante agreed. "He knew the outer signs of love, without the substance." He looked toward Bogdana. "I know I do not always understand her, but I do appreciate her. And I will strive to be worthy of her."

Adam nodded. "Now I see better how such a vow is good for a man, especially in such a wretched, lonesome place as this, surrounded by every kind of ugliness and filth. It reminds him of purity, of perfection, of nobility. Otherwise he might lose hope and fall victim to all the evilness around him."

Dante kicked his horse lightly, taking his place behind Bogdana as they resumed their march through the woods. Dante took his gaze from her small, powerful frame and looked at the trees above them. Although they were as lifeless as before, and the pine scent in his nostrils as pungently nasty as before, everything seemed somehow less threatening or maddening to him, less like an experience of real evil and pain and more like a picture of such a scene. Dante had been reminded that the reality of these things lay elsewhere, and he muttered his thanks for this small, indistinct revelation.

Chapter 25

I heard on all sides lamentations uttered,
And person none beheld I who might make them,
Whence, utterly bewildered, I stood still.
Dante, *Inferno*, 13.22-24

Shortly after seeing the vultures, Dante noticed movement in the trees ahead of them. This time, however, it was not high up in the branches. Radovan looked back and gestured toward the motion, so all of them were aware of the possible attackers. He and Dante drew their swords as they continued to make their way along the path.

As they approached the movement, Dante heard the moan of the dead, though it seemed softer and more labored than usual. More like an exhausted whisper of despair, rather than the gnawing drone of hunger Dante had grown used to in the last two days. The moving shapes were clearly two dead people, but by this time in the day, the forest had grown quite dark, so Dante still could not make out what these corpses were doing. They weren't approaching them, but seemed to remain where they were, though their arms and legs were moving. The dead people's movements increased as Dante and his companions got closer to them.

They emerged in a small clearing, where they could finally discern the situation of the two figures. On the other side of the clearing there were two human forms hanging from a branch of one of the trees. They were suspended from the tree limb by ropes around their necks, with their arms and legs free. There were two small logs on the ground near their feet. They must've climbed up on those and then kicked them away, Dante thought. They appeared to be a young man and woman. The man was bigger, though neither of them had been very large. They were both thin and pale, with black hair, and dressed in simple, peasant clothes. Both had torn clothes, with their sleeves soaked in blood, and the young woman had a gaping wound on her neck as well. As he got closer, Dante could see the two were quite young, probably a bit younger than Bogdana.

Dante and the others dismounted and came closer to the unfortunate couple. As the living approached, the two dead people grew more agitated. The ropes around their necks kept their moan from rising to the kind of hungry, enraged roar Dante had heard before. Instead, it remained a steady and despondent wheeze drawn and expelled through their clenched teeth. Their limbs flailed about, which set their bodies to swinging, causing them to bump into one another. Sometimes it almost appeared they were trying to embrace each other, but the illusion quickly passed, for in the next moment, their movements would pass from groping and pulling on one another, to something more like slapping and clawing. The man, being affixed to the branch at a point closer to the trunk, occasionally bounced off the tree, his hands reaching for the trunk for a moment, but in the next instant he'd kick at the tree and send his body swinging back away from it. In a better, saner world, with tiny figures made of wood instead of human corpses, the whole spectacle would've sent Dante into fits of laughter.

"Why have I lived long enough to see this?" he asked in a low voice, as they watched the grotesque show before them. "I used to love puppet shows when I was a boy. I'd beg to go see them. I would beg God to keep me from seeing this, except I think somehow it must be His will that I look."

"You watched the puppet shows to learn something?" Adam asked. "They were probably fables, with a moral?"

Dante looked at him. As always, everything was compacted and distilled by Adam, as if the sickening, overwhelming human degradation and despair in front of them could be sterilized and boiled down to a lesson. He gestured to the two wriggling corpses with his left hand. "This has a moral? This? What? That all is death, and never-ending pain? The hopeless, tortured existence of a beast caught in a trap? The pointless gibbering and contortions of an idiot beggar left to die on the street?" Dante's jaw clenched and unclenched. "I don't think such a lesson is from God. It must be from somewhere else."

Adam seemed to know it would be better now to lower his gaze, out of respect for Dante's righteous anger, and for the suffering of the dead in front of them. "Yes," he said quietly, "the lesson is from somewhere else. It is from this hellish hole we have been driven into. But God is even here, friend. I know you know that."

There was a pause as Dante considered what to do.

"How did they even get like this?" Radovan said.

"They must've been bitten and didn't want to turn into the undead," Adam said. "They thought killing themselves would stop it, but they were wrong." He glanced over at Dante.

Dante returned the glance. "Death solves nothing. Death changes nothing," he said, barely opening his mouth. His words felt very cold on his lips. Adam looked away, nodding slightly.

Radovan did not appear to notice the exchange between Dante and Adam. He shook his head. "They should've known better. Everyone knows you'll turn once you're bitten, even if something else kills you before the plague does."

Bogdana finally moved from the group, going to the saddle of her horse to retrieve the hatchet. "They were young," she said as she returned. "They didn't know. At least they did it in such a way that they couldn't hurt others." She looked up at the contorted faces as the dead twisted in their madness and frustration. Their movements appeared one moment like a tragic, graceful dance, and the next like the spasms of a sick and mortally wounded animal. "They probably helped each other to do it. Maybe they were lovers. Maybe each of them only wanted to help the other avoid more pain and shame and guilt. They were scared, confused, in agony. Look at them. They still are." She turned back to Dante and the others. "I've seen enough yesterday and today to know which people to condemn and despise, and which to pity and help. I'm beginning to wonder when you three are going to catch on."

Dante blushed, not quite understanding how he deserved the sting of her reprimand, but knowing nonetheless it must somehow be right and for his good. Even as her speech wounded and embarrassed him, it gave him much more strength and resolve than was offered by the coldly rational words that had dropped from his lips a moment ago.

"All right," he said. "What do we need to do now? Why do *you* think we are here, now, in this horrible place?"

"Why, to get them down, of course" she answered. "To finish what they started. To do what they wanted to do, rather than what they foolishly tried to do the wrong way at the wrong time."

Adam nodded. "She is right. Judgment is not the point here. Mercy should be our only concern."

"So there is mercy, even in this hell?" Dante asked.

"Perhaps here most of all," Adam said.

"You already said God is here," Bogdana said. "So love and mercy must be here. But God does not often do merciful acts on His own. That is our job." She turned to Radovan. "Can you do what needs to be done, while they're still hanging? Can you reach high enough?"

Radovan appeared to consider it. "It would help if someone held their feet. If they would stop swinging back and forth, it'd be easy enough. Up under the chin. It'd be over in a second. If they even feel pain."

Bogdana offered the handle of the hatchet to Dante. "I can't very well climb the tree. Take this and cut the branch they're hanging from when he's done."

Dante sheathed his sword so he could take the hatchet with his right hand. He looked at the grim piece of iron and nodded.

He hadn't climbed a tree since he was a boy. It was much harder than he remembered. His hands and feet kept slipping, especially his feet, since there were no branches close enough to the ground for him to step up onto. As he struggled up the tree, he noticed he did not hear the pathetic sound of the dead anymore, and the branch had stopped swaying around from their exertions. Dante glanced over his shoulder to confirm the others were finished with what they needed to do, and, seeing that they were, he hacked at the branch. Hanging on to another branch with his left hand was an awkward position, and he couldn't get much force behind the blows. After a few minutes of hard work, he was panting and both his arms ached, but he had done enough damage to the branch that it no longer supported the weight of the bodies. Dante looked over his shoulder again, and saw the branch's burden rested on the earth. Bogdana was cutting through their nooses with a knife.

Dante dropped to the ground and joined the others. Radovan broke the branch from which the bodies had hung into smaller pieces, while Bogdana and Adam kicked piles of pine needles on top of the corpses. The layer of needles on the forest floor was almost as unbelievable and monstrous as Dante had imagined. It was nearly up to their ankles, so in just a minute they'd created a huge pile by clearing a circle around the bier.

Radovan tossed the two logs the people had used in their final act on top of the pile, then knelt down to start the fire. "Should we say something?" he asked softly. "I know some people believe suicide is a very grave sin."

"Despair is a very grave sin and a disease," Adam said. "Suicide is some people's ineffectual treatment of that disease. As you have reminded us, daughter, we only know what bodily disease these people suffered from. We do not know whether their souls were sick. We have freed them from their bodily torment. We can only have faith God will save them from any spiritual anguish."

"I remember a story. I don't know where it is in the Bible," Bogdana said as she stepped closer to the bier. "I heard it a few times in church, and I liked it because it seemed so simple, even a little funny. A widow keeps asking a wicked judge to help her, and he does not. But finally she wears him out, and he helps her. The story ends by saying if an unjust man will act this way, how much more can we expect from our righteous God? I think that's true. He is strong, and we are weak. He is perfect, and we are not. If we have done what little we can, we know He can do so much more. That isn't even faith. It's just common sense."

The tiny woman knelt down, her hands on her thighs, palms up.

Though her enormous belly made her movements more difficult and slower, Dante thought she moved with an exceptional grace and confidence, as though what she were doing was both necessary and beautiful. As he watched her, Dante had the strangest notion that the Blessed Virgin must've looked like this when she prayed during her pregnancy, when God Himself was inside her, giving her terrible strength and unutterable wisdom. The thought was rendered more fascinating and vivid to him as he remembered the frescoes of the Virgin he had seen in the Scrovegni Chapel in Padua, shortly after they had been painted in 1306. They had included one of a pregnant Mary visiting her pregnant cousin Elizabeth. Dazzlingly beautiful, the paintings were nothing like the captivating reality before him. Now such images seemed to him stilted and artificial, whereas here was the breathing reality of a peasant girl who was filled with the Spirit of God. The paintings were merely human products, no matter how talented their artist. Now he beheld an icon fashioned by the one, true Divine Artist. Dante had to blink and shake his head. The vision was so intoxicating and incongruous, there in that foul, polluted clearing, with nothing but disease and death for miles and miles around them.

Bogdana leaned her head back. "We do not know their names, Lord," she prayed, "but You do, as You know their hearts. They died, but You can never die. Their bodies failed them, but You can never fail any of Your servants, who call on You night and day from this pit. We know You are their redeemer. Amen." She lowered her head, as did Dante and the others, before Radovan sent the sparks into the bone-dry, ash-grey needles, which immediately took light.

They stayed a few moments as the pyre roared to life. Dante watched the plume of grey smoke as it cascaded up into the branches above. He wondered if the smoke would mingle with the clouds, which were exactly the same color, or if it would sneak past them to find the sun, which must still be shining somewhere, in some place that for now Dante could only imagine.

Chapter 26

Clearly to manifest these novel things,
I say that we arrived upon a plain,
Which from its bed rejecteth every plant.
Dante, *Inferno*, 14.7-9

By the time they left the fatal clearing it was nearly too dark to continue, but still they went on. After a while, the clinging smell of the burning bodies was replaced by the smothering scent of the dry, dead forest. The trail turned to the right, and Dante and his companions emerged from under the trees, marching out into a plain that spread out before them. It was too dark to see the plain's full extent, but as far as Dante could see in the twilight, everything was blank, grey, and flat for some distance, except for the black shape of the forest now behind them.

The horses' footfalls had become completely silent, and Dante looked down to see the animals' hooves were churning through a layer of the finest ash he'd ever seen. The ash was so fine, its color such a sickly grey, it looked like flour that had been ground from some mixture of blasted, diseased plants. The dust's fine texture meant that, in just a few steps, their horses' hooves had sent huge clouds of it swirling up, engulfing them in a burning, stinging fog. Although the air around them had already turned cool in the night, the ash seemed unnaturally warm to Dante, as if it had just been swept from the bottom of an oven or kiln. The fog quickly became so thick Dante could barely see the rump of the horse ahead of him, and Bogdana's back was completely lost to sight.

"We can't go on now!" Adam shouted from the rear. "Come back, you three!"

Dante waited till he could see Bogdana had turned her horse, then he pulled his around and started to retreat to the edge of the forest. They stopped there, coughing and brushing themselves off as they dismounted.

"We'll stay here. Right at the edge of the forest," Adam said. "The plain will be hard enough to cross with daylight, but in the dark it would be impossible. We could start to go in circles and get completely lost. Once we can see the sun in the morning, we can head more or less west and cross the plain quickly. It's not that wide, east to west. Let us make camp here, quickly. Stay close. We'll build a fire. Nights are very cold here."

Everyone hustled about with the preparations, gathering firewood and breaking out the provisions from the saddles. No one was ever more than a few steps away from one of the others, however. Once they were seated around the fire, things seemed safer, though Dante would not say he felt normal or relaxed, just slightly less threatened and sick at everything around him.

Everything was silent, except for the crackle of the fire. Dante knew this was good—they could hear any intruders as they approached—but it still filled him with the kind of foreboding he'd felt constantly for two days, a seething dread at a world that was unnatural and monstrous in every way, and yet always made a terrible, predictable kind of sense, no matter what horror he saw next. He chewed their modest rations—dried fruit and meat, nuts, and some bread—and passed the water bottle to Bogdana, who sat leaning against him, for it had suddenly gotten quite cold. Dante knew her solid, reliable body was the only thing that kept him from shaking in fear, just as he knew her need for him was the only thing keeping him from weeping in despair. If a man had love and a purpose, he lacked nothing necessary. These things were stronger than the flesh, stronger than its pains or pleasures. Dante still had doubts as to whether or not the weak flesh would be strong enough for him to survive another day in this hell.

"I've never been this far up the valley," Radovan said as they ate.

"I did not know this desert plain was here. How did it get like this?"

"Centuries ago, a huge fire swept through the forest," Adam explained. "It is said it burned for months, leaving this huge scar across the valley where nothing ever grew again. It almost seemed like a barrier, to keep people from going further up the valley. But eventually they returned and forged ahead, up to the higher, rougher plateaus we will see tomorrow. There is even less life up there, but only stones and torments, and the people who thrive on such pain and strife."

"Why then do they go up there?" Bogdana asked.

Adam shook his head. "As I say, they thrive on it, and every creature in the world goes to where it can survive, where it can live the life it was meant to. In a peaceful, well-watered valley there are gentle creatures and beautiful flowers. Under a rock there are worms and venomous things that cannot abide the light of day. It is no different with men. They say they go further up the valley to mine the jewels that are hidden in the mountains there, but I think that is a lie they tell to themselves and to others, to make themselves seem less incomprehensible. I think they go there to get away from other people, and their laws, because that is how they want to live. Tomorrow you must see what that kind of life is like. I am sorry, but it is the only way for you to survive."

They were all silent for a moment, then Adam spoke again. "And what did you know of the valley before the other day, my son?" he asked Radovan.

"Not much at all," the younger man said. "I knew there was valuable timber and mining here, and that's why people kept coming back, even though it was terribly dangerous, what with the undead plague constantly breaking out every couple of generations. People want what is here so much they are willing to risk their lives for it."

"Where were you from?" Bogdana asked.

"Not from any of the towns near here. My family lived in the city. My father was a tailor. He taught my older brother to take up the business. He taught me enough to help out when I was a boy, but we knew the business was only big enough to be passed on to my brother. I thought to join a monastery. I liked the discipline, and working hard at something, on your own. It seemed noble, I suppose. But I didn't have the head for it. I could read a bit, but I didn't like all the praying and singing. I had heard of the army, and how it would always be necessary to keep a large, well-paid one in our country, with the threat from this valley always looming. All the boys in the city are told how brave and just our leader, Lord Mihail, is, and they all want to grow up to be soldiers and knights like him. I remember seeing him in parades in our city, and he looked so chivalrous, so noble and strong as he rode by, with his armor, sword, and lance. Even if I could never rule our country, I thought I could be as good and righteous as he, killing monsters and saving people from them, like he did. I suppose it was childish, but I believed it and it gave me something to work for."

He fell silent for a moment before continuing. "So I joined the army, and for a few years, it was an easy life. They fed and paid us a lot, for what little we did, most of the time. But then this plague came. I always thought I was hard, fearless. And I was, for the fighting. So long as the dead were attacking, I could kill them as well and as easily as any man could. But more and more I saw ones that were wounded, unable to stand up or fight. Or they were children. Or we were attacking villages where some people were still alive. I didn't ask to be an executioner, and I wasn't ready for it. The commanders would tell you all the people were going to die anyway, and this was more merciful. It had to be done, but you just can't make yourself do that. Either it comes naturally, or you have to stop doing it before you go mad. I suppose some can just not think about it." He paused for a breath.

"The first night, after killing many people, living and dead, we drank a lot. I think for some of the men, that was enough. It dulled their memories and their consciences to the point where they could do it again. But I couldn't. I couldn't stop thinking about the people we'd killed, their faces, their eyes, all the blood and tears and snot running down their faces, as they're hit over and over. People shouldn't be so weak and easy to kill. If they were harder to kill, then you could just do it. But they die so easily, they make it impossible for you." He looked up. "It's funny, I didn't have the head to be a monk, but I thought too much to be a soldier in this wretched war against the monsters. I'm just not cut out for anything in this world." He dropped his gaze, brooding.

"You fought for that woman," Dante said. "You tried to help her."

"Yes, I tried." He spat out the words. "And I failed. The only good thing that happened there was that useless dictator being annihilated, and that wasn't my doing. I could've taken credit for that, if I had still been in the army, loading the trebuchet that crushed him. Instead all I did was watch more people die and kill each other senselessly. That's all I can do is watch more bad things happen."

"You came with us and helped us," Bogdana said. "I don't know how far we could've made it without you. Thank you."

"You're welcome. I just hope it results in something. I hope I don't fail you, too."

"Everyone fails, many times," Adam said. "Whether you have the strength to carry on is the measure of your bravery. We all know that you do, my son. You needn't judge yourself the way you do. You stopped doing evil and started doing good. What more would you demand of yourself? Success? That is a matter of fortune, not virtue."

Adam turned to Bogdana. "And you, my daughter? You lived close to the valley before? You knew something of its threat?"

"Yes. I've lived near the valley my whole life," she began. "I had heard of the plague since I was little. We knew to be careful. My parents had lived through a plague, and they always told us to be careful. But it makes us too wary sometimes. You see someone hurt and you stay away at first, afraid that they're one of the dead. Someone staggers and falls, maybe they've had too much to drink and they throw up on themselves, and someone bashes their head in, thinking to save the village. But all he's done is kill his neighbor and made some woman a widow. People shouldn't live like that."

She sighed before she resumed. "It's what I loved so much about my husband. We'd grown up together, though he was a couple years older, and he'd always been so gentle and trusting." She tilted her chin up, to indicate Radovan. "He was big, like you. A huge, strong man." She held her hands out, turning them over a couple times to show her palms, then the backs of her hands. "And his hands! I never could believe how big they were when he'd grab me—always playfully, never rough. He could pick me up so easily, or toss our boy so high up in the air. I could never think of him hurting someone, just to try to protect himself or possibly avoid the plague. He'd have to be sure there was no other way before he could do harm to anyone. He was perfect. And our life was hard, but it was good."

She looked down. She was sitting right next to Dante, leaning against him so he couldn't see her face. He could smell her — a living thing of sweat and blood and breath. He could also hear in her description how happy she'd been, and he wished, more than anything else, she was still happy like that, even if it meant she would never meet or know him. Perhaps he would've watched her from the road, playing with her son or kissing her husband, and he would've smiled with joy to see such a happy and pretty peasant girl, and that would've been a better existence for both of them. But that was not the life they now had, and he knew he must be glad of this one, too, as bitter as it was.

"And, like you, that all changed with the plague," Bogdana continued. "My husband came crashing through the door of our little cottage, holding our son. They had seen an injured man in the fields, and of course my husband had gone to help him. He probably didn't see the bites at first, and even if he had, you know there are wolves and bears in the woods. He would've thought the man had been attacked by one of those and needed help. I know he would've thought that before he'd think he should run away and ignore someone in pain, someone who might need his help. But the man was already dead. My husband could overpower him easily, but you know how they are if they take you by surprise, and you don't get them first with a weapon. He bit my husband terribly on his arms and neck, and our little boy tried to jump in to help his father. He wouldn't have known not to do that. Perhaps it was my fault. I didn't always remind him of the danger, the way my mother always harped on it with me when I was little. She'd hit me with her hand if I ever went near a child or other person I didn't know, or if I went to the door to answer it, or if I was ever out of her sight in the woods. But maybe she was right." She had to stop, and her small body shook with silent sobs.

"You needn't say more," Dante told her. "We know. There's no need to say the rest."

She inhaled and drew herself up, sniffling in all the mucus her weeping had loosened up. "No, it's all right. It's good to talk about them. It's good to tell people of goodness and innocence and bravery, when all they see is wickedness and hate and pain. It's good to remind them that, just three days ago, people still helped each other, rather than tearing each other apart like beasts. So, my husband and son were both bitten, before my husband could tear the man off of them and beat him to death. My husband, as big and strong as he was, was weaker from more bites. He probably wouldn't last the night. He was panting and wheezing from carrying our son all the way from the fields, and normally it wouldn't have winded him at all to do that. Our son was still small, only four. My little boy wasn't as bad off, just one small bite on his arm. He didn't even cry. But it would be the same in a day or two—a terrible death, then back up and trying to kill me. Either one of them would get me or I'd have to kill them. I didn't know what to do for them.

"But my husband, he'd thought of it already, even as he dragged himself back to our home to die. He'd thought what would be best for me, what would cause me the least pain. He wanted to spare me as much as possible, keep me from seeing them suffer. He told me to take a basket of food and go to our neighbor's barn and hide in the loft there. I asked what he was going to do, and he said he'd take care of it, to just trust him. I kissed my son on the forehead. There was too much blood on my husband for me to kiss him, but I wept for him, and he knew how I felt. I thanked him for taking care of it, because I knew I couldn't do it, and I promised to make sure our baby would survive. I stood outside and he locked the door after me. There was no one around, so I thought I should stay there, in case he changed his mind or needed me for something. I waited, and the roof started to smoke, then the door. I never heard anything from inside the house, even as the flames engulfed the whole building. Even if he had ... taken care of our son before he started the fire, my husband must've still been alive through all that, and he never cried out, or tried to escape. He took all that responsibility, all that suffering, on himself, rather than cause me pain or guilt."

She leaned more of her weight on Dante. He thought the story had taken much of her strength. "I waited in the barn till the next day, when our neighbor's wife came in and tried to eat me. That's when I broke out of the barn. I saw the whole town was being destroyed. I thought I wouldn't be able to keep my promise to my husband, and I've never felt such guilt, such despair. After he had kept every promise to me, and saved me from so much, I thought I had failed him utterly. But I kept fighting, and killed my neighbor, after I had seen you. You got me out of there. And then I met you two, and you helped as well. You are all very brave. If I hadn't known my husband, I'd say you were the bravest men I've ever known. I can never thank you enough."

"No need, my daughter," Adam said. "We can take turns sleeping now. You three may go first. You look very tired."

An icy wind began to blow, swirling the ash around them like a dirty, grey blizzard, except the sickening snow stung like a maelstrom of ground glass. Dante drew his knees up and pulled a blanket over his head, crossing his arms in front of himself to pull the fabric tight across his cheeks, leaving just a gap for his eyes. He watched the others do the same, their motions slow and stiff, the way ghosts or people in dreams move. They could've been four survivors on the Anatolian plains, with the ashes of fallen Troy raining down on them as they bided their time waiting for the inevitable, fated rebirth of their people. Or they could've been four of the damned on the outskirts of Gomorrah, the salty, toxic exhalation of an unknown, jealous God wearing away every trace of them, as they waited for a sunrise their burning, tear-filled eyes would never see. The feeling of Bogdana's body pressing against him could not tell Dante which of these two worlds they now inhabited. It only told him that he could endure either.

Chapter 27

Of naked souls beheld I many herds,
Who all were weeping very miserably,
And over them seemed set a law diverse.
Dante, *Inferno*, 14.19-21

Dawn came, though one could not say for certain that the sun rose. Instead, daybreak was just the time when the grey all around them brightened to the point where Dante could see indistinct shapes again. All he could see of his companions were three irregular mounds of ash, like stunted pillars of salt that had dared to look back on a better, happier world. Their world was cursed, and Dante knew it was their duty to gaze upon it, or else suffer worse for their doubt and disobedience.

Bogdana was the first to rise, the mortal crust cracking and falling from her like a chrysalis. The condition of the horses was much less terrifying than that of their riders, since they had been tethered under some of the nearby trees, partly shielded from the ashen snow. After a quick drink of water and some more of their provisions, they mounted their horses. With blankets wrapped around their heads as cowls, they looked like Arabs set to cross the desert, on their way to trade for European or Chinese treasures, or to slay the infidel Christians. A light, sultry wind was blowing steadily from the north, so the dust kicked up by their horses billowed off to the left, leaving their view ahead clear enough for them to navigate. Even though this helped them, Dante could not think of the wind as anything but unnatural and, in some strange way, vindictive. It seemed like a begrudging aid to them, breathed out from something that both envied and punished their ignorance and weakness.

They trudged on for what seemed like the entire morning, but looking back at the lighter spot in the clouds where the sun ought to be, Dante could see it had not been long at all. Then Dante saw, off to their right, another cloud of dust approaching. It seemed to be angling toward them, heading south or slightly southeast, as they made their way westward. Given how visible both their dust clouds were, it made no sense to try to flee from this new group, whoever they were, so the four continued on their way, watching as the others drew closer.

Eventually, Dante could discern a cart pulled by two mules. The cart stopped near them, and both groups waited for the dust to clear enough for them to see each other and speak. As Dante pulled back his cowl, he saw a man and woman at the front of the cart doing the same. Although the pair had been mostly upwind of the dust billowing out in front of their vehicle, they were still thoroughly encrusted, as if they suffered from leprosy. When they had brushed themselves off, Dante could see the two people were middle aged, with the dark hair and ruddy complexion of everyone in the valley. Both looked beaten and worn, though the woman might have been pretty once, with the flashing eyes and long brown hair of many of the women Dante had seen here. The couple's haggard appearance looked as though it predated the outbreak of the living dead, something more simmering and deep-seated, like a plague of its own. Surveying the cart, it looked to Dante like the contents of a home: some furniture, boxes, bundles, and a small cage that contained clucking chickens. Three small heads popped out then disappeared among this pile of household goods. Though Dante couldn't help but feel a little encouraged at the first sight of living children in days, he also felt depressed that they too were lost in this deadly wasteland, perhaps with even less chance of escape than he.

"Hello," the man in the cart said. "What news? Where are you headed?"

"We're trying to make it west, across the scar," Adam replied. "Then further up into the mountains. We hope to escape the dead and the army that way."

The man shook his head. "I don't think we'd ever make it, especially with my wife and the children. The ascent is difficult. Have you seen it? Do you know what kind of men are up there, sir? Bandits and murderers are the nicest of the lot. The ones they send out as a welcoming committee when you first arrive! Then if you survive those, you get to meet the really nasty ones. The ones who like hurting you not just to take your things, but just for the sake of hurting you. No, thank you! We're trying to get to the south side of the valley, across the scar. The woods are supposed to be thicker there, and I think we can hide. It's worth a try."

"Maybe," Adam said. "We've seen fewer dead this far up the valley, so perhaps if the army relents or doesn't come this far, then you'll survive."

"I hope so, sir. Please pray for us, and we'll do the same for you."

"Of course we will," Adam said.

Hearing one of the people in the valley mention prayer and hope shocked Dante much more than many of the horrors he'd seen in the last couple days. There again was that terrible quality of familiarity. In just two days he'd grown so used to brutality and blasphemy of every kind that the invocation of God or faith or goodness sounded to his poisoned ears like something grating, harsh, inappropriate, and embarrassing. He had expected the man to curse them or make threats, and this gentler, more civilized exchange did not comfort or encourage Dante, but only confused and disoriented him, almost as if the man had begun speaking in a language unknown to him—or worse, forgotten by him.

Having heard an unexpected expression of piety, Dante then noticed a wooden icon among the items in the cart. It was a painting, mostly in brown and gold, of an elderly, bearded man, holding up his right hand, his thumb bending his ring finger down, with the other three fingers extended. The painting was situated in an odd way, right at the front of the cargo, facing forward, so that it almost appeared like a third passenger on the driver's bench between the man and his wife. Its placement and seeming ostentation only perplexed Dante more, though at least it helped make some sense of the man's earlier expression of religious sentiment.

As Dante contemplated the icon and the odd exchange, the man's wife shot out her left arm to give her husband a solid blow on the side of his head. From the way he didn't flinch or move, it seemed it was as uninteresting and ordinary to him as it was to Dante. Things had returned to normal in this environment, which was further confirmed when the woman swung her right hand around to slap her husband in the face.

"Why do you talk so?" she growled after the attack. "Why do you continue to utter such useless horseshit?" As if on cue, one of the mules picked that exact moment to drop three round balls of dung into the dust in front of them. The woman laughed, though it wasn't a happy or healthy sound, but seemed even more forced and out of place than her husband's religiosity. "See, even a dumb brute knows what you're saying is shit! What makes you think I'll pray for these people? And don't say that you and the children will pray for them: I couldn't care less what you do, and I'll be damned if I let my children waste their time on your foolishness! What makes you think these people would even care? We haven't seen anyone as senseless as you in days, and perhaps these ones aren't as foolish as you, either!" She leaned forward so she could look at Dante and the others. "Are you as crazed and foolish as this wreck of a man? Then tell you what. He'll pray for you, but I don't want something as useless as that." She leaned back and swatted her husband once more; the blow was backhanded and casual this time. "Ask for something useful next time, why don't you?"

"What do you want?" Radovan asked. Dante thought the younger man looked a little more shocked at the woman's words and actions than Dante felt, and he took some comfort in this. "We have a bit of food and water and can share those."

She waved them off. "Why prolong the agony? Unless you have a way out of this mess, I don't really want anything of yours."

"Please, dear," the man said. "I meant no harm. I thought perhaps these people still had hope, and I wanted to share it with them. Let them know there were still others who cared and prayed for them."

"Oh, I know you care," the woman said. "And I couldn't care less if you do. It's just how that really bothers me. But really, why argue with these people? I got myself into this. I had to marry this dolt and get myself dragged to this wretched valley. But you were too much of a coward to go further up the valley, where the real riches were. So you stayed here and chopped down tiny, twisted trees, like the stunted gnome of a man you are. You dragged them into town and sold them. Probably for less than they were worth, I'll wager. And now you want to hide in the trees while we all wait around to die. Lovely."

"Please, dear." Dante heard the man's voice quiver. "Don't talk like that. Saint Andrew helped you find me. You said so yourself, once." He gestured to the icon between them. "And he blessed our union. We have three children. Many other people can't have them, or their children die, and they're very sad. I know things are hard, but don't talk like that."

"Oh, don't even remind me of this silly icon!" She spat on the painted wood before smacking her husband. "My family had money, you fool. Not a lot, but some. Otherwise you wouldn't even have this decoration to heap all your silly hopes on—a stupid, little idol, as dumb and useless as you are." Two more blows fell on her husband, one from each of her hands. "And as dead as we're all going to be soon." Another blow, this one a closed-fist punch that turned his head around and sent blood flying out the side of his mouth. "And what did you have? Hopes. Big dreams. Love. And worst of all, *piety*." Dante shivered at how she said the word. It sounded like it caused her real, physical pain to make the sound.

Apparently the woman had gotten herself quite worked up, for she leaped down to the ground and kicked at the dust, sending a cloud billowing up around her till Dante could barely see her. He could only make out an occasional foot or hand, flailing out of the swirling storm of hate and rage. "All that belief and love for the Lord of all! The mighty King of creation! King of this… this… *shit* is more like it!" She must have snatched up the animal dung in her frenzy, for a crumbly, moist glob hit her husband in the face. "I believe in one shit, the shit almighty, maker of shit and more shit!" Saint Andrew's serene, unchanging visage was the next to be defiled with a projectile. "I believe in the shit, the only begotten shit of the shit, true shit from true shit!" She'd started to cackle at her blasphemy at this point, when the third handful hit Dante, though he'd raised his arm in time to be spared the full, facial assault of the woman's fury. "And I believe in the shit, the giver of shit, who proceeds from the other shit!"

The attack and the cursing stopped. Dante brushed himself off, and looked over to see the woman's husband wiping his own face. The man cleaned up Saint Andrew, though the only way he had to do so was with his sleeve and some spit. Dante thought the man was muttering the whole time he cleaned the icon. Probably praying for forgiveness, because even his cleansing was dirty and profane, Dante thought.

The figure of the woman slowly emerged as more of the dust drifted off. She stood there, staring at all of them, fists clenched at her sides, panting. Her husband hung his head, seemingly waiting for her, though he said nothing. She raised her fists, very slowly and deliberately and with a terrible, lonely kind of grace. For a moment, the area around her seemed to brighten, almost imperceptibly, and Dante decided the woman had most definitely been very pretty at one time, perhaps not so long ago. She tilted her head and Dante thought she looked above her husband, past him, past Dante, past all of them, and into the silent, unmoved clouds above them. From where she faced, Dante supposed she might be looking at that brighter patch of cloud hiding the sun.

"I would do anything to shut you up!" she howled. "But you won't! I'd kill you, but I can't! You never leave me alone! You never shut up! But you'll never change me. *Never*! I'll always be what I am, and I'll always hate you, deny you, curse you, spit on you! I'll never come crawling, begging and cringing like a beaten dog! I'll hit you and hurt you every chance I get! I'll die, but everyone dies! It proves nothing! And that will be my revenge. That will be my triumph. To hurt and hate and ignore you and all your *shit*! *Forever*!"

Her pitch rose on the last two words, and she elongated the final syllable, making it into a shriek of rage and agony that tore through the valley with all the hideous strength of a doomed, proud race. Dante wondered if Joshua's trumpet had sounded any different to the people huddled in Jericho as they prayed to their little, stone idols. He wondered if the screams of those crushed under the Tower of Babel had any less outrage and anguish in them. And with an empty feeling in his chest, Dante wondered why such a cry did not bring the mountains' stones crashing down on them, if such pillars were held up only by love and justice, and not by the kind of brute, soulless force that could noiselessly withstand the assault of so much power, passion, and pain.

All six of them stayed there, motionless, for some time. And the children, Dante presumed, were huddled somewhere in the cart, perhaps used to scenes like this, or perhaps learning a new and awful lesson about how the human heart worked. Then the woman slowly lowered her head and fists, and climbed up on to the cart next to her husband. The reins slapped the mules' backs once, and the cart creaked into motion, sliding off to the south with its cargo of human misery. Dante watched them for a moment longer, until the dust engulfed them forever.

Chapter 28

A greater fear I do not think there was
What time abandoned Phaeton the reins,
Whereby the heavens, as still appears, were scorched.
Dante, *Inferno*, 17.106-108

They rode on in silence after their encounter with the unhappy family, until the land rose up before them in a high, rocky bluff. It extended across the valley, north to south, so if they were to proceed further west, they would have to climb it. It looked far too steep for the horses.

"Is there a trail somewhere?" Dante asked, as he unwrapped his face and brushed himself off.

Adam looked north and south, then at the peaks that loomed above the bluff, further to the west. "To the south there is."

They proceeded to the south a short ways, staying close to the base of the cliff. They stopped when they saw the line of a trail snaking back and forth across the cliff face. The trail was a very steep switchback, and it was so narrow it was barely discernible from where they were. Although it was more navigable than the bare cliff face, it was clearly impassable for horses.

"This?" Dante asked.

Adam dismounted and the others followed. "Yes," he said. "This is the trail to the next plateau. The one to the final plateau is even steeper, though it's not as high."

"I thought you said people live up there?" Dante asked as he got down. "How can this be the only way up?"

"There aren't many this far up, and they live very simply, if wickedly," Adam replied. "We must learn simplicity from them, and avoid their wickedness. Take only necessities—water skins and a little food. Eat what you can now. We only need to survive until tonight. We will decide our fate by then, as the people here have decided theirs."

Dante slung two water skins over his shoulders and filled his pockets with food. He rolled the blanket up into a small bundle with a few other items, like flint and knives. Tearing a piece of bread off with his teeth, he handed the rest of the loaf to Bogdana.

"But you said there were mines up here," Dante said. "How can they bring their goods down and sell them?"

"They mine for jewels, so they can carry their gains on their own backs," Adam said. "It would be different if they mined iron or copper—useful, substantial things. But with such small expensive cargo, they don't even need pack animals to help them in their existence, like normal men would. Just their own intellects and desires are enough to drive them on. And men who are totally impervious to beauty are perfect for plucking such tiny fragments of it from the darkness."

Bogdana patted the neck of her black horse. "What will happen to the horses?" she asked.

Radovan and Adam were already starting up the trail. "The two from our monastery are trained to return to it. Without us to burden them, they should be there before we reach our goal," Adam answered. "I suspect the other two will know to follow them. Animals are better about that."

Bogdana followed the other two up the trail, and Dante fell in line behind her. He looked over his shoulder. The horses were already churning up a cloud of dust to the east, heading back the way they had come. He looked up the trail, at the height they had to scale, and felt fairly sure the animals had a better chance on their journey. The trail was little more than an irregular ledge, slightly wider than a person's foot. One had to lean toward the cliff face to keep from falling over, or hold on to rocks. Sometimes there were gnarled trees and shrubs that grew there, many of them dead, and their roots and stems offered some handholds.

After toiling up the bluff for some time, they stopped for water.

All of them were panting from the exertion. Dante looked down, and the height made him feel sick and dizzy. He'd never been especially afraid of heights, but balconies or frequently-used trails were one thing—those were made by civilized people to minimize a person's fear. Hanging on to a dead tree root over a plain of ash several miles wide, with ominously described horrors above them and shambling hordes of the dead below them, that was something else entirely. That was a situation to kindle a mind like Dante's to the most horrible flights of speculation—to thoughts of avalanches, earthquakes, and volcanoes, as well as swooping attacks from giant birds of prey, screeching ghouls tumbling down the slope, or even tree roots coming to life and wrapping around his wrist and neck, then tightening and leaving his strangled body forever on that desolate, cursed mount of slaughter. Dante closed his eyes and breathed deeply. The only sound he heard was the faint whispering of the wind. He looked to Bogdana, and the sparkle in her eyes when she glanced back at him was enough to banish his terrors for now.

They had only gone a short ways after their water break when they again stopped. "Look there," Adam said as he pointed up. "What are they doing?"

Dante looked to where he indicated. Four birds were circling above them. The wheeling birds spiraled down toward them as they watched. They were not small birds, but they also weren't big enough to be the kinds one would normally associate with this behavior, like eagles or vultures. If Dante's fantasy of an aerial attack were coming true, it was not being launched by gigantic, mythological creatures. However, looking down to where his boots overhung the edge of the trail, then past them into the chasm below, Dante thought of how it wouldn't take a harpy or a sphinx to knock him off this tiny ledge.

The four of them stayed still on the ledge and watched the birds as they descended. The animals made no sound as they came closer. Finally Dante could see that they were owls, as little sense as that made for a group of birds flying in the daytime. Dante thought how owls were the birds of Athena, but also how the Bible declared them unclean, and associated them with defeat, death, and desolation. But whether he took his symbols from Athens or Jerusalem, all such knowledge seemed pretentious and pointless to Dante right then, there on that silent, forlorn cliff. Warning, curse, blessing or prediction—none of those seemed certain, and all seemed possible.

The birds continued their descent, and Dante could see the creatures' large, unblinking eyes looking at him. With their strange, unnatural bodies, they could even keep their eyes fixed on him throughout their spiraling flight. Their stare was neither chilling nor comforting; it wasn't even penetrating, as though Dante were being searched or violated. He did feel as though the birds saw everything. It just didn't bother him or reassure him, because it didn't seem to matter to these beings what their all-encompassing gaze took in, and therefore it didn't matter to Dante if they saw every detail of him and went on examining him forever. All-seeing eyes without judgment or approval behind them might as well be made of glass.

As the birds passed below them and tilted their heads to focus on some spot on the valley floor, Dante turned to the pair of eyes that most mattered to him in the world right now.

"Four of them, four of us," Bogdana said.

"Yes, but we don't know what that means, and you said just knowing that they mean something was enough for you," Dante replied.

"Well, perhaps it is enough for me. But I don't like it. Let's get out of here. Who knows what else is watching us?"

Dante felt sure, as he always did, that something was watching. But for the first time in his life, he was not sure what it was. Perhaps, as with Bogdana's earlier evaluation of portents, it did not matter: they knew they were not alone, and that was enough.

Chapter 29

There is a place in Hell called Malebolge [Evil Ditches],
Wholly of stone and of an iron colour,
As is the circle that around it turns.
Dante, *Inferno*, 18.1-3

They were panting and sweating by the time they reached the top of the cliff, but after only a short rest, they started moving once more. The trail led back into a forest on the plateau. Most of the trees here looked less sickly than those they had seen before crossing the scar, but given how many trunks Dante saw fallen on the ground, he wondered if some strange disease made them topple over, dead, even while they appeared relatively robust. By now it had become commonplace to Dante that there were no sounds, no animals or birds, no movement other than their own steady footsteps. The air seemed cooler and less dry up here, but not necessarily healthier, and certainly not more vibrant. It could have been the dank, pestilence-filled vapors of a swamp. At least the trail here was wider, so Dante could walk next to Bogdana, with Adam and Radovan ahead of them. Although they kept looking all around, after a few minutes of walking, Dante felt a bit more relaxed.

"I've never been up high like that," Bogdana said as they walked. "I didn't think I'd be so frightened."

Her weakness was as captivating to him as her strength and seeming invulnerability. "It's hard if you're not used to it," Dante said. "I've been many places, but with the trail so narrow, and everything so strange and dangerous here, it was very frightening."

"You were scared?" She must've been very frightened on the cliff, as he had never heard her voice like this, as though she actually expected or needed him to be strong.

"Well, not so much." Or did she want him to express vulnerability? He cursed himself inwardly. Now he wasn't sure which was the right response.

"But something bothered you. I can tell. If it wasn't the cliff, what was it then?"

Dante breathed deeply. He had been thinking as though she were a Florentine woman and this was some game to test him, in which he had to give a right answer for the flirtation to continue. But she had just been trying to find out how he felt. He wondered how long it would take him to get used to such honesty and reply in kind. "I don't know. I've felt like hell since we crossed that cursed desert of ash. Who knew there were such places on earth?"

She nodded. "It was awful. The dust got into my mouth and nose; it still burns. But you have seen many horrible things in these three days. Was it the woman who bothered you?"

Her intuition was as unnerving as it was enchanting. Or rather, it was enchanting because it was unnerving. "Yes, I suppose it was," he said quietly.

"Why? We've seen many evil and sad people. Why did she upset you so?"

"It's just what she said was so violent. Others said wicked or selfish things, but she was so out-of-control, so bursting with anger, lashing out at everything. I hadn't seen or thought of someone being so enraged, so much like an animal."

Bogdana shrugged. "Many people lose their tempers all the time. And many men are much more violent than she was. Perhaps it was because she was a woman. Is that what shocked you more?"

Dante had to concentrate to keep from missing a step or faltering. He knew this was as true as it was obvious, and unstated because it was both. Though perhaps he should've known better by now, Dante slipped back into treating her question as some kind of test, as though he was supposed to protest that no, he would never think such a thing. Or was he supposed to agree and explain how beautiful and gentle a woman was supposed to be, perhaps even state explicitly that Bogdana was such a lovely, demure creature who could never do and say such things? Dante was fairly sure that was the wrong answer, since the first thing the beautiful woman beside him had done when they met was to bash a man's brains into the ground. He blushed and tried to hide his growing agitation and confusion at having to give an honest and unadorned answer.

"Well, yes, I suppose it was. It did seem worse and more shocking, since she was a woman."

"You must know women can be angry. I know men get away with it more than we do, but you must've seen it before."

"Well, yes, but it was all so vulgar, gross, so *ugly* with her. Women aren't supposed to be like that." He'd let the last part slip out. It was honest and it felt good to be unguarded, but he knew it sounded wrong and indefensible as soon as he said it.

Bogdana arched an eyebrow and gave a small smile. He only caught it out of the corner of his eye, avoiding her glance as much as possible. "You thought us too *pretty* to say and do such things?"

"No . . . yes . . . Stop twisting my words around!" He'd meant to sound plaintive, to make her stop, but it came out as petulant, even spiteful.

Her smile dropped immediately. "Don't be angry," she said very softly. They walked a few steps. "I'm sorry. Please forgive me."

He wanted to embrace her, to weep into her long, beautiful hair and beg her forgiveness, but he would've restrained himself even if they'd been alone, in some place where corpses didn't walk about and women didn't examine men's feelings and thoughts in such uncomfortable ways. So he just walked. "No, no, you didn't do anything wrong. I've never been so sad and confused as I've been here. It's like going mad."

They kept walking. "I didn't mean to mock you. I just wanted to know why you were so upset. I've heard many women say such things as she did in the desert. But now I think about it, there were never men around when they would talk so. You weren't used to it. It seemed as strange and frightening to you as the cliff did to me."

"Yes. I suppose that's what did it," Dante said.

"Perhaps it is good, in a way, to see these secret sorts of wickedness we hide from other people all the time, out there, where people are normal. But I'm sorry it caused you pain."

She slipped her hand in his and squeezed. She even let her hand stay in his for a few steps. Dante thought of how different this gesture would be in Florence. So fraught with conflicted meanings it would be empty, even painful, like eating tasty food when you knew it was going to make you ill later on. But in the silent forest of death, the gesture only signified what it made visible and concrete—that two people chose to be connected to one another, that they wanted to be one instead of two. It was both more and less than it would mean in an Italian city, and Dante thought how strange it was this dark, desolate place revealed more and concealed less than the sunny streets of Florence.

Chapter 30

Upon my right hand I beheld new anguish,
New torments, and new wielders of the lash,
Wherewith the foremost Bolgia [ditch] was replete.
Dante, *Inferno*, 18.22-24

As they walked through the silent woods hand-in-hand, Bogdana suddenly pulled away and gave a tiny yelp. Dante reached for her as she turned to lean against a tree. Adam and Radovan also heard her, and they rushed to her side as well. She bent down, grimacing in pain as she drew in long gasps through clenched teeth.

"Is it your time?" Adam asked.

He seemed to Dante to be the calmest of them. Having been through this before, Bogdana looked resolute, not confused or frightened, but definitely distressed. Probably not from the physical discomfort of childbirth, but at the prospect of giving birth in this horrible place. Radovan looked the way Dante imagined he did at that moment—open-mouthed and terrified at the mystery of life, and panicked at the possibility of seeing a naked female body, especially one doing something for which only it was equipped. Something that had nothing to do with a man's pleasure or interest, and something so overflowing with agony and impurity.

"No. Not here, not now," she panted. "It'll pass. I know it will."

"Women have given birth in worse places, I'm sure," Adam said as soothingly as he could. He turned to Radovan. "My son, please keep an eye out for unwanted visitors." Pale and sweating, Radovan eagerly nodded at this suggestion and turned away from the heaving woman.

He looked almost on the brink of fainting, so much so it seemed to Dante the command had been more for the young man's well-being than for the rest of them.

Still holding on to the tree with one hand, Bogdana gripped Dante's shoulder with the other. The pressure she applied seemed inhuman, like it would drive him to his knees it was so powerful. Her brown-eyed stare locked on his, and he knew there was no arguing with her about anything at this point. She had become completely primal, physical, unaccountable for anything other than the needs of her body at that moment, and for the other body and spirit for which she was solely and completely responsible.

"Then I feel very sorry for them," she said, her breaths coming faster and more shallow, her teeth still clenched. "But I will not let that happen. Just stand here with me one moment till it passes."

They had no choice but to obey, and after a while, Bogdana's breathing slowed, and her grip on Dante gradually eased. She stood back to her full height and looked at them as she caught her breath and regained her balance. "Thank you," she said. "My first time, I had pangs the whole day before I gave birth. But we must hurry. My baby will not be born in this valley."

Dante wanted to hold her by the arm, coddle and comfort her, but it hardly seemed appropriate in their situation, so they walked side-by-side on the trail. Suddenly, Bogdana gave another yelp, and he thought her birth pangs had started again. But when he looked at her, he saw her head turned, her hand over her mouth and nose, retching. He looked ahead and saw that Adam and Radovan were not hurrying to her this time, because they too were coughing and heaving, with their hands covering their mouths. Before he could react, Dante was assaulted by the foulest odor he'd ever experienced. It was not like the stench of the dead, or the burning he'd smelled in various places the past three days. This smell was utterly of the living, but from the most disgusting and diseased parts of life, as though all the shit of a city's sewers had backed up on to the street during a summer flood and sat there in the sun to stew for a few days. Then when hundreds of people had been led through the sickening slurry, they vomited out the soured contents of their stomachs, adding it to the sun-baked sewage for some more simmering in the still, cloying heat. That was the kind of scent assaulting Dante now, stinging his eyes and nose and making him gag. Through his tear-filled eyes, he could see Bogdana was retching as hard as he was, but having heard how much more sensitive pregnant women were to smells, he was surprised she wasn't doing much worse.

The nausea subsided enough Dante was able to get the blanket he'd used as a cowl and wrap it around his face like a scarf, providing some kind of protection against the smell. He helped Bogdana do the same, while Adam and Radovan did so as well. With that little protection, and with their getting used to the noxious fumes, they were able to proceed. As they went, they were further molested by swarms of green flies whose numbers seemed to increase with each step. A bit further, and Dante saw tents of various sizes and shapes among the trees ahead. There were so many it was like a small city under the trees. The four stopped when they heard voices and shouting.

The large tent nearest them might have been white or beige at one time, but now it was thoroughly spattered with black and brown, from the ground to nearly the top. The smell and flies seemed to intensify near this one, and the shouting was coming from here. As they watched, the sides of the tent would fly outward in one spot then swing back, then fly outward in another spot, as though people were fighting inside, pushing one another against the canvas. Among the shouts Dante could now distinguish the moan of the dead, crescendoing sometimes to the pained, outraged roar they made. Above this steady drone a living voice hovered, occasionally punctuated by other, violent sounds.

"Oh, Alexis, you'll have to stop this foolishness!" There was a thwack and a roar. "God almighty, you always did have a hard head!" A grunt and another thwack were followed by a wet slapping sound, a splash, and gurgling. "Christ, by my mother's eye teeth, you crazy whore-loving fool. Stay down. Ugh! Now you got it all over me. Stupid, whoreson bastard!"

The next thwack and cursing brought two men crashing through the tent flaps and into Dante's view. The first one out of the tent was a dead man. His skin was mostly grey, though around his head and neck there were several gashes of red. The left side of his face was completely smashed in, revealing teeth and bone in places. His clothes were dripping everywhere with some foul slop of piss-soaked shit.

The dead man was followed out of the tent by his living assailant, who was only slightly better for wear. He was a tall, lean man with long, grey hair and beard, carrying a short-handled shovel in his right hand. At some point in their fighting, his arms had also been smeared with the latrine's contents. He brought the flat side of the shovel down again on the dead man's forehead, finally causing him to fall back on the ground. But as with the other dead people Dante had seen assaulted, this one writhed and moaned, still trying to get up. The living man stood over the struggling corpse.

"If that damned head is so hard we'll just take it off completely!"

He planted the edge of the shovel below the dead man's chin, put his right foot on the shovel's blade, and pressed it down through the flesh and bone of the neck. The dead man's hands shot up to claw at the handle of the shovel as his blood spilled out on to the ground. Then there was a wet, cracking sound and his arms went slack and fell still, sticking out straight from his sides. There was no underbrush in this sick, dead forest, so Dante could see the jaw was still moving. He shivered and looked away.

The grey-haired man finally noticed them. "Oh, hello strangers," he shouted to them in a surprisingly friendly tone. He tossed the shovel back by the entrance to the tent and looked down at the body and head, then back to the four newcomers. "Just a moment. Can't leave this lying around!"

He looked around, as though trying to decide what to do with the remains. He picked up the arms and laid them across the body, then he kicked the head a couple times till it lay next to the left elbow. Folding the corpse's legs under it, he made it about as compact as it could be. Then he picked up an end of one of the fallen tree trunks, dragged it over, and let it drop on top of the dead man. There was a crunching, splintering sound. Dante had no idea whether it was from the rotten wood cracking or the dead man's ribcage or skull being crushed. He shivered, but did not look away as the man hauled another log over and dropped it on to the body as well. The man kicked some twigs and leaves on to the pile then walked over toward them.

"Sorry about that!" he said as he came closer. "I should've kept a closer eye on old Alexis there. He was acting kind of funny when he came in this morning, but he said he was just sick and hungover. I knew something was up, so I told him to stay away from my girls and come back later and maybe I'd let him have a turn. He was looking really dodgy when he went to take a shit. When he was in there so long, I just knew he'd gone and died. So I went in to take care of it. The damn fool had gone and fallen in, so now I have shit all over me!"

Dante and the others couldn't help but recoil and hold their blankets tighter to their faces.

The man laughed. "Not from around here, eh? Sorry. I'll go wash up then. Come on."

"Are you just going to leave it there?" Adam asked. "Not bury or burn it?"

The man looked over his shoulder at the wood piled up on top of the body and shrugged. "Why? People should know not to poke around in things, especially around here. And I doubt it makes any difference to old Alexis now. It'll all settle down soon enough, become part of the dirt, and him with it. That's the lot of all of us, and today was his turn."

He started walking away from the latrine, with Dante and the others following him. Thankfully the stench and flies diminished somewhat as they went. As they walked by the various tents, more bodily odors wafted over them—the tangy, musky scent of sex mingling with the sour, rotten smell of human waste; neither was improved by the combination. All of this cacophony of odors was accented by the sounds of lust—the heavy, rhythmic grunts of men and the higher, more erratic shrieks and squeals of women. Dante could see that most of the occupants of the tents were none too careful about closing the flaps all the way, letting the dark world around them behold every contortion and quiver of their abused, debased bodies. They copulated in every possible position and combination, doing so with all the discretion and grace of dogs. Some seemed to have the urgency of canines as well, though most made their motions lazily and carelessly, as though nothing much mattered to them.

Dante tried to turn away, and he also thought of shielding Bogdana's view from such vileness, but they were in the midst of one vast whorehouse. There was virtually no way one could avoid the sickening spectacle all around them. The ground in front of his feet was the only place Dante could look and be spared some of the embarrassment he felt on behalf of those committing such shameful acts, even though they seemed to feel nothing but deranged abandonment. And even when he chastely looked down, the chorus of cries and groans continued to assail him.

The man led them to a large, round stone that seemed to define something like a town square for all the tents around them. It hadn't been carved or fashioned to look like a well or fountain, but that seemed to be its function, as water bubbled out its top, trickled down the sides, and ran out in a little rivulet that ended in a mucky, swampy area nearby. The stone was bulbous, more or less spherical, and someone had decorated it to look like a giant breast, adding an aureole around the top. All over the sides there were also crude pictures of genitals coupling with other genitals, mouths, or anuses, the artist having reduced his subjects to just these few, simple parts.

The man knelt down and washed his hands and arms in the water running off from the stone fountain.

"What is this place?" Radovan asked as the man splashed in the water.

"Really new here, aren't you?" the man said. "This is our camp for those who work in the mines up here." He winked and gave them a knowing, conspiratorial glance. "Well, for those what need a camp and all its diversions, eh?"

"But why don't you clean that vile place up, if you decide to live here?" Adam asked, unwrapping his scarf now they were further from the main source of the stench.

"What, our shithouse?" the man said, looking over his shoulder as he rubbed his sinewy forearms under the water. "Why bother? It'll just get dirty again. Besides, it doesn't really belong to anyone, so no one wants to do it. Just let it be till we can't stand it anymore, then move a little further away from it. There's plenty of room here."

"All this was not here the last time I climbed this far up the valley," Adam said. "There were some mines, but never a camp this big. When did all this start?"

"Not so long ago, back when my hair was black," the man said. "It's too cold to be up here in the winter. Well, a few bosses and special workers stay all year round." Again he gave them a sideways look. "But come spring each year, the regular lads climb up here, rebuild the camp, and go to work. And if men are working in the mines, they need booze and food and whores down here. I own a few girls. Make good money here, then go down to the valley in the winter and spend it all, then back at it the next spring. Quite a life, eh?"

"Yes. Quite," Adam said.

The man finished washing. He stood and shook his hands off. Without soap the improvement was not as great as they might've hoped for, but he was now much less noxious. Although Bogdana still kept her scarf wrapped around most of her face, the man nonetheless gave her an appraising look, thoroughly examining her face and body. Oddly, despite his profession, his gaze seemed much less lecherous than some of the men they had met down in the valley. They had looked at her with base, animal craving, while in his look there was only reasoning and calculation, estimates of cost and benefit, the quantifying of things that should never be weighed and measured. Dante gritted his teeth and thought how much better was the drooling leer of a wolf than the unblinking stare of a reptile.

"Yes, quite a life," the man repeated, still eyeing Bogdana. "Not for everyone. But perhaps you'd like to try it, just for a little while, eh? Here, let's go to my tent for a minute. It's right over here."

He walked to a small lean-to near the fountain. It consisted of a sheet of canvas suspended between the ground and a tree branch, leaving it open on three sides. Under the awning a large chest was set in the middle, apparently to be used as a low table. Next to it was a stool. On top of the chest were various items: a wooden tumbler, some dice, a crust of bread, and a small cat o' nine tails.

"This is where I like to do business," the man said, apparently proud of his small domain. "It's shady and away from the smell. I can sit right there and keep an eye on my girls and the rest of the camp. That's how I knew poor Alexis needed to be taken care of. I'm sorry there aren't enough chairs for everyone, so I'll just stand too." He reached down to pick up the cat o' nine tails, swinging it to let its thongs flop across his left palm as he spoke. "I usually use this little one to keep off the flies, but some of the lads like a girl who can use a bigger one. And not how you'd imagine, either, I'll wager! The littlest, mildest fellow in the valley will come in and lay down serious money if he can bloody up a girl real nasty like, make her scream and cry and beg: I usually have to sit in on that, to make sure he doesn't permanently damage any goods. And then another time, a big, hulking brute will come in when none of his friends are around, and he'll pay for a tiny wisp of a woman to paddle him good." He laughed. "I don't sit around for that. I figure the girl can handle it herself, and there's no harm in it."

He paused and gestured to Bogdana with the whip. "So, I guess what I'm saying is it takes all kinds to make a world, and money makes the world go round. And I think a lady like you, as pretty as you are to begin with, and in your condition to boot—I think you could make a lot of money real quick, with some lads who might like something different. Something more like a mommy for them to play with, to tell them everything's going to be all right, or that they've been bad, or whatever it is they want to hear while they're doing it. And it's not like you're going to get pregnant!" He chuckled at that. "So what do you say? One day?" He lowered his voice. "Half for you. That's a lot better than I ever pay my girls. You could be out of here tomorrow morning with more money than practically any woman in the valley!" He held up his index finger. "For one day's work!"

Bogdana grimaced. "How can you say something so disgusting?"

Dante stepped between her and the pimp, who held up his hands in a placating gesture. "Easy, easy, friend" he said. "I was just making a business proposition. I didn't threaten or insult her, so don't get all in a huff."

Adam put his hand on Dante's shoulder. "No, there's no need for violence," he said. "But how can you think of such things—money and sex—in a place like this, at a time like this? Don't you know the dead are rising, destroying everything in the valley?"

The stranger smiled and his eyes flashed. "Oh, my, you are so new to all this. Where did you say you were headed?"

"To the top of the valley," Adam said. "And over the pass through the mountains."

"I see," the man replied. "Then I expect you'll see plenty of the dead up and about in this part of the valley. So yes, of course I know about the dead. All the more reason to make money while I can. All the more reason for the lads to have some fun while they can. We're all going to die any day now, and you'd deny us some fun or profit? Why does that make sense to you? Really, even if the dead weren't going about killing people, where's the harm in what I do?" He waved dismissively with his right hand as he spoke. "Oh, never mind this pretty little mommy here. Maybe she's the wife or daughter of one of you and you're squeamish about that. Too prissy for my taste—I'd pimp any girl if she didn't put up a fuss—but I know some men don't like it when it's one of their own women being rented out. But just forget that for a minute, and think of how it is for some regular woman. Women let men get between their legs—or wherever else the man might want to go—and they get what they want from men, whether it's honor or children or a roof over their heads. My girls just do it for money, and everyone's honest about it!"

"Everyone is open about what's being sold, and for how much," Dante said. His tone was very flat and even. "But I don't think that's the same as being honest."

"Oh, stranger, so much splitting hairs, so much debate over words!" the man said, laughing. "All right, let's suppose 'honest' isn't the right word. Tell me what is wrong about my girls and me making some money off what they have between their legs?"

"People want sex for all different reasons," Dante said. "Some reasons are selfish, some aren't. You offer it to them only for the selfishness of their pleasure and your profit."

The man snorted. "Please! I just show them how everything they do is selfish, so they may as well admit it and be practical about it." He waved them off. "But really, why argue about it? I have money to make, pleasure to sell, and you have—well, whatever it is you have. I suppose you have to get somewhere, by the way you talk. Keep heading north through the camp and you'll find the path up to the highest plateau. I don't know anything about any pass. You're the first I've heard mention such a thing, but perhaps you know where to look. You'll see many men who aren't as nice and fair-minded as me, so keep to yourselves. I can only say goodbye, and that I'm sorry we couldn't do business."

The four of them left the pimp sitting on his stool, whistling a jaunty tune as he flicked the flies away with the cat o' nine tails.

"Do you have this expression in your language: 'Crazy as a shithouse rat'?" Radovan asked Dante as they walked away.

"Yes," Dante replied.

"Well, if we survive this madhouse, we can say that we've seen the real thing, and it really is crazier than anyone else."

Bogdana smirked at this, and even Adam couldn't repress a smile. Dante did not think it so funny, though he smiled a little, because he appreciated the attempt and the need to lighten their sour, depressed mood.

"All right, all of you," Adam said. "I think we've seen quite enough of this mad, evil place. We need to get this poor woman out of here, so let's go."

As he strode away and the hideous odors and sounds receded behind him, Dante could only glance sideways at Bogdana. Her beauty and goodness were not to be contemplated in such a diseased place. After a few steps, he felt it had gotten quite chilly around them. Despite Radovan's quip and Adam's admonition, Dante knew there was no madness here, nor was there any excess of animal spirits and drives, but only a cold calculation that fed on the heat and life of everything it infected, a dark shadow or spirit that twisted and poisoned the bodies it possessed and animated. Dante found himself wishing he could again behold such innocence as animals and madmen possessed, beings incapable of the kind of sin he saw all around him.

Chapter 31

Wisdom supreme, O how great art thou showest
In heaven, in earth, and in the evil world,
And with what justice doth thy power distribute!
Dante, *Inferno*, 19.10-12

They moved among the trees and tents, which in this part of the camp were not being used for the exercise of lust. Most of them seemed to be empty at the moment, their owners or occupants probably away in the mines for the day. Given the pimp's description of his neighbors, Dante was glad not to meet anyone.

After a while, Dante heard a voice ahead of them. It wasn't raised in anger or alarm, but flowed with cadences of encouragement and demand. Dante caught words here and there: "My brothers . . . let us not miss this opportunity . . . Do not delay. The Almighty is full of wrath. And justice."

They continued toward the preaching, coming to a clearing where there were a number of crude, wooden benches, most of which were empty. Dante counted six men sitting on them. Off to the side, away from the benches, five bloody, filthy, emaciated bodies were stacked in a pile—three on the bottom, two on top of those. They were stacked like firewood, face down, with their feet on the side facing the clearing; Dante was grateful not to see their faces, though seeing their feet seemed almost worse, dehumanizing them even more.

The men seated on the benches were facing a man dressed in a bright yellow robe who stood at the other side of the clearing; he was the speaker Dante had heard. Tall and with a shock of white hair, the man appeared much better kept and groomed than anyone Dante had seen for days. The way he moved and the way his eyes sparkled, he exuded a glib, polished kind confidence and reliability. Stuck in the ground on either side of him, two torches burned. By his dress and demeanor, he seemed to be some sort of priest, preaching to the small audience. He stopped his speech or sermon when he saw them.

"Please, join us, strangers," he said.

His listeners shifted in their seats to look at Dante and the others, then returned their attention to the man in priestly garb. The congregants were all older men. They looked lethargic and bored, though they did seem to be trying to pay attention to the speaker. Perhaps they had some remnant of decency left, even in this place, and had come seeking solace or forgiveness for a sinful life that was now threatened by the living dead. Or perhaps it was not decency, but simply fear. Looking at their dirty, tired faces, that seemed the more likely motivation for their apparent interest in some kind of religion.

"Thank you, sir," Adam said as they took a step closer, though they remained standing behind the last row of benches.

The man resumed his speech. "As I was saying, this terrible plague of the undead is a punishment for our sins. A punishment upon the ungodly and disobedient, like the plagues sent upon Pharaoh and Egypt. Do you agree, men?"

Four or five weak "Ayes" and "Amens" went up from the small crowd.

"Do *you* agree, strangers?" the priest asked Dante's group. His smile of perfect, white teeth seemed more accusatory than welcoming, though it was compelling and strangely attractive in its own way.

Adam nodded to Dante, as though deferring to him to represent the group on this matter. "I believe this is because of our sinfulness," Dante said.

The man nodded. "Good. And like the Egyptians, many of the godless will die from this plague, but the faithful, like the Israelites, will not be harmed." His voice rose and he raised his hands above his head. "The angel of death will pass over you if you are faithful, if you do not let your hearts be hardened!" Again there were some half-hearted words of approval and agreement from the audience.

The priest lifted his gaze up to the lifeless sky. "We have no door-posts to mark, Lord! We have no lamb's blood to mark our dwellings with! But we commit our brothers' bodies to the cleansing fire!" He took up the one torch and stepped over to the pile of bodies. Touching the fire to them, they took light immediately, the flames dancing across the soles of their feet. The stench of the burning flesh assailed Dante; worse still were the sounds of fat sizzling and skin crisping and curling back. The smoke this time was thick, black, and greasy. Thankfully the wind was not blowing back toward the clearing, or they'd all be choked and driven out of there.

The minister had returned the torch to its place and addressed his audience. "We will send this smoke up to our just and merciful God! Let it serve as a beacon, as a signal fire to guide the angel of death away from the tiny remnant of the faithful. You are fortunate indeed to be among that remnant, my brothers. Now perhaps you will be spared. But for such restraint and kindness, the Lord requires a commitment, a sacrifice, a sign of some generosity on your part, in gratitude for His abundant grace."

He picked up a basket off the bench closest to him and moved among the men, each of whom threw a coin into it, though they seemed to Dante to grumble and hesitate as they did so. When the priest approached him, Dante raised his hand and shook his head. The man didn't bother to offer the basket to the other three. He grunted, turned, and made his way back to the front of the congregation.

"I sense a most disturbing lack of faith here," he said as he shook the basket, making the few coins clink together. "Most have given little. Some have given nothing. No one has given as much as they could. The Lord helps you pull riches from His earth, and this is all you can give back? This is sinful. Perhaps you don't deserve His protection."

The priest paused and seemed to be thinking. When he resumed, his tone had softened. "But perhaps I haven't made the rewards clear enough. You need more encouragement. You are sinful and hard of heart. Perhaps some concession is better than a threat. Tell me, have you sinned?"

Dante could see the six original congregants were confused at this question, obviously unsure what response they were supposed to give. After waiting a moment and seeming to relish their discomfort, the priest supplied the answer. "Of course you have! I've seen you whoring and drinking and fighting! I saw some of you doing these things just last night!" He lowered his voice. "And more importantly, God saw you too. And God and I both know you'll sin again tonight! Confess!" There were some murmurs from the six men. Dante looked at Adam and scowled.

The priest nodded his approval of the vague and noncommittal admissions of guilt. "Good," he said. "And what if the dead came, right after all your godless, filthy sinning? Would you have time to repent? You might not!" Again his voice began to rise as he got back into the rhythm of his sermonizing. "You could feel a cold, impossibly strong hand close on your neck even while you were in the very midst of sinning! And when those avenging teeth sunk into your sinful flesh, it'd be too late to repent! So repent now, my friends! Repent for the sins you're about to commit! I can offer you forgiveness for these before you sin, so you'll be safe! Can you do this? Can you commit to this kind of repentance and accept the safety it offers?"

This time the preacher's vivid speech and enthusiasm seemed more infectious to his meager congregation, for their acclaim was more vigorous and lasted longer than their earlier exclamations. He raised his one hand, while with the other he again shook the basket. The audience, other than Dante and his friends, now seemed excited and committed enough that they came forward on their own to throw more coins into the container. The preacher nodded his approval and set the basket back down as the congregation returned to their seats.

"Better, much better," he said.

Their attention had been so focused on the priest, Dante did not notice the man staggering in from the side till he had come quite close to the minister. Some of the men let out a gasp and pointed, and the priest turned to see the man approaching him with outstretched arms. But he did not seem surprised or frightened by any of this. He just put the palm of his right hand on the man's forehead and held him at arm's length, while he gestured with his left to his congregation, indicating for them to stay away. Dante thought this very strange, and looked closer at the assailant. He did move slowly and stiffly, and moaned a bit, but there was something not quite convincing about him being a dead person, something alive about him. Perhaps the eyes were too shiny, or his motions were too fluid, or the red stains on him were too bright, looking more like mashed berries than like dark, dried blood. Whatever it was, Dante was convinced the man was alive and the "attack" was staged. He looked at Adam, this time rolling his eyes. When he looked at Radovan, the younger man returned the expression.

The men of the congregation were yelling in fear and waving their hands, but the preacher continued to play his act. "If you have faith, you can say to this mountain, 'Be pulled up, and cast into the sea!' And it will be done according to your faith!" he shouted. "If you have faith, you can say to the wind, 'Be still!' And the storm will cease and you will be saved! And if you have faith, you can say to the dead, 'Rise!' And they will rise again!" He gave the supposedly dead man a shove, and the actor fell backwards. He lay there on his back, making some convulsing motions and moaning. The charlatan extended his hands over his accomplice, palms down, and shouted louder than before. "Be gone, spirit of uncleanness! Let this poor man live once more!"

The actor on the ground gave a choking, strangling sound then he went slack. His death rattle was probably the most convincing part of the whole show, and made Dante shudder. Then the man on the ground lay silent and still. Not even Dante could resist the urge to crane his neck and see what he'd do next. The original group of six looked enthralled by the performance. The man on the ground blinked and slowly rose to a sitting position, where he looked around with a shocked, stupefied expression, as though just waking up in a completely unexpected, unfamiliar place. The minister helped him to stand, and presented him to the audience.

"With faith, we have power, even over death," the priest said triumphantly. Then he lowered his voice and scowled at them. "But if you lack faith, you are doomed. And the Lord knows your faith, based on your generosity." He extended a hand in the direction of the basket, into which more coins now flew.

Adam and Radovan hustled Bogdana and Dante out of the clearing. "Let's go," Adam said in a low voice. "This is mad, base, and vulgar."

Their escape did not go unnoticed, however. "You there!" the priest shouted after them. "Do you still lack faith?"

"I agreed with you about the source of the undead plague," Dante said. "We have our own way of dealing with it and are eager to move on."

He had considered openly exposing the man's deception, but as jubilant as the old men looked as they fawned on the supposedly "saved" man, Dante doubted they would've believed him. And as surrounded as they were in the tent city, it hardly seemed advisable to raise any alarm or confrontation with the strange, wicked inhabitants. Better to sneak out quietly with as little attention or debate as possible.

"Then you lack faith," the minister replied. "We will pray for you that your faith increases. But you are going down a very dangerous, deadly path. Others may not be as tolerant of your faithlessness as we are."

The other three were already out of the clearing. "Thank you for your prayers," Dante said and slipped out after them.

Walking away from there, he marched beside Adam.

"It's funny," Adam said as they walked. "I assumed the farther we went up the valley, the more isolated and removed from civilization, the less people would be interested in money. It seems I was wrong."

"I'm not even sure it was about the money," Dante said. "He liked the power, being the center of attention, being superior and more intelligent than those around him. The money was just a bonus."

Adam nodded. "I think you're right."

They walked in silence for awhile before Dante spoke again. "Now I have been cursed at for praying for someone, and cursed for not joining in an impious prayer."

"Such are the ways of the wicked," Adam replied. "Wisdom and goodness to the vile seem vile. Filths savor but themselves."

"Should I have said more to him? Tried to counter his evil plans?" Dante asked.

"No, of course not," Adam replied. "There is no point in debating with the truly, habitually evil. They must be watched, observed, learned from, but you needn't try to correct them. If we were far from here, in a normal town or city, you should have pointed out his wickedness to save his victims from being cheated, perhaps even to teach him to stop and behave better himself. But here? I fear those he cheats are nearly as much to blame as he is. They want to believe his foolishness and madness. They wouldn't want real faith and hope. It would demand too much of them. So they get what they can for their worthless coins, which otherwise they would spend on other sins. They deserve each other." He gestured toward Bogdana, who walked a few steps ahead of them. "Besides, we have other people to care for."

Dante nodded, thinking some of Bogdana's practicality had crept into Adam's thinking. Perhaps different kinds of wisdom and goodness could magnify and influence one another, the way different kinds of evil so frequently did. It would be nice if it worked that way, though there in that depraved city Dante didn't let himself hope for such a blessing, resigning himself instead to the terrible reality and potency of sin.

Chapter 32

Here pity lives when it is wholly dead;
Who is a greater reprobate than he
Who feels compassion at the doom divine?
Dante, *Inferno*, 20.28-30

They walked on, past more empty tents and dead campfires. Occasionally they would see someone walking about nearby, or looking at them from inside one of the tents, but no one came close or spoke to them.

After moving north like this for some time, their path took them near an old woman sitting on a stool under a tree. She beckoned them to come nearer. Like the pimp, she had an old, battered chest in front of her to use as a table, and above her was suspended a canvas sheet to provide some shelter. On the chest was a human skull; a pile of smaller bones, like those of a chicken or other small animal; some melted stubs of candles; and a small metal bowl with curls of incense smoke snaking up from it. All around the woman were gourds and bottles and earthenware jars. Though the incense was stinging at first, once he got used to it, Dante found it made the area around the woman more pleasant than any place he had encountered since climbing the cliff.

The woman herself had long, grey hair pulled back into an irregular bun. Her dress was made of various fabrics, brightly colored, and was very loose fitting, making her exact size indeterminate to Dante's eye. As she smiled and gestured to them, though, Dante thought she moved with the comfort and ease of someone well-fed, even luxurious, despite her humble and slightly sinister surroundings. She seemed quite cheerful and alert, with sparkling blue eyes and a bright smile. She did not seem at all demanding or accusatory, unlike the priest or the pimp. Nodding a greeting to her, Dante breathed in the scent of the incense more deeply, feeling a bit easier.

A throaty, animal snarl shook him from this reverie. Grabbing the hilt of his sword, Dante turned to see a dead person tied to a nearby tree. The creature was sitting on the ground, baring its teeth and growling at them, its head bobbing and straining forward as it did so. It had been a male, and it looked small, only a boy. The old woman also turned toward it.

"Be still!" she shouted. As in the hut the previous morning, this undead person appeared more obedient than usual and calmed down somewhat at the woman's voice. It stopped its struggles and stared at them sullenly, its growl reduced to a grumble.

The woman turned her attention back to her guests. "I'm sorry," she said. "He gets excited. Don't let him bother you. He's quite secure. And quite useful, as you'll see." She smiled at that, and even under the circumstances, she still looked calm and reassuring to Dante.

Dante looked at her, then back at the dead boy, studying him more closely. He was shocked to see that although the boy was sitting with his face away from the tree, his arms and legs were wrapped around the trunk, with his feet and hands tied together, binding him to the tree. Dante saw no buttons on his bloody shirt under his chin, and it slowly occurred to him that the front of the boy's shirt must be pressed up against the tree. His body was turned toward the tree, embracing it, while his face was turned away from it; his head must've been wrenched all the way around when he died. Dante knew of violent convulsions, of nearly unimaginable wounds in war and in accidents, but he had never heard of or seen a human body desecrated quite like this, and certainly not one that was still moving and making sound, however unintelligible and bestial.

"Why do you keep him there like that?" Dante asked. "Was he a relative? Someone you knew, and you couldn't bear to kill him a second time?"

The old woman continued to smile kindly. "No, no, nothing like that. All my family is dead, completely dead. This boy wandered into camp a while ago. He was quite easy to catch. That's why I asked one of the men if I could keep him. He could barely get around, with his head like that. If he saw someone and tried to walk toward them, he'd start out going away from them. And if he tried to right it and walk backward—well, he was a little too clumsy and he'd end up just falling over. So we tied him to the tree there, so now he can help me in my work. The tying was easier, too. His arms and legs aren't bent back uncomfortably. They're just out like he's hugging the tree. He can just sit there, all peaceful. It's all quite lucky, isn't it? I call him my little sphinx. I think it fits his personality, and bent up the way he is, he even looks something like a sphinx."

"We don't understand," Adam said. "Lucky for what? What do you need this poor creature for, now that he's dead and tied up?"

The woman nodded, still smiling. "The luck was that I could put him to use, even tied up. I could give him scraps of dead things to eat. They like those. Did you know that? Most people don't. I know, they don't like them as much as what they really want, but we all make do with less than we want, so why not them, too?"

She produced a small, dirty, blackened carcass. She held it by its long, thin tail, so it must've been a rat, though she or someone else had bludgeoned it down to an unrecognizable piece of fuzzy jerky. Getting up, she held it before the dead boy's mouth. "He really likes little birds, but they're hard for me to catch. He doesn't mind rats, do you, my boy?" She moved the foul meat a closer and he got a hold of it with his teeth, then pulled it in further with his lips and tongue. She waited patiently, holding the tail, as he set up a sickening chorus of crunches and grunts. When he'd gotten most of his meal into his mouth, she let the tail drop, and Dante couldn't help but watch it disappear into the boy's mouth, looking like a real person eating pasta, or a bird eating a worm.

"So little by little, with some feeding and some kind words, he's come to trust me. I even think he likes being here and helping out."

"Yes, that's nice you could make him calmer," Bogdana said. "But how does he help you? What is it you need help with?"

"Ah, yes," the woman said, looking more serious. "I know you are new here. I know much, but sometimes I forget others do not know all I do. My name is Manda, my friends. All my life, I have had the gift of a keen mind's eye. An eye that can see into the future, a mind that knows what others do not, but wish to. When I was young, I was nearly as beautiful as you, my dear." She smiled and nodded toward Bogdana. "So I ignored my second sight, and did what others expected of me, gave others what they wanted from one so beautiful and desirable. I married and raised children. I was happy, in a way, though it seemed nothing special to me. And when my husband and children died in the plague—probably before you were born, my dear—I was still young enough to try my hand at the world's oldest profession, much to everyone's satisfaction and gain. But as I got older, I knew there was no use in that. Men no longer desired or paid for my body, so the time had finally come for me to profit from my mind. And I have done moderately well. Let me show you."

Manda motioned them closer, and Dante took a step forward, though he constantly glanced over at the dead boy who continued to watch them. The woman took up the small pile of bones and cast it back on the table, inspected them, then leaned her head back, eyes closed, and took a deep breath through her nose. She opened her eyes and looked at Bogdana. "You, my dear, you are fleeing after your husband and," she paused and nodded, "child were killed. Just one child, correct?"

Bogdana nodded. "Yes, my husband and son were killed."

Dante watched her features. She didn't look surprised or convinced, but she didn't look as skeptical as he felt. Manda's supposed second sight hadn't even told her the child's sex, and the number of children was a reasonable guess, based on Bogdana's age. So far he saw no keen eye at work.

"Yes," Manda continued. She turned to Radovan. "And you, young man, you were in the army?" Dante thought this obvious enough from his clothing. "And you left, not because you were scared, of course, but because you hated killing so many people. Perhaps they asked you to kill someone you knew? Is that it? You saw a friend or family member among the crowds you were ordered to kill?"

"No, just ordinary people," Radovan said quietly, looking down.

"Good, I sensed such great kindness and mercy in you, and I assumed it must be for someone close to you. Forgive me, young man: I live here among such wicked men, and your compassion went beyond what I have come to expect, and even extended to strangers. You are truly blessed and virtuous indeed."

This was a brilliant, skillful touch, Dante thought, trying to use a bad guess as further confirmation of her statement, then turning it into a fawning compliment. The woman clearly had great insight into human nature. Radovan looked slightly more impressed than Bogdana had, but mostly he just looked ashamed at his participation in the slaughter, embarrassed to have it brought up again.

Manda turned to Adam. "And you, sir, you are one of those monks from the monastery on the island." As Dante noted before, with his distinctive clothing this seemed no great feat of prognostication. "You have come along with them to help them. You are going to lead them across the pass that goes over the mountains to the west."

"Yes, I am," Adam said, still in a composed voice, though his face, especially his eyes, gave away his surprise, and Dante felt that way as well. This seemed something more than just good guesswork. "You know of the pass?"

"I have heard of it," Manda said, apparently staying a bit evasive as to the source and timing of this information. Had someone already gotten ahead of them, while they were distracted by the corrupt priest, and reported what they'd said to the pimp? Or was it a rumor she'd heard decades ago? Or was she claiming to have gotten it from some source beyond the human realm? Whichever scenario seemed more likely, Dante dreaded it when the woman turned toward him. "And you," she said, "are from far away." Dante relaxed, as this seemed obvious enough from his accent. "You have suffered greatly at the hands of your countrymen, your own people, and now you wander, always an exile, never at home."

Dante struggled not to reveal how shocked he was. Here was

something quite specific, though he had long wondered how much of his suffering was visible on his tired, damaged face. Perhaps his fate was known to all who observed him carefully; or perhaps something more was at work here.

"Yes, that is true," he said.

Manda nodded, looking quite serious, though still comforting in a way. "And you loved once. You lost her."

Dante's struggle to remain composed increased greatly at this statement. Though it was much vaguer than the previous comment—"lost" could mean any number of things—it struck him much more deeply, for he had always hoped that pain was one he could control, direct, reveal, and draw strength from as he wished, and not one that would just be on display to any observer, manipulated and exploited by any charlatan or enemy. He felt dizzy and even angry at the woman, though he only whispered, "Yes, I did."

Manda smiled and more of her kindness seemed to return. "Well, there's always hope where there's love. I have lost much, but I don't know if I've ever loved. I envy you. You are very lucky to have loved so much." She looked sideways at Bogdana, as she seemed to continue to address Dante. "And perhaps you will love again, eh?" Dante blushed more at this innuendo, though he had already come to accept that this part of his story was not particularly difficult for others to intuit.

"Thank you for telling us your story, and for sympathizing with ours," Adam said. "But we still don't understand how this dead boy helps you."

"Oh, well, I found out that he has some of the second sight, too," Manda said. "Of course, it's very dull in his present state, and needs interpretation. But he can still answer questions that I can't. Really hard questions. The kinds people most want to know the answers to. That's why I called him the sphinx. So he's very valuable to me."

Dante was returning to his belief the woman was a complete fraud.

"But how does he answer?" Bogdana asked. "And what kind of questions?"

"I helped him remember how to speak a bit," Manda said. "It's really very remarkable, and so lucky for me. The kinds of questions? That depends on the person asking, my dear. The men up here are so simple and vulgar—they ask when they'll die or where to find more jewels—nothing they need to know, and nothing I care to tell them. My little sphinx answers better questions. Tell you what. You all seem like very nice people, so go ahead and ask him one question for free. Go ahead." She gestured to Bogdana. "You, my dear, I sense have more questions than the others and are more open to the answers."

"No, really, I couldn't," Bogdana said. Dante thought it was the most unsure and nervous he had seen her. "It isn't right to ask such things. And I don't believe it's possible."

"Then you have the right attitude," Manda said, coaxing her, flattering her more. "That is good. But what if belief has nothing to do with it? You'll get the same answer whether you believe or not. And of course it isn't right, but so many people come to me thinking it is right, and they always believe it's possible. And they're always so upset, no matter what the answer. It seems my sphinx and I can never satisfy them. But you have the right attitude. So go ahead."

"Really, please, I don't want to," Bogdana said, the frustration in her voice increasing. "You may ask a question for me, if you like. Why don't you do that and we can be done?"

Manda nodded. "That is a good choice, my dear," she said. "I expected something so wise from you. But let me show you first that he really can answer." She turned to the boy, who seemed to become more calm and attentive when she looked at him. "Sphinx, is my name Manda?"

"Yerrh," he growled. It was hardly human speech, but it did seem timed to her question and not a random groan, so Dante had to restrain a gasp at the shocking display.

"And this pretty woman here," Manda gestured to Bogdana. "Is her name Manda?"

"Nahhh," the boy sighed.

Dante watched the whole exchange as closely as he could. There might have been some signal from the woman to the dead boy to show him which response to give, or there might not have been. Even if she had taught him to make different noises based on signals from her, that in itself would be quite a feat, given the ferocity and ignorance of the dead that Dante had witnessed in the past few days.

"All right, sphinx," Manda said. "This woman here. Did her husband and son die recently?"

The boy hesitated, and Dante still could not see any definite gestures being made by the woman. "Yerrh."

The woman cast a glance at Bogdana before she asked the next question. "And have they gone somewhere better now?"

The boy did not hesitate. "Yerrh."

Bogdana continued to stare at the boy as Manda beamed at her. "Was that a good enough question for you, dear?"

Bogdana looked at the ground. "It was an excellent question, but I already knew the answer."

"Oh, I knew you did," Manda said. "As I said, you're not like the foolish ones who ask so many useless questions. But it was still nice to hear, wasn't it?"

"Yes. I suppose it was. Now can we go?"

"Of course. I wasn't keeping you. You probably should hurry. This place has a way of slowing you down, making you stay put, when at first you intended to leave or do something different and better. So you should go."

"Goodbye, my sister," Adam said.

"You don't want to ask which of you will make it over the pass?" Manda asked as they turned to go. "That is a very expensive question, but I could make you a deal."

"Of course not," all three men said at almost the same time.

Manda nodded and smiled. "Then you are as wise as she. You are lucky to have one another. Everyone else in this wretched valley—that would be the first thing they would ask. I'd get so much money from them for such a silly question. And no matter what my sphinx told them, they'd be so hurt and angry. They might even give up trying to go over the mountains entirely. Such madness and folly. You are all very wise."

As Radovan and Adam stepped away, Bogdana took Dante aside. "Pay her something," she said. Her voice was quiet, but there was not a hint of pleading or weakness in it. She was not making a request, not even a demand, but a statement of what needed to be done.

"What? How can you say that?" Dante whispered back. "How can you say we should pay for her tricks?"

Bogdana looked sideways at the other woman, who had the discretion and good sense to be busying herself with her bones and bottles, rather than intruding on her clients' negotiations. Bogdana looked back to Dante. Though her steady gaze was probably enough to decide the matter, he could also see in her eyes the respect and love that would not let her demand something from him just on authority or by threat. "You shan't pay for her tricks, and she didn't even ask you to, unlike the wretches we met before who threatened us for money, or even bargained for my body. Forget her tricks for a moment. Condemn them if you like. You'll pay her because this is what she's been reduced to. Suppose she does see things. How would anyone keep quiet about that? I think I'd go mad. And suppose she's making it all up, telling people what they want to hear so she can wring a few pennies from strangers, because she couldn't sell her body anymore. You really think she made the worst choice in the situation, and we should judge her?"

"She could be making up the whole thing about selling her body," Dante said, though he didn't sound that convinced even to himself.

"Of course she could be," Bogdana shot back. "But look at her. For God's sake, she lives under a tree next to a dead boy, because he helps her make a few extra coins with the ugly little trick she taught him. I don't think that chest is full of gold and jewels. Now give her something and let's be on our way."

Dante lowered his head and walked back to the woman, laying a silver coin on the chest. He didn't say anything, and Manda seemed to sense it would be better if she didn't either. She also kept her eyes down as he left the coin and walked away.

Bogdana took Dante's hand and pulled him away. "Maybe I was

wrong about her, but then let the blame be on me," she said to him as they caught up to the other two.

"There needn't be blame on you," Dante said. "There's plenty of blame and hate here. You make it more bearable."

She didn't hold his hand as they walked, but her presence beside him made his body feel lighter and stronger, even as his head felt heavier, always clouded and disrupted by the mysteries she would throw in his path.

Chapter 33

Thus, not by fire, but by the art divine,
Was boiling down below there a dense pitch
Which upon every side the bank belimed.
Dante, *Inferno*, 21.16-18

After a while, they had left the tent city and were again following a trail northwards through the sick, stunted woods. As they marched on, Dante felt it getting warmer around them, though it had been much cooler in general since they climbed the cliff. At the same time he was hit by a heavy, burning smell, tinged with a sour, sulfurous scent. Not like the assault on their senses they had experienced earlier, but a steady, permeating atmosphere, still and oppressive because of the lack of wind. He also saw movement ahead of them, and heard sounds, including the moan of the dead.

They emerged out into an open area. Ahead of them there was a wide ditch full of steaming tar across their path. The acidic stench was not as bad as the putrid latrine, but it stung Dante more the closer they got to the source. Across the pit there was a rickety-looking bridge made of ropes and wooden planks. To the right and left some bleached, dead trees were partly submerged and leaning over into the simmering, black pool. Apparently the pit had expanded, swallowing up more of the forest. Dante noticed his feet felt warmer, as though the ground under them was heated; it even felt soft and spongy as they stepped forward into the clearing.

The motion came from five men standing nearer to the pool of pitch. They were whooping and waving their arms. Four of them were large men, wearing armor and carrying pole arms. The fifth wore what looked like a military uniform, and had a sword at his belt. All of them were waving at three dead men on the other side of the tar pit. As Dante and the others watched, the dead lurched forward, sinking into the pitch, oblivious either to the danger or to the bridge right next to them. The men luring them on laughed and continued to yell to them. The steps of the dead men became pitifully slow as they struggled against the viscous liquid. With each step they dragged their feet up, now covered with a clinging blanket of the thick, black substance, then moved them slightly forward, where they would sink in further than before. On the next step, their feet would not come as far out of the steaming soup. The stench assailing Dante increased as the dead began to roast, stewing themselves in their insane march toward the living flesh they desired so much. Their faces grimaced, their lips drew back to reveal their teeth, but their narrowed eyes remained fixed on the five men. Their moans did not vary in tone or volume.

When the three dead men were up past their knees, and not making much more forward progress, the five armed men turned away from them, noticing Dante and his companions.

"Beats going over there and hacking them apart, doesn't it?" said the man with the sword, apparently their leader, as the five men approached Dante's group. "Now they'll just sink in, and we'll be rid of three more of them." He looked back at the trio. Their moans did seem to be rising in volume and tone as the boiling liquid reached their waists. Dante could even imagine he heard a note of agony in it, a slight screeching quality. "Of course, you have to listen to them for a long time. Sometimes it takes them hours to sink all the way." He shrugged.

"Yes, that's quite resourceful," Adam said in an even, non-committal tone. He pointed with his staff at the bridge. "Is that the way to continue further up the valley?"

The man with the sword looked at the bridge, then back to Adam. "Why yes, it is," he said. "But I'm afraid we've been told not to let anyone across. Have to contain the plague, you know. Perhaps if you came back in a few days, everything would be cleared up by then."

Dante stepped forward. This man seemed somewhat closer to the kind he was used to dealing with in Italy. "Sir, my name is Dante," he began. "And you are?"

"Malok," the man said with a slight nod of his head.

"Very good, Malok," Dante continued. "It's our pleasure to meet someone like you, out here in the wilderness. I'm sure we can come to some understanding in this situation. My friends and I are in something of a hurry. And, as I'm sure you know, time is money."

Malok raised an eyebrow. "Yes, well, it's always good to find someone who knows how the world works, especially out here in such a backward, uncivilized place."

"Oh yes, it is. I know." Dante smiled, just a little.

Malok turned to his companions with the pole arms. "Could you four go wait by the bridge?" The four of them left, talking amongst themselves.

Malok turned back to Dante. He put his arm around Dante's shoulder and led him away from the others. "Please, let us take a walk over here."

Dante again noticed the disturbing sponginess of the ground, but let himself be led, nodding his approval. "Yes. It's good to have privacy when talking to another man of the world." Dante lowered his voice. "The others are nice enough, especially the girl, if you know what I mean." His stomach heaved as he gave a sideways, conspiratorial look to Malok, and accompanied it with a leer, but he played his part. They both chuckled. "But they're not so sophisticated. They might not understand how exceptions can be made. How they *should* be made for the right people. For the right price."

"Oh my yes. So true. Now, you were saying something about the value of time? Perhaps something about how much a few days' wait might be worth to someone? Someone in a hurry?"

Dante still had some silver coins, though he hardly wanted to spend all of them on this rapacious weasel. He was glad he had his remaining money distributed throughout several bags and pockets. He brought out one handful, the one he thought would be enough to get them through this. "Let's see… all four of us are in a hurry." He counted out four coins into his right hand. "The woman's in an extra hurry, and I do so want to keep her happy." Again the leer, and Dante burned with shame that it didn't make him feel as sick as the first time. "So she'll keep me happy!" They chuckled as another coin dropped into the pile of four with a cheery clink. He looked over his shoulder, to where the three dead men could still be seen, their arms sometimes waving out in front of themselves, sometimes groping upwards toward the planks of the bridge. They had sunk quite close to it, and one of them could nearly reach it. "Those dead men should probably be gotten away from the bridge before we try to cross it. There are three of them, yes?"

"Yes, three." Malok glanced back at them, but immediately returned his attention to the pile of coins in Dante's hand. It clinked three more times.

"So, I think that's a pretty good estimate of what a wait like that might be worth?" Dante said. "Don't you? I mean hypothetically, of course." He let the coins jingle a bit. "Not that anyone would ask for, or offer, something so crass. I mean it just as a discussion of how something like that *might* work. If it came up."

"Yes, that discussion sounds about right," Malok said in a soothing, affable tone. "Of course, the person might have to share with others. That would definitely make it more costly."

Dante laughed. "Oh my, yes, but only if the person were foolish enough to discuss his arrangements in front of others! A really shrewd operator would know to go off in private for the negotiations, wouldn't he?"

Malok joined him in the laughter. "Yes. Yes he would. That would make things go much better. No need to worry about whether the amount might divide evenly. Say, by five." He paused, still looking at the coins. Dante could tell he'd watched carefully if Dante had any left in his other hand. "Still, a really shrewd man—not a greedy one, mind you, just a shrewd one, a man who knows what his time is worth—such a man might still want the total to come out divisible by five."

Dante nodded. "Yes, a shrewd man might want that." He let the last two coins drop from his left hand to the pile in his right. He made a flourish of showing his left hand was empty. "An even ten is such a nice, hefty amount, isn't it? My, they're getting quite heavy in my hand." Dante dropped his hand slightly to the side, and quite dexterously let the ten coins slide off and into Malok's pocket. "Oh, there, that's much better. Doesn't that seem much better to you?"

Malok clapped Dante on the shoulder and turned him back toward the others. "Oh yes it does. Now let's get to work on that valuable time we've been discussing." He parted from Dante and approached his men standing by the bridge. "Hey you lazy dogs! I have a job for you. Get to the edge and poke those crazy bags of bones till they get down in the muck where they belong. Get to it!"

The four men with pole arms grumbled at these instructions but followed them. They stabbed at the three dead men, sometimes digging into their lifeless chests, sometimes hacking at their flailing arms. As they did so, Dante moved his friends closer to the bridge.

"Come on," he said. "We should be ready to cross as soon as possible. God knows if these creatures will honor the agreement I bargained for."

As they edged closer to the tar pit, one of the dead men managed to grab the head of one of the pole arms and pull on it. Though the blade sliced into his hands, the smile on his face seemed not to show pain but some triumph and pride at accomplishing something to harm his tormentor. The man wielding the pole arm was pulled off balance and fell forward into the hot muck. He was able to catch himself with his right foot, but that sunk in nearly up to the knee, so now he was caught in the pit. He screamed in pain and let go of the weapon, waving his arms to try to keep his balance so he didn't fall further into the deadly mire. His back foot slid into the pitch as well, though only up to the ankle, making his screams redouble.

The dead man who had disarmed him now considered his prize, and his expression looked more like a grin. He seemed to understand enough to move his hands from the blade, to avoid mutilating himself further. He didn't think to turn the weapon around and hold it by the right end, however, or his attack that followed might have done much more damage. As it was, he started batting and poking the weaponless man with the hilt of the pole arm, causing him to howl and curse more, though the attacks did not do any real damage.

As the other three men dropped their weapons to help pull their fellow out of the pitch, and their leader cursed their incompetence, Dante pushed his friends forward. "Go, go," he said in a low but urgent voice. "Go now, while they're distracted. One at a time. Hurry! You first!" He pushed Bogdana toward the bridge.

She hesitated. "Now? On that?" She looked terrified. "I thought I was scared on the cliff! This looks much worse!"

"You and Adam are the lightest," Dante said in as reassuring a tone as he could, though he hardly felt calm or confident. "You should go first. We'll be right behind you."

Bogdana took a deep breath and clambered up the couple of wooden steps and on to the planks of the bridge. A better-constructed rope bridge would have two ropes for the person crossing to hold on to, but this had only one. She held on to it with her right hand and extended her left for balance, trying to scamper across as quickly and nimbly as possible. Her weight made the whole structure sag dangerously close to the tar. It would have been a frightening crossing, even if there weren't a dead man underneath the bridge, trying to grab at the nearest plank as it sank down closer to his reach. Bogdana gave a yelp as she skipped over the dead man's clutching fingers, then scurried on to the other side. She turned back towards them; after looking pale and aghast for an instant, she smiled and waved them on.

Adam was the next across, followed by Radovan. As the bigger man bounded across, the bridge dipped down further than before, so that the dead man succeeded in getting a hold of one of the planks, holding the bridge stretched downward in the lowest position, even after Radovan reached the other side. He turned back and saw what had happened, looking as though he was going to return and try to get the dead man to let go.

Dante waved him off. He didn't want to shout and draw attention, but there was no choice. They'd all be to safety in another moment anyway.

"No, no!" he said. "Stay there! I can make it!"

The commander now noticed their escape. "Hey! Where are you going so fast?" he called to them. For the moment, he remained by the other four, as they were still busy trying to extricate the wounded man, their work hampered by the clumsy blows of the dead man, and also by the fact that another of them had gotten stuck up to his ankles in the pitch as he tried to help.

Dante climbed the steps up to the bridge. The dead man's struggles were making the whole thing shake. It sounded like the supports and ropes were straining from his efforts. Dante imagined being trapped on this side of the bridge, answering to the violent, dishonest men who had just seen two of their comrades injured because of him. He ducked his head and ran.

The dead man had gotten a hold of the bridge now with both hands. He couldn't fit his head between the planks, but he stuck his mouth and nose through as Dante leaped over him and ran the rest of the way to the other side.

The four of them walked quickly from the tar pit, trying to make it to the nearby tree line without further incident, but the commander of the bridge guards again called to them.

"Hey," he said. "Are you just walking away? Get back here! All this shit you caused should cost you extra!"

Dante looked over his shoulder to see both the men had been freed from the pitch, and now the two uninjured ones were menacing their commander.

"Extra?" one of them said. "They paid you? Where's our share?" The two larger men began swatting and shoving their leader between them, as Dante turned and ran into the woods.

They moved at a fast pace, Dante looking over his shoulder for signs of pursuit, but eventually he calmed down and they walked more normally.

Adam was beside him. "You seemed quite skilled at negotiating with that man," he said to Dante.

Dante frowned. "Bribery was one of the things I was accused of when they drove me from my city," he answered. "It wasn't true, but you pick up some of the skills and habits of people like that when you have to deal with them. And they seem the same all over, wherever I go—simple, ugly, petty. I'd feel better if I could just hit them, stab them, because they're so vulgar, but sometimes it's not possible, and you have to wallow in the filth just like them, if you are to survive."

Adam nodded. "Yes, I think we should prefer violence, even though it is ugly and harmful, to their falsehoods. But you used their wickedness against them. I doubt any of the rest of us could've gotten past them. We were lucky to have you with us. Rejoice at that, my son. Now, let us make haste."

They walked on in silence, the ground sloping upward slightly. It seemed to Dante to be turning even colder than it had been before.

Chapter 34

They had on mantles with the hoods low down
Before their eyes, and fashioned of the cut
That in Cologne they for the monks are made.
Dante, *Inferno*, 23.61-63

The temperature had dropped so much that Dante and the others resorted to wrapping their blankets about themselves once more. The trail had bent in what seemed to Dante a southwesterly direction. The peaks at the end of the valley were now quite close, rising above them just to the west. They looked even blacker and less forgiving than when he had first seen them. He scowled at them and returned his attention to the trail.

Ahead of them Dante saw two figures approaching, walking along the trail in the opposite direction. They moved slowly, but their motions appeared fluid and calm enough that they seemed more alive than dead. As they got closer, Dante could also hear their voices, so they clearly were not more of the dead come to attack. But Dante had long since realized this did not preclude anyone here from having hostile or malicious intent towards them.

As they came closer, Dante could see the figures were men in robes, and their cloaks were much more regal-looking than the humble, coarse blankets in which Dante and his companions had wrapped themselves. The golden robe of the preacher who had supposedly resuscitated the dead man was flashy enough, Dante had thought, but these were so outrageously ostentatious, they would have embarrassed the Benedictines at Cluny. The robes Dante now saw on the two men were purple with gold embroidery throughout. The embroidery included swirls and patterns of the most expensive and intricate kind. Even a prince would pause to wear these, they were so gaudy. These seemed more like what would be worn by someone who intended to dazzle and distract the weak-minded. Someone like a barker in a carnival or circus, calling out to people, trying to gull them with unlikely promises that they should know better than to trust, but which they let themselves believe because it gives them some pleasure. Dante also noticed the robes' edges were lined with the luxurious, warm fur of the red fox, and he had to admit a pang of envy for the warmth and comfort they must offer in this desolate place.

The men themselves were middle aged. The one was of average height and build, his companion a little shorter and stockier. Both wore their dark hair quite short. They were smiling as they approached.

"Hello, strangers," the taller one greeted them.

"Hello, sirs," Adam said. "Is this the trail that leads to the highest plateau in the valley?"

"Yes, it is," the shorter man replied. "Just up ahead, you'll see the last part of the trail that goes right up the cliff. You can't miss it, but it's a tough climb. Lodar and I had a terrible time with it, both ways. My name is Catalin. Who are you people?"

"Just refugees, fleeing the plague," Adam said. "We will cross over the mountains and be free of this place."

The one called Lodar raised his eyebrows at that. "Really? I never heard of such a thing. Well, Catalin and I could barely make it all the way up to the mines, so I doubt we'd make it across the mountains. Just not cut out for that kind of work!" He pointed to where two logs lay near each other on the ground in a V shape. "You'll need to keep up your strength. Let us rest here a bit and have some food and drink. We have plenty, right Brother Catalin?"

"Oh my yes, Brother Lodar," the other said, as he sat his bulk down on the one log. Lodar and Dante sat on either side of him, on the same log, while the other three sat on the remaining log.

"You are monks?" Dante asked, as the two robed men produced

a rather surprising amount of provender from enormous pockets in their cloaks.

"Yes. We've just come from preaching to the miners higher up in the mountains," Lodar said. He took a bite from a chicken leg and passed it to Dante. Dante took the smallest possible nibble and gave it to Bogdana. She looked to Adam and Radovan, who nodded, then she instantly took the whole thing apart in two bites. "Telling them the great value of piety in these dangerous, difficult times, exhorting them not to give in to carnal temptations. We counseled them all to abstain from women and wine. Some of them responded with a godly fear and a proper gratitude." From somewhere in their robes both he and Catalin sent up a jingling sound, at which they snickered and slapped each others' knees.

Catalin took a swig from a wineskin, grinning as he handed it to Dante. "Well, those miners up there that take to preaching. Or talking. Or have money. Some of them just aren't as jovial as we are, if you know what I mean?" He laughed harder than before.

Dante took a small sip from the container. It was spiced wine, and he was grateful for the surge of heat it sent through his drained, exhausted body. Besides the monks' sodden rapaciousness, he'd also noticed how both of them stole careful but hungry glances at Bogdana. Dante handed her the wine, which she took only a tiny sip of before passing it on to Adam.

"Yes, I'm sure many of them don't wish to hear such austere preaching," Dante agreed, holding his disdain in check.

Both the monks looked sideways at him as they chewed on more food they'd taken from their pockets. Catalin smiled less, though his rosy, cherubic cheeks still expressed some mirth. "You're not from around here? You don't know about the miners up there?"

Dante shook his head. "No. We just know there are mines further up the mountains."

Catalin nodded as he chewed. He seemed to consider what to say, then smiled more when he'd decided. "Let's just say you should all be careful up there. They're an ugly, unpredictable lot, that's for sure. But you all look intelligent, and I imagine you've seen your share of brutes and thieves, if you've made it this far up the valley. You should be fine."

"Speaking of thieves," Lodar said, "did you see our colleague Nicholas? Wears a golden robe?"

Dante had just taken a bite of black bread, so Adam answered. "Yes. We heard one of his sermons."

Both monks guffawed at this. The wineskin had come back around and they each took a long swig after their raucous laughter. They looked quite flushed now. "That old slickster. That shameless quack! You didn't give him any money, did you?" Lodar asked them.

"No, we refrained from making a contribution," Adam said.

"Good, good," Catalin said. "As I said, you all look intelligent. I didn't think you would've. But you got to give it to the old trickster. He puts on quite a show! And it works out well for us. He's getting too old to do all this walking and climbing, so we take our show on the road, and he stays down there and lives off the fat of his sheep, and no one gets jealous or upset. Good, eh?"

"Oh, quite good indeed!" Lodar agreed as they drank more wine. This time they did not pass the skin back to the others.

"But I bet that greedy bastard Malok took a big bite, didn't he?" Catalin asked. He looked mischievously over at Bogdana and giggled. "Oh, excuse my language, my dear!"

The man's girlish twittering, and the way he looked at her, made Dante want to punch him in the face. He supposed it would be pretty much expected and acceptable in this wretched place, but he fought down the urge as he swallowed the bread and handed the loaf on to Bogdana.

"Yes, he did," Dante said.

The two monks laughed and continued to drink. "Well, no offense to him," Lodar said. "We all have different fish to fry, different sheep to fleece. He's just making a living."

"His colleagues didn't seem too pleased when they found out he hadn't shared," Dante added with some satisfaction.

The two monks paused for a second to look at one another then burst into more peals of laughter, followed by more gulps of wine.

"Oh, my, you've made my day." Catalin gasped when they'd calmed down a little. "I always told him to be careful, not to get too greedy, but who listens to me?" He clapped Lodar on the back. "You got to cut your friends in, right? Otherwise they gang up on you, turn on you, and then all your money won't help you! Right, friend?"

Lodar stood up and hauled his stouter companion up after him. They clasped each other for a big hug then turned to the others. "Well, friends, I hope this was as refreshing to you as it was to us!" Lodar said. "But we should probably be going."

"We wish you luck, getting where you want to go," Catalin said between hiccups.

"You as well," Adam said as the four of them also stood.

Dante watched the two monks' backs moving toward the tent city, and he could hear one of them—he thought it was Catalin, and again his fists clenched and his head burned with anger—say in a soft voice: "What a sweet, little thing. Too bad her friends don't have more of a sense of humor. How can people be so serious in a world like ours?"

"We should pay Nicholas a visit tonight," the other replied. "I bet he'll have some of that nice muscatel you like so much. And he adores this spiced wine, and we have a lot of it, so we can trade."

"Oh, you're right! That'll be splendid!"

Their voices and laughter faded away after that, leaving Dante with his angry, violent thoughts. Such imaginations were slowly fading when Bogdana put her hand on his shoulder to pull him away and get him moving forward again.

"At least they had good food," she said. "Ignore the rest of their foolishness."

"Yes, they were good for something, I suppose," Dante agreed, though he could never have her sprightly, graceful tone. Dante turned and followed her, still wondering how people as different as Bogdana and the two deceitful friars could both be so happy and content, while he only knew doubt, anger, and sadness.

Chapter 35

Who ever could, e'en with untrammelled words,
Tell of the blood and of the wounds in full
Which now I saw, by many times narrating?
Dante, *Inferno*, 28.1-3

They continued on through the woods and soon emerged into an open area right at the base of the cliff. In the clearing ahead of them were several dozen wooden, X-shaped crucifixes. On all of these, men writhed in undeath, moaning and straining at their bonds. As they watched the grotesque spectacle of these cruelly tortured undead, Dante noticed another dead man on foot, approaching them. Radovan shouted a word of warning as he and Dante drew their swords, the three men positioning themselves between the monster and Bogdana. Dante saw out of the corner of his eye that she still had the hatchet, for it had suddenly appeared in her hand.

As the creature came closer, however, Dante could see it had a leather collar around its neck. Then he saw the collar was attached by a couple links of chain to an iron pole about four feet long, the other end of which was held by another man. The man holding the pole was alive and was guiding the dead man by yanking the pole one way or the other. He looked big and strong enough for the task, and was clad all over in leather, probably as a precaution against the thing he was handling.

"Easy there, Bert!" he shouted as he pulled back on the pole, jerking the dead man to a halt about six feet from them.

The dead man stayed where he was, eyeing them but not making any other aggressive movements, swaying slightly and looking more surly than vicious. He'd been tall and lean in life; he'd probably looked sullen and hungry even then. The corpse leaned forward a bit and sniffed at them. Dante could imagine a slight smile on its dry lips. He wondered what it was like to be a dead man who was treated like a living dog, and what there could possibly be in the experience worth smiling at.

"No need to go biting everyone!" the dead man's handler said as he looked over the four newcomers. "So long as we're sure they don't mean any harm. Right, Bert?" The name even sounded like that of a dog. "I'm Peter. You've already met Bert. So what are you four about?"

They all stepped back a little. "We mean no harm," Adam said in a placating tone. "We were told there was a passage up the cliff somewhere here, and we were looking for it. We just wish to continue on our way."

"You have some business up there? With the boss?"

Adam cast a glance back at Dante, but he had no guidance to give; bluffing and bribery only worked when you had enough information on which to base your statements. Now they had nothing to go on and were reduced to guessing.

"The boss?" Adam said in an innocent tone, a voice that betrayed his ignorance, but hopefully also showed how harmless they were.

"Yes, Lord Ahriman. He's in charge here. If you're going up there, I thought it must be to see him. You don't look like just regular folks."

"Well, we certainly mean to give all our respect and obedience to the Lord of this place," Adam continued. "But we have no appointment with him. We are just climbing up and over the mountains, to escape the plague of the dead. We won't be any trouble to him."

Peter nodded and grunted. "That's good to hear." He tilted his chin toward the crucified men. "You see what we do with trouble makers."

Dante and his companions looked back to the crucifixes.

"Yes," Adam said quietly, "we see your… retribution at work here. We are very law-abiding, I assure you. Now may we proceed on the path? Is the way up the cliff just past these… criminals?" Dante thought the revulsion in Adam's voice sounded a bit too clearly, as he described this scene of sadism and butchery as a kind of justice, these men as criminals, when their "crime" may well have been nothing more than finding themselves in this foul, evil place.

Dante kept a close eye on Peter, who seemed not to detect anything suspicious in Adam's tone. "Yes. It's not far from here," Peter said. He took a step back, dragging the dead man with him. "Go on ahead. Bert and I will walk behind you. We want to make sure you keep up a smart pace here. This place is for the locals to gawk and learn a lesson. We don't really like strangers hanging around here too much. Strangers get ideas when they see how normal folk live. Ideas are bad."

Short of fighting, there didn't seem much choice but to obey, so they moved ahead. Dante brought up the rear, closest to the dead man. He could hear Adam and Radovan speaking in low voices just ahead of him.

"What is wrong, my son?" Adam asked.

"That name, Ahriman. It was the name of an evil man from our capital, a member of the ruling family," Radovan replied. "But he was killed years ago. It's not a very common name, so I don't know why the lord of this place would have the same name."

"I'm sure the lord of such an abominable place is very evil too," Adam said. "But it can't be the same man if he was killed."

"He was. Everyone knows he was."

"Then don't worry about it," Adam said. "We have more immediate problems."

They walked among the victims on the X-shaped crosses, all of whom were variously mutilated beyond the wounds of crucifixion, each one with some extra gashes in its flesh, some enough to reveal their insides. Like everything else here, the sight of the ruined, defiled human form barely shook Dante any more. He could observe with detachment and only a tiny bit of curiosity that all the viscera, ripped skin, shattered bones, and torn muscle were oddly bloodless and dry. All the different parts, their operations obscure or unknown to the human mind, parts meant to be hidden from prying eyes and the ever-present sun, had now been torn loose to hang outside the mortal cages like useless scraps of leather or cloth.

"What did these men do?" Dante asked, turning to address the man behind them.

"Trouble makers, I tell you," Peter replied. "Rabble rousers. These are what you call your sowers of discord. I heard one of the smart fellows calling them that when he read out the charges against them. Stirred up the workers and miners to rebellion. Insurrection, mutiny—can't have that sort of thing. Filled their heads with ideas that they shouldn't be doing what they do, or they should demand more of a share of the profits, or they shouldn't have to work in such dangerous conditions."

Dante thought they had picked a most ironically appropriate form of execution for the men, considering the most famous crucified man had also preached to the oppressed and downtrodden.

Peter had become quite animated in his defense of their killing field. "Like anyone has a right to all that," he continued. "Like any of us ever get to pick what goes on around us. You just make do. That's how me and old Bert get by."

"Live and let live," Dante said. He immediately cursed himself inwardly for the remark, as it seemed hard to believe it could be taken as anything other than sarcastic or ironic, though he said it in a bland, even tone.

Thankfully, Peter had reached that stage of a self-justifying rant where almost anything other than outright attack was taken as confirmation and agreement. "Yes, exactly," he said more loudly. "Bert and me don't bother anyone, and we expect others to do the same. And if they don't, well, that's their bad choice. That's on them."

They had come close to the most mutilated man Dante had seen yet among the crosses. His skin and hair looked darker than most of the other inhabitants of the valley, as though he had journeyed here from some land to the south—a Greek or Turk or Persian. Someone had split him open from under his chin to his crotch. He must've been quite alive when they did so, with blood still flowing, as his clothes and the wooden cross were soaked in his purplish gore. It looked like someone had smashed a bushel of overripe plums and smeared them all over, then let them sit in the sun to fester and cook down to a blackened tar. His insides, from his throat to his colon, had tumbled out from the horrific wound and now hung between his legs. The man's crazed, agonized writhing set the innards swinging, brushing up against his knees as he struggled. Dante shivered to remember that he had once seen the bloated, burst carcass of a horse by the side of the road, and it had revolted and sickened him more than this display. He felt that another day here, and he would belong to this place completely. Too accustomed to darkness and screams of misery, he would be unfit to return to a place where there was sunlight and laughter.

"That's the worst of the lot," Peter explained. "Damn foreigner with his filthy, heathen ways. Didn't talk right. Always had out his holy scriptures. I don't even know what they were. Jew or Mohammedan or popish or devilish mutterings. They're all the same. And not for normal folk. Telling the workers how God wants freedom for all people. Have you ever heard such foolishness? Have you ever seen where God wants things any different than the way they are?"

"Things are the way they are for a reason," Dante said, satisfied this time that his irony was safely innocuous.

"That's what I'm saying!" Peter agreed. "If God wants things different, He'll make them that way! No sense stirring things up and upsetting people and making them act all foolish. Work's work and business is business. God wants it that way. I mean, that's just obvious. Good common sense, that's what we need. And these boys here just didn't have any."

If the split-open man had been the most thorough and grotesque mutilation Dante had seen, the one he came on now had some sick element of whimsy to it. This dead man didn't move on his cross at all, because his head had been severed from his neck. His left hand was nailed to the arm of the cross, along with the smashed remains of a lute, the neck of the instrument hanging mournfully down by its strings. His right hand was also suspended on the cross, but someone had tied the hairs of his head to the fingers of this hand, so that it now hung from them like a lantern. The jaw and eyes moved, though no sound came from it.

Peter laughed at this one. "Now, the boys had some fun with this one, I admit, and maybe they went a little too far. But this is what I'm talking about. People who have no common sense. This fellow here fancied himself a poet. Can you imagine? A poet? A bard? What else did he call it? A troop… troubadour? In this world?" He laughed again. "You might as well say you're one of those philo-somethings. What are they called? Philosophicators?"

"Something like that," Dante said. "Very foolish indeed."

They had thankfully come to the end of the animated charnel house. Dante and his companions turned back toward their guide. Though Dante had grown disturbingly inured to the valley's horrors, he didn't know how much further he could go on with a dead man sniffing at his heels, and he hoped they would now be dismissed and sent on their way. Alone.

"What did you say you were again? What kind of work do you do?" Peter asked, as he jerked Bert around and away from the four travelers.

"I'm an apothecary," Dante said without pausing. Though it was clearly a much better answer than "poet," the man's eyes looked as uncomprehending as Bert's. "I make medicines."

Peter nodded. "Now see, there's some common sense. Something useful. You'll see a tent up ahead, before you come to the path up the cliff. Maybe they can use your help. They have lots of sick and wounded people there. Now hurry along."

They left that place, Dante feeling quite certain he could help no sick person, perhaps not even himself. The doctor for his wounds was as silent and inaccessible as he was powerful and knowledgeable.

Chapter 36

We step by step went onward without speech,
Gazing upon and listening to the sick
Who had not strength enough to lift their bodies.
Dante, *Inferno*, 29.70-72

As the man had indicated, they soon came to a large tent by the side of the trail. Even before they saw the pavilion, they heard the moans coming from it, though these sounded like the cries of living people in pain, not the hungry voices of the dead. They soon smelled the sick and dying as well. The sour scent of decayed flesh and human filth assailed them. Though it was still chilly here, the tent was open on the side facing the trail, probably to try and get some fresh air for the patients. Dante could see several small braziers with smoke trickling up from them. He caught the earthy, slightly acrid smell of burning herbs: another attempt to purify the diseased air.

The patients lay on the ground. From the way they wailed incoherently and writhed on their dirty blankets, many of them appeared to be feverish and delirious. Moving among them were three women in long, black robes and black scarves wrapped tightly about their heads. The scarves even covered their noses and mouths, so only their eyes could be seen. Dante noticed the three women limped when they walked. At first he thought they were just shuffling so as not to step on the patients, but after a while he could see all three of them had a definite limp. One of the women spotted Dante and gestured for the four of them to come closer. She stood over a frail, old man. He wasn't moving and his skin was grey. His mouth hung open, and although there was bloody drool dried on his neck and chin, his lips were now dry and cracked.

"You, the big one!" she said, as she pointed to Radovan then to the man at her feet. "Put your foot on his chest. Hold him down. I should've kept a closer watch on him, but we have so many. Please, hurry!"

Radovan looked at Dante and the others, then did as the woman had instructed. As she went to the other side of the tent, the dead man's eyes opened. He clawed the boot and leg holding him down. His feet kicked around randomly before he got them planted and tried to arch his back or roll over. Radovan had to lean forward to keep the struggling man pinned down, but by then the woman had returned with an ugly iron pole sharpened on one end. She held the point just above the man's right eye and shoved it down. His roaring howl was instantly cut off, as the woman put her weight into it and pushed the spike all the way down. The man's arms dropped. There was a slight wheezing sound as his whole body seemed to collapse in on itself like a spider in a flame.

The woman took the spike and leaned it against one of the tent poles. She draped a blanket over the dead man's face, then leaned herself against the tent pole as well. She sighed.

"Thank you," she said. "I'm Myra. It's hard with just the three of us. There were more, but two ran away, and the other got sick."

She was a small woman. Covered as she was, it was impossible to guess her age. Her hazel eyes appeared tinged with fatigue and sadness, but were still bright and alert. She was probably a few years younger than Dante.

"You have taken vows, my daughter?" Adam asked.

Myra looked at her robes. "These? Well, sort of." She looked around at the sick people. None of them seemed attentive to the conversation. "Why don't we take a step into the fresh air for a moment?"

She led them away from the tent. She closed her eyes and inhaled deeply. As cold and sterile as the air was, it was much better than in the tent.

"There, that's better," the woman said. "I'm not supposed to say it in front of them, but no, I'm not a monastic. I wasn't even really a believer before this. They make us wear these clothes. It's all a disguise or costume." She pulled the covering from off her face. "That's not really part of the outfit. That's just for the smell and diseased vapors." Her mouth was small, her cheekbones high; like the rest of her, her face was slender and drawn, but still full of life. "Anyway, they think the sick people will like it better if there are religious women caring for them, and it'll keep them calmer. The ones who can still move about would be quite a problem, if they thought they weren't being treated properly. They could get everyone worked up, and then the bosses would really crack down and kill lots of people. So I suppose it's for the best."

"I don't understand," Dante said. "Who makes you do this?"

"Who? Lord Ahriman's men, of course. The ones who run all the mines and everything else in the valley."

Bogdana stepped forward. "How did you come to be here in this terrible place?" she asked.

"How? Oh, there's nothing special to it. My family was poor. I started selling my body. I heard the pay was better for working girls up here, so I came, but then I found out what they wanted you to do was disgusting. I wouldn't always do what the men asked. My pimp said I complained too much and he beat me. They wouldn't let me leave and go back down to a regular town, one with normal men with normal vices. Men who just want you to do what their wives won't, not men who expect you to do things no decent person should. They wouldn't let me go, but they wouldn't let me sell myself up here, either. So they hobbled me. Smashed my one foot with a hammer. They do it to all the girls they want to work in the hospital. It heals, mostly, but you can never walk right again. Makes it harder for us to run away. Nearly impossible for us to climb back down the cliff. I suppose they mean for us to spend the rest of our lives in this wretched hole." Myra stretched her arms out to her sides, then over her head, before bringing them back down and taking another deep breath. "The air is nice. I wish the sun would come out."

"What they did to you was awful," Bogdana said in a quiet tone. "You must be so sad, and angry at them."

Myra shrugged. Then she smiled, just a little. Like her eyes, the expression looked fragile and exhausted, but still full of life. "Oh, at first," she said. "But not for very long. It was my own fault for coming here. My own fault for what I did before, too. You know how your mother always tells you not to do something, or you'll be sorry. And it turns out she's right, but you didn't listen. It hurts to be like this, and no one likes to hurt. It frightens me, even, what might happen. I think of that especially when I fall asleep. But angry or sad? No, not really."

"Not angry?" Dante said, nearly as mesmerized by the black-clad woman's equanimity as he was by Bogdana's beauty and simplicity. "I would be very angry, perhaps even angry with God. You have so much faith that you do not feel this way?"

Myra looked at him and smiled more broadly. "Yes. As I said, that's sort of the funny part. I had no faith before this. Didn't really think much about it. I mean, you know how you think about it when you're a child. Then you grow up and you're not interested in such things and don't think about them. You think you're too busy with more important things. But since I ended up here and saw real suffering and death all the time—now I see what I had to be grateful for. I even have a little hope, somedays. I think I'll find another of the girls, and we'll become friends. Trust each other, look out for one another. And if her other foot is the one that's broken, the opposite from mine, then we can lean against each other, and perhaps we'll be able to make it out of here. I like to think of that. Sometimes I feel quite certain it'll happen one day soon."

"You may be right," Dante said. "And until then, at least you do some good for the sick people here. You're not like the evil men who put you here."

"I suppose, though I do very little, other than put them out of their misery when they pass." Myra gestured to the clothes she wore. "These are less of a disguise than to call myself a nurse. I really can't do anything for them. I feel worse about lying to them about that than I do for wearing these clothes."

"Are they all sick with the plague?" Dante asked. "They've been bitten?"

Myra shook her head. "Oh no, very few with that," she said. "Those people would die or be killed before they ever got here. But we still have to be prepared for when sick people pass. They usually get back up, even if they haven't been bitten. Mostly we just have regular sick people here: disease, fever, injuries. So much can go wrong and hurt people. I guess I always knew that, but now it seems overwhelming. It makes my problems seem not so bad. Mostly I worry about the children. I really don't know what will become of them."

"Children?" Bogdana asked. "You have children here?"

"Only a few," Myra replied.

She put the covering over her mouth and nose and led them back toward the tent, taking them around the one side of it, where three children squatted on the ground just outside the pavilion. They looked to be about four to six years old: two boys and one girl. They had made up some game with rocks and sticks and nutshells and were playing it in the dirt. The children glanced at them, seemed satisfied they were neither a threat nor offered anything interesting, and continued with their game.

"Are they sick?" Adam asked. "Why do you have them here?"

"No, they're fine, so far as I can tell," Myra said. "I'm told it happens during a plague. Some children will escape from the monsters that killed their family, and they'll keep running, till eventually some of them end up all the way up here. I don't know what to do with them. I don't want them near the sick, but I can't just set them loose. God knows, up here there are plenty of men who would do terrible things to them. So I just keep them here and feed them. Perhaps if I ever leave, I'll be able to take them with me. I hope so."

"They are lucky to have you here to protect them," Adam said. "I think you have found another part of the reason for why you are here. Our way is too difficult to take them right now, but keep them here a bit longer. I think someone will find you here and take them to safety. Perhaps you as well. Have faith."

"Where did you say you were going?" Myra asked.

"Up and over the mountains," Adam said.

"Oh, yes. They are far too small to make that journey, if there even is a way up there. I've never heard of one. And I certainly can't make it. But I will pray for you."

Dante could see Bogdana's eyes glistening with tears as she silently embraced the other woman. Then the four of them left, hurrying on to a fate as uncertain as hers, Dante again simmering with shame that he approached such a fate with much less hope than the small, maimed woman.

Chapter 37

For where the argument of intellect
Is added unto evil will and power,
No rampart can the people make against it.
Dante, *Inferno*, 31.55-57

"There, up ahead," Radovan said, as he pointed to the cliff face rising above them to the right. "That must be it."

Adam looked up. "Yes, that's it," he agreed. "We're very close now."

Dante followed their gaze and saw a thin line going straight up the embankment. As they got closer, he could see there were metal posts driven into the stone, and between these ran some kind of rope or chain. Thankfully, although it was steeper, this ascent did not look as tall as the one they had climbed earlier that day, rising perhaps fifty or sixty feet above them. As with everything in the valley, it seemed more than enough to kill them, however.

Dante felt Bogdana pressing on his shoulder. "That?" she said. "There's no way I'll make it."

He put his hand on hers and squeezed it. "I'll be right behind you," he said. "You've got to make it." Dante thought if she lost hope he'd have no chance of continuing, so he had to keep her spirits up.

From up ahead they heard a loud roar, and Dante saw a gigantic figure standing at the bottom of the path up the cliff. It did not seem to be approaching them, but remained where it was. As they got closer, Dante could see it was a huge dead man. Like the other dead man Bert, this one had a leather collar around his neck. The collar had two chains attached to it, and these were fastened to two large stones near the cliff face. Although he was hunched over now, he was obviously an enormous creature. Dante had heard the Frisians were giants such as this, and he wondered if this unfortunate man had come from such a faraway place only to die in some gruesome, violent way, and then go on to toil in endless, restless futility. Incredibly, this dead man also held a huge wooden club in his right hand, beating the ground with it as he eyed the intruders. Dante had grown used to such ferocity in the dead, but he had never seen them capable of wielding tools or weapons before. It thoroughly chilled him. Not only for the increased danger, but also because it meant the man might retain some of his intellect, and therefore some of his humanity, all of it trapped in this enormous husk of hunger and madness. Dante imagined this was how Goliath looked, and he knew he was no David, either as to faith or skill at arms.

They got closer to the giant and surveyed the situation. The creature snarled and reached for them; if he were still breathing, his frenzied, determined straining at his leash would be strangling him. Dante looked past him at the trail. He could now see it was a black, iron chain that ran between the posts up the cliff face. Also, there were grooves worn into the stone, almost like steps, so it wouldn't be quite as daunting as it had looked from a distance. If anything, climbing down would be harder, since one would be walking backward while facing the cliff. Their difficulty now was they couldn't get to the bottommost end of the chain leading up the cliff without going through the giant corpse now guarding it.

Radovan had his hand on his sword hilt. "This isn't going to be easy," he said. "They're not supposed to have weapons."

"Or be that big," Dante muttered.

As they watched, the giant held his club above his head and gave a roar. Not just another completely inarticulate noise of rage. It almost seemed like words in some primitive, forgotten language. It sounded to Dante like, "Raphel may amech izabi almi!" Dante could hear Bogdana gasp behind him at this apparent attempt at speech. Garbled as it was, it was a whole sentence of some kind, uttered on the creature's own initiative, and not just a one syllable trick as they had heard Manda's "helper" perform.

"Good Lord," Radovan whispered. "It can speak. We really are doomed."

Adam stood between Dante and Radovan and put his hand on the latter's shoulder. "Easy, my son," Adam said. "Those who live and die the cursed life remember many things. This one remembers something about language. It can do him no good, but only torment him further. You may feel some shred of pity for him because of it. But do not fear him. We will attack him together, all three of us, and we will prevail. This is where you prove yourself men."

Dante looked to Radovan, and both of them drew themselves up. "You distract him," Radovan said. "I'll try to attack him from behind. We'll have a better chance."

Dante nodded. He hardly liked the idea of being the decoy for such a formidable opponent, but he knew Radovan would have the better chance at striking it a fatal blow.

"You there!" Dante heard a man call from somewhere nearby. "What are you doing?"

They turned from the monster to see a live, more normal-sized man approaching them. His face was greasy and scarred, with a thin, scruffy beard. He carried a spear and wore leather armor. Adam gestured to Radovan and Dante to get their hands off their swords, then he called to the man. "Nothing. We just wanted to climb up the trail. We meant no harm."

The man stood near them now. "Well, see that you don't," he said. "Or I'll have to let Nimrod here off his leash to bash your heads in. Then I'll have to get him back on his leash, and that could take some doing, so we don't want that, do we?"

"Oh no. Nothing of the kind," Adam agreed meekly.

"So, you want to go up the trail, eh? What for? I don't call Nimrod off for just anybody. There's no sightseeing in this valley!"

"Lord Ahriman sent for us," Adam said without any pause. Dante cast a sideways look at him. Adam gestured to each of the four of them in turn. "A new guard, a new apothecary, a new alchemist, and a new maid and… whatever." Dante thought it was risky, filling in too many details, but there was no turning back now.

The man leered. "I like plenty of 'whatever,'" he said. "But she looks a bit well-used."

"Well, her timing wasn't perfect," Dante agreed. "But she's so pretty it seemed worth the trouble. I'm sure she'll be quite enjoyable once she drops the extra baggage."

The man snickered and let his eyes roam from Bogdana's face to her breasts. "I suppose." He stuck his spear in the ground. "Well, I can pull Nimrod out of your way, but it'll take some work. I call him Nimrod because he's so big and strong. Makes a great guard, so nobody goes up to Lord Ahriman's unannounced. But it makes getting him out of the way a bit tricky."

"I see," Dante said, pretending not to get the implication.

The man was not a wily one; Dante had sized him up quickly. He was too used to people being overwhelmed by the threat of this monster, so he wasn't prepared for any refusal or negotiation. And Dante was losing patience with greed in this part of the valley.

"I mean, it'll take a lot of work," the man repeated. "And the worker needs to be paid. Or the work doesn't get done."

Dante got out one silver coin and held it up between his thumb and forefinger. "And what if the worker works for a very important man? A man who must be obeyed and not questioned. Then the worker won't want to delay that man's visitors, will he, by trying to wring something extra from them?"

The man's eyes narrowed. Dante could tell he was shamed and wanted to do something about it. Dante could also tell that getting paid this much was better than he usually did, and therefore he'd settle for it. The man took the coin.

"All right," he grumbled, as he walked over to one of the stones to which the giant was affixed. He looked over to Dante. "Go over there." He pointed further away.

Dante saw a third big stone with a metal loop attached to it. Dante led the other three to stand by it, as the man detached the creature's chain. Half untethered, the giant immediately lurched toward them, but the second chain on him kept him moving in an arc without getting any closer to them, like a dog chained to a tree or post. The man with the chain then walked over to them and attached it to the rock closest to them, and the giant was trapped in a different spot, away from the trailhead.

When the creature was once more restrained, he let out another wail with his club held high. "Pape satan, aleppe!"

The man who unchained and rechained the dead man shook his head as he conducted the four travelers over to the trail. "Oh what is it now, Nimrod?" he asked. "Satan? Yes, I suppose we'll all be seeing him soon enough. You especially, the way you've been acting. Now be still." He pointed them to the chain and steps up the cliff face. "Just haul yourselves up. It'll be colder when you get up there. It's always colder up there, for some reason. Be on your way."

Radovan started up the path. As Dante had suspected, it wasn't as difficult as it looked at first, and the young man made good progress. Adam followed, with Bogdana after him, and Dante brought up the rear. About halfway up, Bogdana lost her footing and sent some rocks skittering down on Dante. He turned his head as the tiny avalanche pelted him. When it was over, he looked back up to see Bogdana peering down at him. Her foot that had slipped was still scratching the cliff face, trying to find purchase, and her face looked pale and sweaty.

"I'm fine," he called to her. "Please don't look down."

The rest of the climb was thankfully uneventful and brief. Soon they were looking down on Nimrod and his handler. The latter wandered off as soon as they reached the top. Dante thought he probably only stayed that long in order to see if one of them would fall to his or her death, so he could loot the body. The former continued to stare, shaking his club and fist at them. Dante fancied he could catch more snippets of gibberish, in a tone that seemed to him both plaintive and enraged.

Chapter 38

Whereat I turned me round, and saw before me
And underfoot a lake, that from the frost
The semblance had of glass, and not of water.
Dante, *Inferno*, 32.22-24

Dante immediately felt how much colder it was at the top of the cliff, as strange as that seemed after such a short ascent. They again wrapped themselves in their blankets and began moving. The ground was frozen hard as stone, the frost on it crunching under their footsteps. As much as Dante had cursed the deathly stillness they had experienced on the previous plateau, here he quickly found himself longing for it, as howling, icy winds pummeled them. This assault seemed to have a special fury, for it swirled about them, constantly coming at them from a different side, rather than blowing steadily like a normal storm.

There were few trees this high up, so the wind was merciless and inescapable. After trudging for some time, they took shelter next to a boulder and a gnarled juniper tree, so they could get out of the wind and rest.

"I have never seen it this cold in the springtime," Dante said. He rubbed his hands and face, trying to get warmth back into them. His teeth were chattering so much he could barely speak.

"It's always colder in the mountains, and it's still early in the spring," Adam said. "But this does seem unnatural somehow, like a further blight and plague on this place."

"Back there you seem to have gotten the hang of lying," Dante said, stomping his feet before they became too numb.

"Yes, it was useful," Adam said. "Shameful but useful. Unfortunately, it is often much easier to learn new vices than virtues, so this place corrupts everything and everyone in it."

"Myra, that woman at the tent for the sick, did not seem wicked," Radovan said. Dante glanced at him and was encouraged by his still noticing what little goodness could be detected in this pit.

"Yes. She was a rare and virtuous woman," Adam agreed. "But so wounded by all the evil. We must pray she survives a bit longer, until someone can help her."

They tightened their blankets around themselves and continued walking. Ahead of them, the ground was completely smooth and white. They had come to the edge of a frozen lake. Radovan stepped out on to the ice, and stomped on it with his foot to test it.

"Should we cross it?" he asked. "It seems solid enough."

Adam looked to either side at the vast expanse of ice. "Yes, it'll be much quicker than circling around it," he replied. "We don't have much daylight left. Let's go."

Once they were on the ice, it could be seen it was not perfectly smooth, but had many irregularities in it. Hunched over as he was, Dante could observe these closely. In places it looked like ripples in the water had frozen, and there were many shades of blue detectable in the ice. Here and there he could see what looked like strange, indistinct objects within the ice, but it was impossible to tell if these were real, or illusions made by various cracks and bubbles trapped deep underneath them. Ominous pops and groans came from underneath—sometimes right at their feet, sometimes from far away, sounding almost like thunder from a distant storm.

Although the lake was quite large, it was not wide in the direction they were moving, and they crossed it quickly. As they neared the other shore, Dante could see some motion ahead and to their right. As they got closer to it, he saw it was two human forms lying down, partly submerged in the frozen, marshy ground at the edge of the lake. Dante could barely hear their moans over the howling wind.

He looked more closely at them, since they seemed incapable of getting up or attacking. They were two dead men, both caked with frost over most of their bodies, though in some spots there were also smears of dark, frozen mud. Where their skin was visible, it was either covered with frost or a shade of white indistinguishable from the snow. Almost all the tears and gashes in their skin were bloodless and nearly invisible, for the frost had filled those in as well.

The way the two men were lying, it looked to Dante as though they had been grappling together when they fell into the swampy ground. Then they had frozen there in mid-fight. As Dante watched, they continued to wrestle. They didn't really seem able to lift themselves up very much, so they clawed and bit at each other's faces and necks. The one dead man forced the other down and partly climbed on top of him. Dante could now see a gaping hole in the skull of the one on the bottom. Unlike the rest of their bodies the brain appeared bright and pink, especially shocking and livid with no other color present anywhere around them. Inside the broken skull, it looked like part of the brain was missing. The dead man who had forced the other one down now tried gnawing away at the edge of the hole, apparently trying to widen it, since it was not big enough for him to tear out any more of the brain. As he gnawed, the dead man's one clouded eye lit on Dante, but he made no move to leave his grisly feast. His jaw just worked slowly up and down as he stared.

"I didn't think they attacked one another," Dante said quietly, for the wind had suddenly died down.

"The dead remember," Adam replied. "This man must have hated that one with some special, intimate venom. A loyalty betrayed? A promise broken? A special humiliation that could only be delivered by someone he loved and trusted? Whatever it was, that hate now consumes him forever."

The man's teeth scraped along the skull with a small, rasping sound, like someone using a file on wood.

"So hate is stronger than love?" It was almost a whisper when Dante said it.

"Never believe that, my son," Adam said with a note of sternness. "You know not to. You know what hate is, and you know its limits."

Dante drew himself up more, though he still stared into the dead man's eye. Dante stepped closer to the struggling corpses. Still they did not react to him. "Hate is a kind of love," he said as he slowly drew back his right foot. "A twisted, stunted kind of love." He swung his foot forward. The thing's head jerked to one side from the blow, then turned back to resume chewing. Dante kicked it again with the same effect. "A love of pain and hurt and ugliness." Dante stepped away from the horrible, useless things on the ground.

"Yes," Adam said. "And for some people, it is the only love they know. As a man you must look on these pathetic creatures and pity them. But you must also scorn them and spurn their cursed life. It is the only way." The wind picked back up, whipping their blankets around and stinging their faces with sharp needles of snow and ice. "Now let us finish this journey."

They stepped off the surface of the lake and back on to frozen earth. Ahead to the left, Dante could see where part of the mountain had been torn away, as though a bite had been taken out of the black rock. It was a huge quarry, the wasted contents of which had been discarded to the one side in a gigantic pile of dully glistening slag. Where they were walking, the ground was covered with the black, pulverized dregs of the mine work as well. Dante picked up a rock and examined it, noticing several shards of dark red in it. Garnets? Rubies? Dante didn't know enough about gems to tell, but if even a castoff piece like this one had so many jewels embedded in it, the ground must be richer than anywhere else on earth.

As Dante considered such untold wealth, his attention was drawn away by the clink of metal striking rock. He slipped the stone into his pocket without thinking about it, focusing on what might be a new threat. The metallic clanking seemed to be in time to a low, rhythmic chant accompanying it. An explosion shook the ground, as a huge plume of black smoke and dust shot up from the quarry. The clinking and chanting became the only sounds they heard once more.

They were close enough now to see the hundreds of men swinging their picks in the dark pit. As more and more of the miners turned to notice them, Dante saw their eyes were as dead as the stone at which they were hacking.

Chapter 39

He from before me moved and made me stop,
Saying: "Behold Dis, and behold the place
Where thou with fortitude must arm thyself."
Dante, *Inferno*, 34.19-21

Radovan and Dante drew their swords. "There's no way you can tell us we'll prevail this time," Radovan said, as some of the dead men dropped their tools and shuffled toward them. There were a dozen or more in the nearest crowd that noticed them, and hundreds more in the ranks behind them.

Adam moved to stand beside them and planted his staff in the ground. "Of course I can," he said. "And we shall. You see how slowly they move in the cold. We will start running away from the quarry and straight toward the mountains, as quickly as we can. You, my daughter, move as fast as you can and get ahead of us. We will slow them down. It will give you the time you need to escape. You will have to trust your instincts to find the pass, but I know you can do it. The virtuous can find things that the wicked cannot see."

"And us?" Dante said.

"We will prevail. I give you my word," Adam said. "I did not say we would survive. But that is always a part of the blessed death: to die with honor and virtue, purpose and sacrifice. I know you would want that."

"I do," Radovan said.

"I do," Dante said softly, as he hustled Bogdana ahead.

They trotted forward, angling diagonally away from the growing horde following them. She was moving more awkwardly than she had been, almost waddling, but it looked like she could keep up a pace faster than the frozen dead.

"You there!" Dante heard someone shout from the direction of the quarry. "You people! Stop! What are you doing?"

Dante turned to see many men running between them and the crowds of the dead. These men were alive and carrying torches, which they waved at the dead to drive them back into the quarry. Dante heard the crack of whips as well. He and his companions stopped and watched the men round up the dead and return them to their work. In just a few minutes, the clinking of picks and the steady chanting had resumed.

A group of five of the men with torches approached them. The men were all clad in leather armor and fur coats. Besides the torches, they all carried iron truncheons—thick, black, brutish weapons. Dante could also see black leather whips coiled at their belts.

"Now what did you think you were doing?" one of the men said to them. "You interrupted our work. Got them all riled up. I don't care if you want to get eaten alive, but if they got you and went into a feeding frenzy, it'd take us the rest of today and all night to calm them back down and get them back to work. Might even have to put a few of them down, if they got too unruly. You were lucky you didn't cause us more trouble."

"But why don't they attack you and eat you?" Dante asked, looking in amazement between the armed men in front of him and the dead ones swinging picks. "I don't understand. You have them doing work."

The man frowned and shrugged. "Ask me how you get a bull to plow a field," he said. "The beast's bigger and stronger than you and could kill you at any moment. But you beat it, whip it, and get it to mind." He smiled: a very crooked and dirty affair. "And you feed it, of course." He pointed his truncheon at them. "That's where you all might still come in handy, if you don't behave. Now, no one's answered my question!"

The speaker swung his truncheon, catching Dante's right arm just below the shoulder. It was a backhanded blow, so it wasn't as powerful and debilitating as it might have been, but it still drove Dante to one knee with a cry of pain. Dante raised his sword, in case he needed to ward off another blow, but Adam and Radovan stepped between him and the men with clubs.

With his left hand, Dante grabbed Radovan's arm, keeping him from advancing. Dante pulled himself up. "No, please, it's my fault," he said. It was shameful, to be sniffling with his eyes full of tears, but there was nothing to be done about it, the pain was so intense. Besides, it might put off the attackers from more violence if Dante and his friends appeared weaker. "I shouldn't have asked so many questions. It's my fault. I'm sorry."

"Yeah, you ought to be," the man who had struck him said. "Now answer my question."

"We're all sorry we caused trouble," Adam said. "We were just trying to get further up into the mountains. We didn't know you had the dead working here. We didn't mean to upset them or interrupt your work."

"Well, you should be more careful where you go wandering around," the man continued, still stabbing the air with his truncheon for effect. "The world's a dangerous place. And people have work to do."

"We should take them to Lord Ahriman," one of the other men said.

The man who addressed them first nodded. "Yes. I think you're right, Cassian," he said. "Let him deal with it. It's not far. Start going the way you were headed. Go on."

Adam looked to Radovan and Dante and nodded for them to put away their weapons. Dying to save Bogdana from the hungry dead was one thing; dying so that these brutes could get a hold of her was senseless as well as useless. So they sheathed their swords and followed the men.

They were led past many more work gangs—some living, some dead, some striking at the ground out in the open, some being led into the mouths of mining tunnels that would take them further into the darkness to search for cold, sparkling stones. Whenever they passed the dead, the men with torches would shield the dead men's view of the newcomers as much as possible and hurry them along. Finally they came to a huge pavilion. This one was closed all around and had two guards at the entrance. The men escorting them explained the situation to the guards then left. After waiting a few more moments, Dante and his friends were led inside.

The interior of the tent was opulent, though the whole structure retained the feel of a military camp, ready to be broken down and moved to a new location at any time. It was not fit for an emperor, but Dante could imagine a Roman general on campaign lived in something like this. A fire roared in the middle of the area in a large, round brazier, the metalwork of which was quite intricate. The tapestries on the walls were colorful and skillfully done. Their subject matter was mostly battles, especially those including the burning of cities, the slaughtering of children and old men, and the raping of women. It could have been the sack of Troy reproduced a dozen times, so far as Dante could tell. The floor of the tent was covered with furs and rugs, many of the latter with scenes similar to the wall decorations. There were a couple tables and many chairs; all of these looked of high quality, very ornate in their design. The more surprising furnishings were two large bookcases, full to overflowing with ancient-looking tomes.

They were taken before Lord Ahriman, who sat at the one end of the tent, flanked by four more guards. Behind a gauzy curtain nearby, Dante saw two voluptuous feminine forms reclining. The lord's chair was a high-backed one that resembled a throne, though he had forgone any gilt or brocade. It was just a massive chair, as ornate as the others in the room, but not more so. The man himself looked a bit older than Dante, very handsome and well-groomed, especially considering the people Dante had been exposed to for the last few days. His hair and beard were black and closely trimmed, his eyes a cold and striking blue. He wore black pants and a white shirt, over which he'd pulled a voluminous red robe that hung open in the front. If the tent exuded the aura of a Roman general, the man and his garb looked more like a statesman or philosopher—elegant, but restrained, thoughtful, and in control.

Lord Ahriman's demeanor also seemed more civilized than those they had encountered elsewhere in the valley. He waved them over and smiled at them; his teeth were perfectly straight and dazzlingly white. "So, I am told you entered my part of the valley and caused some disturbance?" he asked in an affable tone. His voice seemed oddly welcoming in this place, the exact opposite of his violent servants outside.

"Yes," Adam replied. "We meant no harm. We were just passing through."

"I see," the lord said. "You picked a most peculiar place to come. No one comes up here. There's no way out, I'm afraid."

"There is a pass through the mountains," Adam explained. "We will take it. We won't cause you any trouble."

Ahriman looked thoughtful and a bit puzzled at this reply. "Oh, it's no trouble, really. The men who run the mine were being overly dramatic. They can certainly keep the 'special' workers under control. Or they should be able to, if they're doing their job. But I'm confused about this pass. I have heard of it before. You're one of those monks from that strange monastery, aren't you?"

"Yes, sir." Adam bowed his head with this reply.

Ahriman nodded. "A most unusual lot, to be sure, with most odd beliefs. Nothing I could ever see the value in. But perhaps you know some secret path that we don't. I can't see the harm in your traipsing about the mountains. But you'll stay away from our workers, and be on your way?"

"Absolutely. Without delay," Adam said.

"Good. Then I see no reason to keep you. You may go."

Before they were led out, Adam raised his hand. "My lord, if you please, I mean no disrespect, and don't wish to take up any more of your valuable time, but I wanted to ask about this place. I was up here many years ago, and none of this was here. There were just a couple small mines, and a few miners—regular miners. Is all this new?"

Ahriman smiled again. "We've been here a few years, but our operation has grown a great deal since you were here. Isn't it impressive? And finally putting the dead to some use. That was a real boon."

"Yes, it is… fascinating what you've done here," Adam said.

Dante wondered why they didn't just get moving. Although his arm still throbbed from when he had asked too many questions before, Dante had to admit his own overwhelming curiosity about this infernal place. Dante thought even Ahriman's tone contributed to this longing for more information, as though his voice had a special seductiveness to it, a low softness that made one want to hear more.

"But don't you worry the army will come here and destroy it? They're moving up the valley, you know. I don't understand how you can stay here."

Ahriman's smile had a note of condescension in it now, though it was still quite captivating. "Oh, I'm afraid you don't know our arrangements with the army. The *boyar*, the ruler, is my brother. He would never let the army get above the valley floor, to climb up to either of the two plateaus. All the lands up here are mine. And the people as well, both living and dead."

"No!" Radovan exclaimed. "You can't be! Lord Mihail killed his brother Ahriman years ago, after Ahriman killed their older brother!"

Ahriman laughed, a sound so infectious it almost made Dante want to join in. "Oh, yes. I know he still tells that story!" the handsome lord said. "How many versions of it have all of you heard? That he killed me in single combat? In a huge battle? Threw me off the castle parapet? Lay siege to my castle and burned it to the ground, with me inside it? That we fought on a frozen lake far to the north, where I'd fled, and the ice cracked and I fell through?" He lowered his voice a little. "Did it ever strike you as rather convenient and surprising that all those stories included my body being completely lost? No evidence whatsoever? And did it ever occur to anyone that my brother Mihail, the second eldest of the family, stood to gain from our older brother's death, and not I? Don't all these things add up, and show that Mihail was behind it all the time? That I just did what we both wanted done, with his approval and support?" He gestured to the contents of the tent and smiled again. "And now, with his protection and reward for a good deed?"

Dante could see that Radovan was crushed by this revelation. From his earlier description, this Mihail was some kind of local hero, someone whom boys were raised to admire, even idolize. To take that belief away from someone would freeze and kill a part inside him, much more than the snow and ice outside ever could.

"Where I come from, these things would be noted, and people would figure out what had happened," Dante said. He looked down at the floor, out of shame for what he now confessed of his homeland. "Many would even praise the ones who had done it and call them shrewd, intelligent men who deserve to rule."

Ahriman looked to Dante, raising his eyebrows and nodding. "Then you come from a land of very wise and enlightened people," he said. "Where did you say you were from?"

"I was born in Italy," Dante said.

The lord nodded. "Ah, yes, I have heard of this place. It must be glorious to be among so many people who are honest and direct about what they want, and what they'll do to achieve it. I think I would like it there very much."

"I'm sure you would," Dante said. He cursed himself for continuing the conversation, but his curiosity was now completely in control of him. "I understand why your brother Mihail did this, but I don't see exactly what you gained."

Ahriman gestured to the contents of the tent. "I understand my surroundings might seem humble," he said. "But they suit me. I range up and down these two plateaus, and everyone I see is *mine*. You might think the fawning and groveling would get old eventually—but they don't! And I know, even if I don't always show my hand, how far my power extends. My brother's reign depends on the wealth we provide him from these mountains. The occasional outbreaks of the living dead mean he can keep such a large army at all times, and keep the people cowed and fearful most of the time, or jubilant and grateful when the monsters are destroyed by Mihail's soldiers. But they're never really destroyed, of course. I just keep them here, busy, working away. They have a purpose now. I've even given them a sort of happiness, as meager as it might seem to some. And our youngest brother, Gabriel, wasn't left out, either. He became the leader of the church in our land, and the pews and coffers are always packed. The poor, frightened people need to pray their knees raw and empty their pockets, always asking for protection from the terror of the living dead, or pouring out their gratitude when the plague's been quelled. So my dead are always useful, whether they're working hard or being killed! Just their existence gives me more power than anyone in this land! I rule over the dead. What other ruler can say that, anywhere in the world? It's like in ancient Greece. The world is divided between three powerful rulers: one for the earth, one for the sea, and one for the underworld. I got the underworld. Many might think it dreary, but I find it intoxicating and thrilling."

"How can you brag about this?" Radovan asked. "How can you tell us all this? What if someone found out?"

Ahriman shrugged and smiled. "Who would believe you? And what would they do about it? Surely you've heard rumors before that I was alive, and you disbelieved them. Mothers tell such stories to their children to frighten them into behaving. I am the stuff of legend. I have accomplished the greatest trick of all: I've convinced people I don't exist. They need for me to not exist. They need for me to have been killed by their just and noble ruler. And people always get what they need. Very seldom what they want, but always what they need. And I help them get that. So everyone's happy."

They all fell silent for a moment, and there was just the crackling of the fire and some whispers from the women behind the curtain. Dante glanced over at his companions. They looked as mesmerized by this man as Dante felt. Bogdana was the first to tear her focus away and look toward the door.

"May we still go?" Dante asked.

Ahriman looked surprised. "Of course. I'm sorry if I went on a bit, but you asked. I don't get many visitors from the outside world."

They were led back outside and continued their trek away from the mines, further up the slopes. For the first time in their journey, Radovan was not in the lead of their group, his strength and hope seemingly drained from him. The sun was nearly touching the mountaintops ahead of them. Dante had no idea how they could make it over these peaks. It seemed as though exhaustion and despair might finally defeat them, when violence and hate had not.

Chapter 40

We mounted up, he first and I the second,
Till I beheld through a round aperture
Some of the beauteous things that Heaven doth bear;
Thence we came forth to rebehold the stars.
Dante, *Inferno*, 34.136-139

Dante kept looking over his shoulder as they made their way further into the mountains. He could see, from the corner of his eye, the other three did so as well, clearly fearing treachery and pursuit as much as Dante did. Leaving the camp, they wended their way through piles of blackish slag as tall as two men. In addition to these, there were smaller piles, still as tall as a man, of all kinds of trash from the miners: broken tools and crockery, shattered barrels and other pieces of wood and metal, scraps of food with the burnt bones and flayed flesh of animals. There were even a great many frozen bodies of the miners themselves—naked, most of them tinged with blue and green, all of them used up, emaciated, broken, and randomly mixed in among the other trash with no concern for their previous existence as men.

Perhaps it was because he kept looking back that Dante did not notice the dead lying in wait for them among the piles of rock and other debris. As Dante glanced backward, he heard Bogdana's shriek, but before he could return his attention forward, he was hit from the side by a charging body that carried him down to the ground. All he could see, for an instant, was a bluish face pressed close to his. All he could hear was the rasping growl it made. All he could smell was stale air and rotted flesh, and all he could feel were its fingernails raking across his face. Its filthy claws bit into his flesh and ripped down from his forehead, across his left eye, and down his nose and cheek. Immediately Dante's eye burned from the blood pouring into it. He tasted the bitter, copper tang in his mouth. He let out a scream of pain and outrage at this final attack, this last, grasping, tenacious obstacle.

The thing had a hold of Dante's sword arm. The claws of its right hand were now at his throat, but Dante had instinctively lashed out with his left arm and now had a hold of the monster's throat as well. He might've frozen there long enough for the dead man to tear his neck open with his ragged nails, but Bogdana's scream pierced Dante and lashed him into a fury. His fingers sunk deeper and faster into the dead meat than the claws digging into his own flesh, for his were spurred on by something more than just hunger. The dead man was not larger than Dante, and like all the dead, his balance and coordination were none too good. Dante wrenched his body to the side, rolling the two of them over. When Dante was on top, he pulled up on the dead neck and proceeded to slam the head attached to it into the rocky ground, over and over. Dante only stopped the assault when the fingers around his own neck slackened, the ruined head lolling back like a rag doll's before he let go.

Rising to his feet, he took in a ragged, wet breath through clenched teeth, his head swimming. He turned like a drunk toward Bogdana's screams, and saw her struggling under a dead woman much larger than she. For the only time he'd ever seen, she looked to him frail and overpowered, weaponless and pinned down, thrashing about wildly and furiously, but with the woman's cracked, yellow teeth closing in on her neck. Perhaps it would've made more sense to draw his sword, but Dante was not thinking clearly or logically. Scooping up a jagged, black rock the size of an infant's head, he only thought how they were far too close to let this stop them; how they had been through too much for it to end like this. With an animal roar he charged, swinging the rock upward, smashing it right into the dead woman's hideous maw. The blow threw her a little to the side and made her tilt her head backwards. Dante slammed the rock right down on her forehead, driving it into her skull in an explosion of brain and bone. Then he crouched and launched himself at her, catching her around the neck with his left arm and knocking her off Bogdana.

Dante landed on top of the dead woman. Though she no longer struggled or moved, he straddled her and continued to bring the rock down into the mangled flesh of her head, over and over, till the muscles in his arm burned from the exertion and each blow came more and more slowly. He could feel the blood from the cuts on his face mingling with tears and drool, as he tilted his head back and sputtered in frustration and sorrow, no longer able to look at his grisly work. But still the rock rose and fell, making sad, wet noises in the frozen, dead air.

Finally Dante felt Bogdana touch his shoulder, while her other hand cupped gently around his hand, easing his motions to a halt. "It's done," she said softly. She squeezed, and his hand relaxed. He let the bloody stone drop to the rocky ground with a clack. She pulled him to his feet, turned him around, and led him a few feet from the corpse he had made. He looked down at the ground. She pulled the sleeve of her blouse out a little, past the edge of the jacket sleeve, and wiped the blood from his mouth with it. "We're done here."

The four of them stood there for a moment, panting in the thin air, just staring at each other. Dante could see two corpses on the ground by Radovan, and another near Adam.

"We must make haste," Adam finally said.

They moved again. The further they got from the mining operation, the more familiar Adam seemed with the land around them, guiding them quickly into the bare mountains behind and above Lord Ahriman's camp. Though the rocky landscape looked utterly featureless from a distance, as they moved along Dante could see they were following the barest of tracks — little more than the kind of line scratched on a mountain by the nimble goats living there. It was still freezing cold around them, but at least they no longer had to contend with the savage wind that had attacked them on the frozen lake, and there were no more creatures, living or dead, to assail them. The ground they walked on was frozen and there were patches of snow all around. Higher up the snow was much deeper. Poised on the slopes above them, Dante saw huge piles of dirty, grey snow remaining from the previous winter. Though it was cold this day, the spring time temperatures on other days seemed to have undermined these snow banks, carving them out into strange, undulating shapes, jutting out from the mountain face like claws or wings that defied gravity to pull them down to the valley below. Adam turned back several times and put his finger to his lips, to show they should be quiet, lest they start an avalanche.

The air was thin. They were all breathing hard when they stopped to rest under a rock outcropping. Adam looked around them as dusk crept up toward them. He pointed to another outcropping a few hundred feet ahead of them as he put his hand on Dante's shoulder.

"There, you see that rock?" he said.

"Yes," Dante said.

"The pass is just beyond that, and you'll be on the other side of the mountain, out of this valley of death. Go to that outcropping, to protect yourself when the snow comes crashing down. Just press yourselves up against the rock and you'll be safe."

The other three looked at Adam.

"Where will you be?" Dante asked. "We've fought off the last of them. We can all leave safely. And why will the snow come crashing down? I don't understand." He looked up at the snow above them more nervously than before.

"I will return to the valley," Adam said. "I fear some of these wicked men may try to follow us and find the way out of here. It must remain a secret the evil do not know, do not believe in. It gives us some power over them. The same way not believing in evil gives it so much of its power. God knows, they might try to lead the dead out of the valley if they knew this path, and befoul other lands with their plagues. Besides, one of us should return to save those children we saw before. It is my job to take them back to the monastery and raise them to fight this evil, but first I had to make sure you were safe. So you all go on ahead. The snows are very unstable this time of year. A loud shout and they will come tumbling down and obliterate the path."

"I will go with you," Radovan said.

Adam shook his head. "You are as brave as ever, my son, but you do not need to do this. I will sneak past the men in Lord Ahriman's camp more easily if I'm alone, and I can take the children by myself."

"This land is my home," Radovan replied. He gestured to Dante. "I think you can say how difficult it is to live far from home, in strange lands. No matter how beautiful they are, they have made you sad and sick, haven't they?"

Dante nodded. "Yes, they have, every day."

"Then I will return with you, sir, to the valley. I think you may need some help, for Myra will need someone to lean on as she goes down the mountain."

Adam looked between Radovan and Dante. "I see you two are alike in some ways, after all." He smiled and shook his head. "Well, love for virtuous women is not a very bad thing to have in common, I suppose. Let us go before the darkness overtakes us completely. Farewell, my friends."

Adam pulled Bogdana and Dante to his small but reliable chest. Dante had not felt such a paternal embrace in many years. He was glad the freezing cold had already made his eyes wet with tears, to save himself the embarrassment of his weeping being noticed. Radovan clasped the two separately and more briefly, but Dante felt reassured by his stoic strength, and again gladdened by his virtue and optimism. Having made their farewells there on the barren mountainside, Dante led Bogdana to the rock Adam had pointed out. They turned back to see the other two men waving to them.

"You will always have hope, you who have left this valley!" Adam shouted. As he did, Dante could hear rumbling and creaking all around them. "Go forward! The banners of the King advance!"

The sounds coming from the snow did not crescendo gradually, but all at once turned into a roaring explosion. Bogdana gave a squeal and Dante pulled her close as a thundering, rushing blast of snow engulfed them. Dante pressed his stinging nose and eyes into her hair until the sound stopped. When he opened his eyes, he could only see white for several minutes more, but gradually the world became visible. The trail to the valley was gone, a mountain of snow in its place.

If Adam and Radovan were still back there, he could not see them.

As Adam had described, the trail ahead was clear, leading down through a crevasse free of snow. Dante pulled Bogdana along in the twilight and, in a short while, they had clambered far down the other side of the mountain. As they went, the temperature rose rapidly, turning from winter to spring in just a short while. Soon the terrain also transformed, from a rocky waste to a lush meadow. In the fading light Dante even saw flowers in the tall grass, and heard crickets calling to their mates. Looking at Bogdana, he risked a small laugh at this new landscape, though he feared a fragile spell might be broken and everything around them would erupt in ash and flame. But as they made their way down the mountain, the fields around them now lit by the moon, Dante wondered if it had really been the last three days that were under a spell. It now seemed like an evil dream from which he had suddenly been summoned, like a fever patient finally breaking through the wall of suffering and blindness that had been wracking his body and smothering his mind.

They walked more slowly. The lights of a town were ahead of them, down a gentle slope that they now traversed quite easily. Dante took the jewel-encrusted stone from his pocket and held it out to Bogdana. She took it, turning it over in the moonlight. Its enormous worth could be seen even in the night. She looked sideways at him and smiled. The curl of her lips and the sparkle in her eye were mischievous.

"For me?" she said. "You stole something for me? Is that a proper gift?"

He pretended to look shocked or hurt. "It was on the ground. That's not stealing!"

She shook her head. "You are always so exact and precise, such a stickler." She put the stone in her pocket and slipped her hand into Dante's.

"Well, you have made me less so," he said. "But I think you'll need the jewels, to help you make your way in whatever land this is we've come to."

He felt her hand tighten on his. "And where will you be, Dante?"

"I'll stay near till you're settled, of course, until after your baby is born. But eventually I will go back to Italy. Even if I never return to Florence, I belong in my own country. More importantly, I have a new purpose now. I have something to do that's worthy of you. Something that just has worth, period. It will even have eternal worth. I will tell the world of what we four went through. Hundreds of years from now, people will know of your virtue, and Adam's wisdom, and Radovan's courage. All the misery you've been through will be for something—for goodness, truth, and beauty. And those will last forever, while the pain is just a memory."

"You would leave me because you have to go off to make me immortal?" Her mouth, and especially her eyes, continued to look mischievous. "Perhaps you're less of a stickler, but you are still a very strange man, I think."

"Perhaps I am. But maybe that is not such a bad thing?"

Bogdana turned toward him and took both his hands in hers. She locked her gaze on his. "No. I don't think it's a bad thing at all."

Bogdana tilted her head back to look up at the sky. Dante pulled his focus from her exquisite neck and face, and followed her gaze up to the myriad of tiny lights above them.

"It's good the stars are out," she said.

"Yes, it is," Dante agreed. "It is good there are so many beautiful things in the universe. It is especially good that some of them are much closer than the stars."

In the dark, it was impossible to tell if she blushed at this. Of course, it wouldn't have changed anything, whether she did or not, for Dante would've approved her modesty if she did blush, and admired her confidence if she didn't. He could see, however, that she smiled, though they both kept their attention fixed on the stars. "And when you tell of others' virtues, Dante, what will you say of yourself?"

"Just that I'm very observant. And grateful."

She laughed outright at this. It was the first time Dante had ever heard her really laugh—a full and healthy outpouring of joy, with a ringing, musical quality to it. He imagined that in the empyrean, the blessed laughed like this as they embraced one another—those souls like Beatrice who were beyond pain or jealousy, loss or envy.

"Perhaps you could give yourself a little more credit?" Bogdana said as her laughter subsided. "Do it for me, at least. One who is worthy of me should be more than just observant and grateful, don't you think?"

"All right, for you."

Their gaze met again. When her lips touched his, Dante knew a tiny bit more of the beauty his words could never attain.

BY WILLIAM D. CARL

ISBN: 978-1934861042

Beneath the dim light of a full moon, the population of Cincinnati mutates into huge, snarling monsters that devour everyone they see, acting upon their most base and bestial desires. Planes fall from the sky. Highways are clogged with abandoned cars, and buildings explode and topple. The city burns.

Only four people are immune to the metamorphosis—a smooth-talking thief who maintains the code of the Old West, an African-American bank teller who has struggled her entire life to emerge unscathed from the ghetto, a wealthy middle-aged housewife who finds everything she once believed to be a lie, and a teen-aged runaway turning tricks for food.

Somehow, these survivors must discover what caused this apocalypse and stop it from spreading. In their way is not only a city of beasts at night, but, in the daylight hours, the same monsters returned to human form, many driven insane by atrocities committed against friends and families.

Now another night is fast approaching. And once again the moon will be full.

EDEN

A ZOMBIE NOVEL BY TONY MONCHINSKI

ISBN: 978-1934861172

Seemingly overnight the world transforms into a barren wasteland ravaged by plague and overrun by hordes of flesh-eating zombies. A small band of desperate men and women stand their ground in a fortified compound in what had been Queens, New York. They've named their sanctuary Eden.

Harris—the unusual honest man in this dead world—races against time to solve a murder while maintaining his own humanity. Because the danger posed by the dead and diseased mass clawing at Eden's walls pales in comparison to the deceit and treachery Harris faces within.

MORE DETAILS, EXCERPTS, AND PURCHASE INFORMATION AT

www.permutedpress.com

DYING TO LIVE
LIFE SENTENCE

by Kim Paffenroth

At the end of the world a handful of survivors banded together in a museum-turned-compound surrounded by the living dead. The community established rituals and rites of passage, customs to keep themselves sane, to help them integrate into their new existence. In a battle against a kingdom of savage prisoners, the survivors lost loved ones, they lost innocence, but still they coped and grew. They even found a strange peace with the undead.

Twelve years later the community has reclaimed more of the city and has settled into a fairly secure life in their compound. Zoey is a girl coming of age in this undead world, learning new roles—new sacrifices. But even bigger surprises lie in wait, for some of the walking dead are beginning to remember who they are, whom they've lost, and, even worse, what they've done.

As the dead struggle to reclaim their lives, as the survivors combat an intruding force, the two groups accelerate toward a collision that could drastically alter both of their worlds.

ISBN: 978-1934861110

EVERY SIGH, THE END.
(A novel about zombies.)

by Jason S. Hornsby

It's the end of the world: 1999.

Professional nobody Ross Orringer sees flashes of cameras and glances from strangers lurking around every corner.

His paranoia mounts when his friends and family begin acting more and more suspiciously as the New Year approaches.

In the last minutes before the clock strikes midnight, Ross realizes that the end may be more ominous than anyone could have imagined: decisions have been made, the crews have set up their lights and equipment, and the gray makeup has been applied.

In the next millennium, time will lose all meaning, and the dead will walk the earth.

ISBN: 978-0-9789707-8-9

MORE DETAILS, EXCERPTS, AND PURCHASE INFORMATION AT

www.permutedpress.com

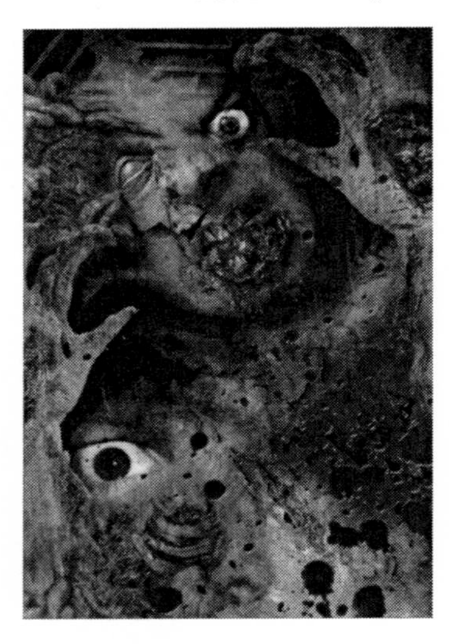

HISTORY IS DEAD

A ZOMBIE ANTHOLOGY EDITED BY

KIM PAFFENROTH

"*History is Dead* is a violent and bloody tour through the ages. Paffenroth has assembled a vicious timeline chronicling the rise of the undead that is simultaneously mind-numbingly savage and thought provoking."

—Michael McBride, author of the *God's End* trilogy and *The Infected*

ISBN: 978-0-9789707-9-6

ROSES OF BLOOD ON BARBWIRE VINES

D.L. SNELL

As the living dead invade a barricaded apartment building, the vampire inhabitants must protect their human livestock. Shade, the vampire monarch, defends her late father's kingdom, but Frost, Shade's general, convinces his brethren to migrate to an island where they can breed and hunt humans. In their path stands a legion of corpses, just now evolving into something far more lethal, something with tentacles—and that's just the beginning.

ISBN: 978-0-9789707-1-0

MONSTROUS

20 TALES OF GIANT CREATURE TERROR

Move over King Kong, there are new monsters in town! Giant beetles, towering crustaceans, gargantuan felines and massive underwater beasts, to name just a few. Think you've got what it takes to survive their attacks? Then open this baby up, and join today's hottest authors as they show us the true power of Mother Nature's creatures. With enough fangs, pincers and blood to keep you up all night, we promise you won't look at creepy crawlies the same way again.

ISBN: 978-1934861127

THE MORNINGSTAR STRAIN

THUNDER AND ASHES

A ZOMBIE NOVEL BY Z.A. RECHT

A lot can change in three months: wars can be decided, nations can be forged... or entire species can be brought to the brink of annihilation. The Morningstar Virus, an incredibly virulent disease, has swept the face of the planet, infecting billions. Its hosts rampage, attacking anything that remains uninfected. Even death can't stop the virus—its victims return as cannibalistic shamblers.

Scattered across the world, embattled groups have persevered. For some, surviving is the pinnacle of achievement. Others hoard goods and weapons. And still others leverage power over the remnants of humanity in the form of a mysterious cure for Morningstar. Francis Sherman and Anna Demilio want only a vaccine, but to find it, they must cross a countryside in ruins, dodging not only the infected, but also the lawless living.

The bulk of the storm has passed over the world, leaving echoing thunder and softly drifting ashes. But for the survivors, the peril remains, and the search for a cure is just beginning...

ISBN: 978-1934861011

MORE DETAILS, EXCERPTS, AND PURCHASE INFORMATION AT

www.permutedpress.com

Breinigsville, PA USA
19 May 2010

238342BV00003B/1/P

9 781934 861318